SOULSTEALER

Book 2: Steven

SHANE BOULWARE

THEORYbee

D1286599

Dear Reader,

Thank you for picking up the second installment of *Soulstealer*!

Set at the same time as Nythan's adventure with Bane in Book 1, Book 2 follows Steven, an imperfect hero who plays an instrumental role in the events of Book 1. Technically, this is a companion novel to *Nythan*. So, while the two storylines and points of view are vastly different, you'll see some overlapping scenes that shed a new light on so many things.

Disclaimer! Like the first novel, *Steven* contains mature concepts, such as: violence, murder, torture, psychotic behavior, and mention of abuse. Sexual scenes and curse words are greatly subdued. **I would still place it as a solid PG-13 and suitable for ages 16 & above.**

I invite you to connect with any of the Soulstealer communities below, and would greatly appreciate a review + rating on Amazon & Goodreads.

Thank you and enjoy!

Shane

SoulstealerBook.com

@SoulstealerBook

fb.me/SoulstealerBook

@SoulstealerBook

It would be **hugely** helpful to me as a self-published author if you **rate and post a review** of *Steven* to Amazon, Goodreads, and wherever else you bought the book.

Your review will **help others** decide to read this book, and your rating will push the *Soulstealer* series to the **#1 spot!** Thank you so much for your support!

Scan the QR codes below or type the link into your browser.

bit.ly/SoulstlrBk2AmznRvw   bit.ly/SoulstlrBk2GR

To Dad & Mom,
Love you both.

All my success is due to God. To Him be the glory.

SOULSTEALER

BOOK 2: STEVEN

Table of Contents

"Faith is taking the first step even when you don't see the whole staircase."

Martin Luther King, Jr.

"If you're going through hell, keep going."

Winston Churchill

"It always seems impossible until it's done."

Nelson Mandela

Chapter 1

Sudden

20 years in the future.

The Soulstealer charged through the doorway and into the dining room.

One of his attendants ran to him. "This way, my Lord!" She pointed to the kitchen. Sounds of yelling and staccato gunfire reverberated from the room he had just exited.

"Out of my way!" roared the Soulstealer, pushing the hapless follower behind him. He dashed into the kitchen and straight to the cupboard's secret exit. The attendant took her place next to three guards, who wore their pale gray masks portraying a face twisted in agony.

The attendant's eyes widened as shots rang out from the doorway. Her head jerked back as a bullet hit her in the forehead. The intruders cut down his bodyguards a half-second later.

Bullets shredded the Soulstealer's legs, and he caught hold of the countertop. He swiveled to steal the breath of life from his attackers when a sword sliced through his neck. The Soulstealer gurgled and collapsed against the kitchen cupboard, grasping at its wound.

One of the assailants, dressed in full metallic purple battle armor, stepped closer, until the low hum of his marred helmet faceplate hovered inches above the dying Soulstealer's face, reflecting the glow of a violet "T" shaped lens in the Soulstealer's eyes.

"By the Ordo Solis, your evil is purged once more, Bane," a deep electronic voice rumbled from the helmet's speaker.

A faint chuckle escaped the Soulstealer's lips, peppering his attacker's faceplate with flecks of blood.

"I rise further."

CHAPTER 2

BEGINNING OF THE MIDDLE

Modern day.

The Ordo Solis, the Order of the Sun. Created by the Catholic Church, from the ashes of the Inquisition, to combat a demon who possessed a human champion and ate the souls of its victims. At the time, the Church proclaimed the demon to be the Living Satan. The Inquisition declared it the Bane of Existence, and the people called it Bane. Nowadays, the public at large didn't think the monster ever existed.

Steven couldn't say what he believed, as every day his bucket of faith sprung another leak. When he was 24, nothing thrilled him more than the idea of defending humanity against an evil enemy bent on sucking the life out of the world. Twelve years later, his passion stooped to an all-time low.

The oversized armchair struggled to fit Steven's big-boned frame as he scowled at the ratty television. It was *his* turn to watch the footage of the Raptor Gatekeeper, who sat and stared at a fireplace for 60 minutes. Not 61 minutes and not 59. Each time, Steven waited until the Gatekeeper left, with nothing of interest recorded once again. He and the only remaining Ordo Solis volunteer did this every night of every day. The same thing, over and over.

And for what? Steven asked himself. *To be the ever-vigilant watchdog that sounds the alarm if Bane returned to threaten humanity.*

He puttered his lips, trying to distract his mind from the truth. Most things the Ordo Solis did seemed like an annoyance, rather than the world-saving role they supposedly fulfilled. It had crumbled into a relic of its former self. The days of being Bane's watchdog ended a couple decades ago; the organization reduced to a tired old bloodhound. Within the past ten years, Solis America membership fell from 50 volunteers to 2. Most of the departed members no longer believed Bane to be a threat to humanity.

Across the Atlantic Ocean, Solis Europe appeared healthy, but only if one compared their total membership count to Solis America. Bane's regional cult there, the Unas, murdered Solis Europe members one by one, and replacements trickled in at a snail's pace. To describe the Unas as bloodthirsty barbarians would be an understatement. Their infatuation with death transformed them into crazed killers. Ritual parties and goth attire served as a continued source of recruitment for fringes of the younger generation. The European public regarded both Solis Europe and the Unas with contempt, labeling them as two cults locked in a bloody feud.

Meanwhile, no one knew what happened to Solis Asia; one day, they stopped responding and hadn't been heard from since. The Sanhetuan Group had their fingers dug into the Asian continent as Bane's regional "support group" there. They operated as reclusive puppet masters from the shadows. Of all the cults, Sanhe proved the hardest to monitor. Over the last hundred years, they became invisible to the Order. If Sanhe ever made contact with the Order's soul-thirsty nemesis, Ordo Solis wouldn't have a way to find out.

Last came the Raptors—a coldblooded cult based in the Americas that messed with Solis America every chance they could. The Raptors used to do silly things like smile and wave into surveillance cameras, set firecrackers off at volunteer homes, and vandalize member vehicles.

Their favorite trick was making the Ordo Solis think Bane had returned. Several years back, they created such a convincing ruse that Solis America initiated the alert sequence to warn the Freemasons and government officials. Journalists uncovered the hoax, and the Order experienced a severe backlash. Most mainstream news organizations published satirical op-eds, and social media ate them alive. The public relations nightmare had yet to end. Steven's cheeks reddened as he recalled memories he'd rather forget.

The Gatekeeper rose from the fireplace chair on video, and Steven swore he saw the guy wink at the camera. Steven gritted his teeth and jabbed the television's off button. The Raptors enjoyed their rivalry with the Ordo Solis like a cat playing with a mouse. Once upon a time, Solis America was the cat, and the various cults of the Bane ran for their lives. Now the cults toyed with the Ordo Solis and, in Solis Europe's case, killed them outright.

We used to be the best of the Order, Steven thought. *Now, we're made a mockery of.*

However relatively harmless Raptor pranks appeared, Steven saw through the ruse. The Raptors believed the Bane would return and prepared themselves for what they viewed as inevitable. Behind the Raptor's silly facade beat a cold heart with terrifying purpose, while the Unas fixated on causing as much havoc as possible, and no one understood Sanhe's motives.

He didn't want to be a part of this game anymore.

Just a little bit longer, for Jeff's sake.

Steven laughed. He needed a vacation from all the crazies.

Chapter 3

The Order of the Disoriented

Steven and Jeff ate Saturday lunch at their usual diner on Lexington and 38th Street. They sat at their favorite red booth near a large window overlooking a busy street. Jeff stood as tall as Michael Jordan. Unlike the basketball champ, Jeff didn't have much meat on his bones, except for the makings of a beer belly. The white handlebar mustache and tired blue eyes showed his age more than the lines on his pale face.

Steven was almost as tall, but with many useless extra pounds all around. He wore his favorite XXL shirt with the original 1960s Star Trek cast. His dark brown hair was pulled back into its usual ponytail, showcasing his smooth caramel-colored skin. Neither man had said a word to the other in the last five minutes. On the table, Steven spun the newspaper he bought on the way to the diner.

He looks exhausted, Steven thought.

Steven had witnessed the pressure take its toll. Jeff's boss demanded he spend less time calling in sick. He spent little time with his young daughter Trista, fought almost every night with his wife Sara, and struggled to pay the mortgage due to the few hours he worked. With the recent volunteer pool dropping from four to two, the time commitment for Jeff and Steven skyrocketed.

Steven didn't blame Raeleigh and Garrett for leaving; they fell in love and decided to move on. Steven wished he'd made the same decision sooner; maybe then he wouldn't feel so guilty about wanting to leave. Jeff struggled to lead the tattered remains of Solis America. Steven would follow him anywhere, but people didn't want to hear about a world-ending myth anymore. Even Wikipedia labeled them as a conspiracy group.

Fortunately, Raeleigh and Garrett stayed long enough to install surveillance in the Raptor's backup rendezvous location. Their visual-only equipment gave them a crude, but effective view into the central area of the bar. At least he and Jeff could continue to monitor the Gatekeeper's unyielding patience for the Bane's return.

When the first meetup spot, Chumley's, closed years back, the Gatekeeper moved around to several sites. It took almost a year of hard investigative work—that none of them were qualified to do—to find the latest meeting place. The closer they got, the more dangerous things became. The Raptors killed Raeleigh and Garrett's dog and set their townhouse on fire. The final straw came when Steven professed his undying love for Raeleigh. Garrett didn't take it well, and his defense mechanism had him proposing to Raeleigh the next day. The newly engaged couple committed to their departure from the Ordo Solis by moving to a small house in Albany, New York, some hours north.

Solis America had so many problems it could've been its own episode of *Jersey Shore*. Steven envisioned just how sensational an episode it'd be, right up to where it ended with humanity's extermination.

Ours is a thankless job, Steven thought.

"So, I watched my days this week. Nothing of note," Jeff muttered, reaching for his black coffee.

"Same."

Jeff took a sip and let out a deep sigh. "What're we doing here, Steven?"

The question caught Steven by surprise. Jeff had proven himself to be the resolute one of the group, always encouraging them to keep the faith. Now his sunken blue eyes and creased face only reflected defeat.

"I…I don't know anymore." Steven picked up one of his fries, then let it clank back down onto the plate. "I've been thinking the same thing." *Maybe this is the out I need. Our mutual agreement to end the fight.*

"I mean, we don't even know if this Satan thing is real."

Steven had never before heard Jeff describe the Bane so nonchalantly. "You're right."

"Perhaps he was at one point." Jeff set his coffee back down, keeping a firm grip on the small black handle. "But after the death of Alexios, there hasn't been one sighting of him. Not one. Maybe that was it. Maybe it all ended with him."

"Yeah, maybe. But then again, if *I* were the Stealer of Souls and had a few hundred failed attempts at conquering the world under my belt, I'd be looking for a change of pace. Hell, I might even go into hiding, bide my time."

He regretted the words as Jeff's face grew stern. The bell attached to the entrance rang. A short blonde woman walked in with her stalky toddler.

"That's what I keep telling myself," Jeff whispered, looking back at Steven. "That the Bane's absence is just a trick. If we stay the course, our faith will be rewarded."

Steven chuckled. "Our faith will be rewarded? How very Raptor-like of you."

Jeff's expression turned sour. "That's not funny, Steven."

Steven shrugged. "Just sayin'."

An awkward silence hung in the air. Steven readjusted his large frame in his chair. "Look, we've been at this a long time. You have a family, and I'm not 24 anymore. Maybe it's time to hang it all up and admit we finally won. We're the only two left. I can't keep going like this."

Jeff looked down at his mug. "What're you saying, Steven?"

"I'm saying…look, Jeff, I'm saying this is a lot of work, and I can't keep it up. I need a break." Steven couldn't help but feel a flash of guilt.

Jeff sat in silence, gazing out at the street as a diesel truck sped past. "How long do you need?"

Steven pursed his lips. "I'm not sure. Maybe a week, a month. Maybe forever."

Jeff's shoulders drooped. "Well, if that's how you feel."

"Aw, c'mon Jeff. This's been coming for a while. Just admit it: we won. The Stealer of Souls is no more."

"I never understood why you called it that, the 'Stealer of Souls.'"

"Cuz that's what it does—it steals people's souls. At least it used to, until we killed King Alexios and it exploded out of his body. It stopped coming back ever since. We exiled the thing, destroyed it, shattered it, ruined it, whatever term you want to use. It's gone."

I don't even know if I believe that, Steven admitted to himself. He didn't know who he was trying to convince...Jeff or himself.

Jeff lowered his head. "You don't know that." Jeff glanced up. "Satan cannot be destroyed, and I still don't think he'd allow his champion to disappear forever."

Steven exhaled. "We've been over this. The only reason the Ordo Solis is still active is because of those lunatics hoping to help it rise again. Which they can't, because the Bane is dead."

"What if you're wrong?" Jeff released his mug and picked up his fork, pushing the untouched lettuce on his plate back and forth.

"Then the world will end someday, which it will anyway. There's a thousand ways for Earth to die off. So let's just enjoy what time we have left. We've done our part." Steven folded his arms across his chest as he leaned back.

"Nine hundred and ninety-nine."

Steven tilted his head. "What?"

"I said...nine hundred and ninety-nine. That's how many ways the world could end if we stay true to our oath. One less than a thousand." Jeff looked up, locking eyes.

"Aw, don't give me that."

Jeff held up his hand. "You swore."

"I remember."

"You *swore!*"

Steven clenched his hand into a fist. "I know!" Immediately, he felt everyone inside the diner stare at their table. Steven shook his head, looking out the window. "But it's too hard now, Jeff. We're by ourselves, and I need to get away from all this."

"Okayyyyyy. How about this: you take some time off and think about if your oath still means anything to you. If it does, come back when you're ready. If it doesn't, then I'll have nothing left but to convince you to never again ride that fugly Harley-imitation you've double-parked outside." Jeff motioned to the glass. "I mean, seriously Steven, how's that even possible?"

They both managed a laugh.

Now there's *my Jeff,* Steven thought.

"Fine," Steven muttered with a sigh. "I'll take some time away. Then make my decision."

Jeff nodded. "Where will you go?"

Steven looked out at his Victory Hammer S. He affectionately dubbed it "the Anvil" after accidentally ramming it into a parked cop car the day he got the bike. He got so scared, he whipped around and gunned down Interstate 95. He got lost for almost half the day and still didn't know how he avoided getting caught.

Damn, I love that bike.

"Dunno, but that's the point," Steven said. "I'm gonna take some vacation days and just ride. No schedule, no worries. Just me, the Anvil, and a whole lot of road."

Jeff smiled. "Fair enough. I'll see ya when you get back?"

"Yeah, I'll see you on the flip side."

Jeff looked at Steven's shirt. "A nerd Trekkie biker. You're a walking contradiction."

"If I'm the contradiction, then you're the walking stereotype. A 40-something-year-old bald guy with a potbelly, spouting all sorts of 'the boogieman's out to get you' conspiracy stuff." He wrung his hands in mock hysteria.

Jeff's sharp laugh cut through all the muffled conversations in the cracked vinyl booths around them. "Yeah, we're all something weird. Let's just hope it stays that way."

CHAPTER 4

A SIGHT UNSEEN

"That's just great, Jeff!" Sara's voice grew louder as her hazel eyes filled with tears. "You promised Trista you'd read to her tonight, and here you are watching your videos again!"

Jeff swiveled his chair toward her, eyes wide. "Okay, okay. I'm going." He stood and headed out of the room.

Sara threw her hands up, tears streaming down. Her auburn hair was twisted in a tired bun with loose strands that threatened to unravel at any moment. "Don't bother," she choked out. "I already did."

She turned to leave, but Jeff grabbed her arm. She jerked out of his grasp, shoving her index finger in his face. "*Don't*...just don't. I can't do this anymore, Jeff. You *promised*." She spun around and marched to their bedroom.

Jeff stood in the doorway. Every year he gave the Order resulted in more time demanded of him. His service to the Order stretched almost two decades, proving to be the costliest period of his commitment. Ever since Raeleigh and Garrett left the Order, it fell to Jeff to spend more time watching footage and writing reports. Fights with Sara intensified. Their daughter, Trista, was just old enough to realize parents screaming at each other meant something bad.

Trista's innocent questions broke his heart. What do you say to a seven-year-old girl who asks, "Daddy, why are you and Mommy shouting?" Jeff didn't know how to answer, just like he didn't know what to do with Sara. He considered the Order's mission of utmost importance. Sara accused him of prioritizing the Order over family. Of *course* he loved his family more, but why couldn't she see that he protected them from a dangerous enemy?

Sara treated his involvement with the Order as someone who would treat a child in the Boy Scouts, one she expected him to "grow out of." She voiced her objections when he didn't, claiming he spent too much time doing Solis stuff. He and Steven needed to keep tabs on the Raptors, keep in touch with Solis Europe, attempt to find someone who could rebuild Solis Asia, fundraise, and liaise with the Grand Encampment of the Knights Templar. Some days, he came home from work only to grind through Ordo Solis tasks until he fell asleep.

Jeff rubbed his eyes, returned to his chair, and spent the next few hours reviewing surveillance. He fast-forwarded through most of yesterday's recording, resuming during the 8:30 to 9:30 evening window to watch the Gatekeeper sit by the fire.

It made it difficult with zero audio and only two camera angles. The first perspective spanned the fireplace and bar, the second from the other side of the room in full view of the VIP entrance behind a bookcase. The owners maintained a strict access list to the VIP section, and the Order no longer had the professional expertise it needed to get inside undetected. Jeff counted them lucky the Gatekeeper kept to the fireplace.

After finally catching up and reviewing today's footage, Jeff turned off the television. He glanced at the clock, wrote "1 AM - nothing of note" in his notebook, and ambled to their bedroom. Sara lay asleep, facing away from him. A pile of crumpled tissues sat on the nightstand. Jeff's heart wrenched as he sat on the edge of the bed, watching Sara's chest rise and fall. Seeing her at peace calmed his shot nerves. He leaned over and outstretched his arm across the king-sized bed to caress her head.

Maybe she's right, Jeff thought. *Perhaps it's time to pack it in.* Solis Asia no longer existed, and each person had their own guess as to how long Solis Europe remained afloat.

We're dying. Some within the Order considered it dead already. Their enemy's leader, Bane, disappeared eight hundred years ago. The world concerned itself with other threats.

Jeff didn't like abandoning something he'd devoted half his life to, but he was a hair's breadth away from losing his family. In the end, what did he consider more important...the Order or his family? Jeff was dismayed he even needed to ask the question.

Chapter 5

Something Comes

Though she didn't believe him, Jeff promised Sara he'd read to Trista tonight, taking no more than two hours reviewing surveillance. He worked his schedule to spend the first hour watching the Gatekeeper in real-time as he arrived, and the second hour emailing and speeding through the day's feed.

The Gatekeeper came into view as Jeff's doorbell rang. Jeff stepped out of his office and got to the door in time to see Sara peering through the peephole. She scowled at Jeff as she opened it, revealing Steven dressed in a Star Trek t-shirt, leather jacket, steel-toed boots, jeans, and a ridiculous purple bandanna around his neck.

Steven waved. "Hi, Sara."

"Steven." She glared at Jeff. "Two hours, Jeff, and not *one* minute more."

Steven grinned and made a whip-cracking motion with widening eyes as Sara returned to the living room.

"Yeah," Jeff muttered, "I'm lucky I'm still in the house. Come on in. I'm watching the Gatekeeper."

"Sweet!" Steven followed Jeff back into the office, setting his backpack down and pulling up a stool while Jeff returned to his chair. They huddled around the television. "Man, we haven't done this in a while."

Jeff cracked a smile. "Yeah, it's been months since we've had a good ole fashioned sit-down. Aren't you supposed to be out cruising the wild?"

Steven shrugged while glancing about the office; empty wrappers and gadgets strewn about. "I was in the neighborhood. I'm still on my vacation time though, so I'll be headed back out for parts unknown."

Jeff nudged him. "You were feeling guilty."

Steven tilted his head. "Yeah, maybe a little. But I was serious when I said that I needed some time away from all this s***. The open road is the open road, and I got an urge I need to satisfy." Steven pumped his fists and rocked his hips.

Jeff laughed while tucking away some unpaid bills on his desk.

"I decided to go south to the Carolinas," Steven continued. "Through Tennessee and Missouri, then Ohio and back here. Tomorrow I'll head out north, possibly all the way to Canuck-land. Who knows? I'll figure it out when I get there."

"Meanwhile…" Jeff began.

"Meanwhile, you're fightin' the good fight," Steven added in a southern accent while eyeing the television. The Gatekeeper lounged in a brown leather chair, watching the fire as he did every day. A small table stood to his immediate right and another leather chair on the other side. His black leather fedora rested on the middle table.

Forty minutes into the video, a young man approached the Gatekeeper. Jeff leaned forward, snatched a notepad and mini pen from his back pocket, and scribbled notes on the paper.

Steven scrutinized the unfolding scene. "Easy, killer, just watch."

The young man tried to sit before jerking still. He stood back up.

"I wish we had audio," Jeff muttered.

"Shhh, just watch." Steven strained to read their lips. The camera angles shot out both ways from the fireplace, giving them the perfect view. The Gatekeeper and his new friend began a conversation. Then the young man grabbed hold of the fedora and set it on his head, tapping the edge.

"Holy s***," Jeff said. "That's the Gatekeeper's hat. He either knows exactly what he's doing, or he has a death wish."

"Mmmhm, we'll see."

They knew what would happen after the Gatekeeper verified the Soulstealer's identity. They had learned about the procedure back when a much stronger Solis America infiltrated the Raptor's former headquarters in Boston. Still, they could only guess at what words the two exchanged. The Raptors guarded the secret with a foolproof method: memorization.

The young man sat in the chair, back erect, and continued their dialogue. He took the Gatekeeper's hat off and returned it to the table, tapping it again. The newcomer said something else, prompting the Gatekeeper to snatch his fedora, stand, and stride toward the VIP section.

The young man made no motion to follow, which they knew wasn't part of the procedure unless the exchange failed. When the Gatekeeper left the room, the young man exited the bar the way he came.

Steven frowned. "That's different."

"What just happened?" Jeff asked.

"Looks like a failed attempt."

"Yeah, but the guy knew what to do."

"Or he was just a dumb drunk. It's probably the Raptors messing with us again."

"How could they know we're still watching them?"

Steven gave Jeff a long look. "Jeff, they've probably been in your house a dozen times this year alone. I'm pretty sure they know."

Jeff drew back, his voice trembling. "That's not funny, Steven. I have a little girl in this house." His eyes darted around the room as paranoia enveloped him.

"C'mon Jeff, they're the Raptors. They have dossiers on every one of us, down to what kind of ice cream we like. We've been playing Spy vs. Spy since we figured out they supported the Soulstealer."

"Is that your new name for it, the Soulstealer?"

"Catchy, isn't it? I came up with it on the ride back. Sounds a lot better than 'Stealer of Souls,' or 'Dracula.' And Satan."

Jeff rolled his eyes. "I guess. We need to get this to Raeleigh; she was always the best when it came to lip-reading." He accessed his laptop and transferred the footage to a thumb drive.

"Think she'll help?"

Jeff nodded. "Yeah, yeah. Something like this…yup."

"Okay. I'll do it. I'm riding through Albany tomorrow anyways."

"I bet, but you sure that's a good idea? The last time Garrett saw you, he was about to punch you for telling Raeleigh she should leave him for you."

Steven leaned back in his chair. "I'll admit I got a little carried away, but it's the truth. Garrett is a douche-nozzle; Raeleigh and I make a better couple than they ever will."

"They're getting married mid-next month."

"Semantics. In any case, I'll take it to them, drop it off, and that'll be that. Easy."

"Fine. In and out, no more issues. We need their help."

"We need *her* help," Steven corrected. "Garrett is, and always has been, useless."

"Whatever. I can pick it up if need be."

"No need, I'll be driving past them on my way back down."

Jeff rubbed his eyes. "I need it a little bit sooner than 'whenever.'"

"Alright, I'll come back before the weekend is over. A couple days should give her enough time to decipher the conversation."

"Fine, just let me know when you've dropped it off, okay?" Jeff handed Steven a thumb drive.

"What? No comms muted? I thought this qualified!"

Jeff considered the Solis Protocol in silence. "Yeah, I suppose you're right. We should really update those procedures. I'm pretty sure the Raptors can't hack WhatsApp."

Steven shrugged. "You never know. Alrighty, I'm heading out. I'll see you when I—wait, can you transfer a copy to mine as well?" He reached into his backpack and pulled out a thumb drive. "I'd like to take a crack at it while I'm on the road."

Jeff hooked the device up to his computer and transferred the file. "Get it to her quick, please. I'll call ahead so that they know you're coming."

"No problemo. I'll see you when I get back." Steven stood and headed to the door with Jeff close behind.

Steven opened the door and looked back. "Jeff, do me a favor. Don't watch it again. Go spend time with Sara. I know you'll be going crazy over the footage, and if that really is the Soulstealer, he'll try again soon. You'll have enough to worry about."

Jeff put his hands on his hips and glanced out the window, his brow furrowed. "We don't even know if he failed though. That could've been it."

"I watched the Gatekeeper's mouth very carefully. He was supposed to say something before he took his hat, and the Soulstealer is supposed to follow him. They're very particular about *that* process."

"But they could've changed it, they—"

"They couldn't have changed it because the Soulstealer only knows the exchange that he *allegedly* taught them. That's the one thing they can't avoid. Just calm down and wait until I get back with Raeleigh's transcript."

Jeff stroked his pepper-colored mustache, eyes glazed over.

"Jeff," Steven said.

"Hmm?"

"Sara."

"Right, Sara. See you soon, Steven."

After Steven left, Jeff closed the door. He turned around and leaned against it, putting a hand to his pounding chest. He couldn't tell which fueled him more: the excitement or fear. Performing the day-to-day tasks made it easy to forget the seriousness of their mission. Now reality hit him full force as the unmistakable signs required he treat this as a serious threat.

Jeff tried to dismiss the thought, remembering Sara. The words from their marriage counselor echoed in his mind. "Be present," he whispered. He wished it was as easy as that.

CHAPTER 6

RUN LIKE THE WIND

Steven sped the three hours to Albany. With little to distract him at 11 at night, his mind wandered to one of his favorite memories of Raeleigh, when he had somehow convinced her to accompany him to a gun range.

"Why again are we doing this?" she had asked, peering up at Steven as they walked through the gun range parking lot. Her blonde hair fell straight past her shoulders.

"Because Jeff said it would be a good idea if we all knew how to handle a gun..." he lied. "Just in case."

Raeleigh's dark brown eyes squinted in amusement. "A-huh..."

He didn't even try to focus on the gun safety attendant, who was sporting a red polo as he covered the basics. It couldn't be that hard, and he remained far more interested in his companion, who listened attentively. He liked that about her; she always enjoyed learning something new.

When it came time to handle their rented handguns, Steven squinted at the heavy metal object, but saw it as an opportunity. "So, what you want to do—"

He was cut off by the *cha-cheen-kuh* sound of Raeleigh's gun, followed by a series of *pops* as the barrel spit fire. He watched in amazement. When her rounds were spent, she inspected the chamber and dropped the magazine like it was a walk in the park.

She winked at him. Before he knew it, her soft hands were on his. "So, what you want to do is, move your thumb and palm to rest under the slide, like this…"

"How…How did you—"

"My dad used to take me shooting all the time," she said, adjusting Steven's fingers to rest in parallel under the slide. "That looks good." She took a step back.

Steven peeled his eyes off her and glanced down at his weapon. He knew enough to realize he had to cock it next, but he would rather die than ask Raeleigh how to do that.

Realizing he should have paid more attention, his nerves kicked in as he fumbled over the top of the gun.

Raeleigh giggled and stepped closer. "Like this." She gripped the top back of the slide near the serrations and pulled it back with a *cha*. She let it go, and the slide slammed to a stop with a *cheen-kuh*.

Steven considered that their first date, though he was quite sure she didn't agree.

His chopper pulled up to the quiet neighborhood where Raeleigh and Garrett had bought their house. Steven rolled his eyes at the mani-cured grass and literal white picket fence. The only thing that looked like it came from Raeleigh was the pink rose garden by the front porch. As Steven approached the door, Garrett "greeted" him from the porch swing.

"Just give me the thing and be on your way," Garrett sneered. His short brown hair was styled like a fifth-grader who used way too much gel.

"Nope. Strict orders. We're here for Raeleigh's expertise, not yours. Speaking of which, what exactly *was* your expertise? Never quite figured that one out."

Garret's nostrils flared, and his lips curled back. Though at five-foot-three, Garrett couldn't do much except glare at Steven's towering frame. Steven always thought Garrett acted territorial out of insecurity, the typical short guy's need to compensate. He glowered as Steven pressed the doorbell.

Raeleigh answered a moment later, her blonde hair pulled back into a loose ponytail. She sported a black Journey t-shirt with cut-off jean shorts, revealing untanned legs. Her lips were a natural light pink, mesmerizing him as she spoke. "Hi, Steven." She stole a glance at her fiancé. "Jeff told us you were coming."

Garrett huffed as he resumed swinging. "Another one of those stupid a** cult tricks."

"Just a bit of lip-reading is all we're asking," Steven said. "I'll be back in a couple days to retrieve your analysis, and that'll be that."

She smirked. "Just a couple of days? How uncharacteristically gracious of you."

Steven matched her smile. "To make sure it's extra thorough."

"Mmmkay. Shouldn't be a problem."

Garrett laughed. "Shouldn't be a problem? We stopped helping them for a reason—"

"Garrett, you were never any help to begin with," Steven countered, howling with laughter. "Raeleigh, on the other hand, is sorely missed. Her talent is second to none." He resisted the urge to wink at her.

In and out, he reminded himself.

Garrett stood and strode closer. "What exactly do you hope to gain by doing this?"

"Oh, I don't know. Maybe save the world?"

"Against a make-believe boogie man."

"If by 'make-believe' you mean a verified historical phenomenon, then yes."

"What'll you do with it?"

"Same thing as last time: warn the others." Steven straightened himself to his full height, making the difference between them even more apparent.

"They won't believe you. Where're you going?"

Steven shrugged. "Wherever I want."

"Are there more copies?"

"Of course. Jeff has the original."

"Yeah, but do *you* have any more copies?"

"You're always asking the wrong question, Garrett."

"Alright, you two," Raeleigh interjected, holding her hand out to Steven. He placed the drive in her soft palm. "Thank you. I'll have it done by the time you get back."

Steven smiled and was slow to drop his hand from hers. "Cool.

Thanks, Raeleigh. You da best." He headed back to his motorcycle and climbed aboard, the leather creaking as he sat. "By the way," he called out. "Congratulations on the engagement. I'm sure that eventually, one day, maybe, you'll be happy."

He swore Raeleigh rolled her eyes as he cranked the bike. Smoke puffed out of the exhaust, and a roar echoed throughout the neighborhood.

She gets it. Oh, how I love that woman.

CHAPTER 7

NOW YOU SEE US...

Jeff couldn't hold back the anticipation any longer. He spent most of his Saturday with Sara and Trista, so Sara indulged his request, giving him three hours to what Jeff hoped would be round two of the young man completing the exchange.

He took way more time than needed drafting an email to the Solis Commandery—the Ordo Solis' headquarters in Europe. Jeff realized he should only send the message after analyzing every second of those videos, as he had made the opposite decision several years before with disastrous results.

I'll figure it out once I see you get accepted, Jeff thought.

He sat in front of the TV wearing his favorite blue jeans and least favorite shirt. Sara had bought it for him and said it was salmon-colored. Jeff still swore it was pink, but he wore it today in hopes it'd make her smile. He glanced at the wall clock—8:00 PM on the dot. Jeff's fingernails dug into the desk while he waited for 8:30. Right on schedule, the Gate-keeper arrived. About ten seconds later, the young man approached him. Jeff wanted to jump up and down.

"C'mon, let's go, boy! Tell the Gatekeeper what he wants to hear," he urged the television. They went through the exact same sequence the night before, but the young man appeared more confident this time.

The young man set the hat on the table and said something, causing the Gatekeeper to narrow his eyes. He picked up his hat and put it on, proceeding to the bookcase door. The young man followed the Gatekeeper into the VIP section, and the bookcase swung closed behind them.

Jeff stared at the screen, dumbfounded, before fumbling for his laptop. "Focus!"

He navigated to the newly minted video file, attaching it to the draft email.

The computer *dinged*, indicating the task was completed, and he heard a knock at the front door. His head jerked toward the sound, only to be greeted by a pistol barrel in his face. A figure wearing a mask depicting a face twisted in agony held the weapon.

Jeff's heart sank, and his face paled; he recognized the mask worn by the Raptors.

"Answer the door," the figure said. His voice sounded artificial, as if altered by some sort of mouthpiece filter. The Raptor stepped closer when Jeff didn't move and pressed the silencer muzzle against Jeff's forehead.

His mind paralyzed with fear, Jeff stood and inched his way toward the office room door. A sharp jab from the muzzle rewarded his efforts, an invitation to pick up the pace.

Time slowed as Jeff walked the few feet to the front door. He looked back at the Raptor in the office doorway, weapon pointed his direction. Jeff's felt the entire neighborhood heard his shaking fingers as they reached for the copper knob. Before he could turn it, the door opened and six or so Raptors forced their way in…each wearing a mask with the face twisted in agony, rage, or despair.

Jeff's vision blurred; his knees buckled. A few moments ago, he discovered an extraordinary secret, like Robert Langdon in *The Da Vinci Code*. He forgot about Langdon getting chased by the secret's deadly guardians.

CHAPTER 8

THE RED HOUSE

Jeff shifted against the duct tape binding him to his living room chair. Sara and Trista sobbed through their gags. Every struggle from his sweet Trista caused Jeff to fall apart that much more.

The six Raptors circled around them. Others went about the house, gently turning items over and breaking things; pictures, chairs, and baskets.

One of the Raptors stepped forward, brandishing a jagged knife. He wove the blade through the air closer to Trista's face, then to Sara's neck. Jeff thrashed against his bindings, shouting through his gag. Another Raptor approached Jeff and put his index finger to his lips in a "shh" motion, while pointing a handgun at Sara's face.

"Mmm-mmm-mmmmmm," Jeff groaned. "Mmm-mmm-mmmmmmm!"

The Raptor behind Jeff relaxed the cloth. "Yes, okay. You have me. What do you want?" Jeff blurted.

"Slow down, Jeff," the Raptor in front of him said. "We'll need to have a cordial conversation if you and your family are to get out of this alive." He guessed she was a woman, even with the mouth filter digitizing her voice.

"I understand. I understand. Just tell me what it is—"

The Raptor holding the knife slashed Sara's lower thigh. Both Trista and Sara's screams were muffled by the gags in their mouths. Trista's petrified stare remained frozen on her mother's leg. Blood seeped through Sara's grey sweatpants and began trickling onto the hardwood floor beneath them. The one standing in front of Jeff clamped her hand over his lips, stifling his cries.

"I *need* you to lower your voice. I won't tell you again."

Sara whimpered in pain. Her eyes looked like she was elsewhere, trying to escape her horrifying reality. Jeff thrashed his head up and down. The Raptor let him go, taking a step back.

Jeff breathed in and out, attempting to calm his panic. "Okay, I'm listening."

"I don't need you to listen," the female Raptor replied, "I need you to talk. How many copies of yesterday's footage are there?"

"Just two. The copy on my laptop and the thumb drive I gave to my colleague."

Jeff's interrogator nodded, and the Raptor in front of Sara slashed her thigh above the first injury. Sara gave a muted scream, her face drenched in tears. Trista's stare moved from her mother's wounds to the crimson knife.

"I need you to be specific, Jeff. Your colleague, Steven, yes?"

"Yes! That's it, that's all there is! Just two copies!" Jeff lied.

The Raptor said nothing for a few seconds. "And how many copies of *today's* footage?"

"Two! The first on my laptop, and the second on the thumb drive!"

"Who have you told about the first contact yesterday and today?"

"No one today, and only Steven and Raeleigh yesterday. I haven't sent the email to the Order; it's still in draft on my laptop." Jeff wished he had pressed send.

"We know. Where did Steven go?"

Jeff paused, but as soon as the female Raptor glanced at Sara, Jeff called out. "Wait! Steven was taking the thumb drive to two other coll—I mean, to Raeleigh and Garrett."

"How long ago?"

"He left last night." Jeff noticed she didn't ask where they lived.

Two Raptors entered the living room, one carrying Jeff's laptop and his notes, the other carrying most of his surveillance equipment.

"Okay, everything checks out," Jeff's interrogator said. "Let's make it more convincing, then our work is done." The Raptors scattered about the house, continuing to trash it in silence. Five minutes later, they gathered back into the living room.

"Is he done yet?" she called out. A tall, hulking Raptor entered, carrying a box full of their valuables.

Jeff panicked. *They want to make it look like a robbery. Which means…*

Jeff struggled against his bindings, feeling the burn of the duct tape rub his skin raw.

"Let's go," the female Raptor said. The hulking Raptor dropped the box and approached Sara, unsheathing his knife. Jeff started rocking his chair.

"Wait!" he cried. "Wait!" Tears blurred his vision. He tried to blink them away, desperate to see his girls. *They can't die. Please God, don't let them die.*

Someone behind him put the cloth back in his mouth. The big Raptor made quick work of Sara's bindings, cutting them all loose. The Raptor picked Sara up and slung her over his shoulder, walking back toward their bedroom. Sara did her best to twist and turn, beating on his back, but the Raptor didn't even flinch. Trista's desperate eyes alternated between her father and mother.

"Jeff, it's best that you tell Trista to close her eyes," his interrogator said.

Hot tears soaked Jeff's cheeks. Before he could speak, the female Raptor drove her blade into his stomach. Sara and Trista cried out to him. The big Raptor handled Sara's boy shorts as he carried her away, pulling them off and letting them fall. As his body convulsed, he craned his neck to see his daughter. A Raptor closed in behind her, a stiletto in hand.

Jeff held his daughter's gaze, refusing to abandon her. He never imagined he or his family would pay the ultimate price. Here he sat, the last of Solis America, about to be obliterated. The Soulstealer had returned with no one to sound the alarm. It finally won.

The images in his brain fogged, and his thoughts slowed. *My…entire… adult life. We…were supposed…to win.* His thoughts ground to a halt as his body lurched forward, staring into the mask of the female Raptor.

"We rise further," one of the Raptors said.

"We rise further!" she echoed with the others, breathing into his face. "We rise again."

CHAPTER 9

RAINS OF STATEN

Steven sped toward Albany, having explored the back roads of the northern United States. He felt re-energized, but still not back to normal. Jeff needed him back in the Ordo Solis, even if they all believed it was just a token cause.

In his rush to leave the small bed and "no breakfast" this morning, he forgot to pick up a printed newspaper. He veered off at the next exit and stopped at the nearest gas station. He picked up the latest edition of the *New York Times*. The headline read something about the President, a nuclear deal, and a multiple-family homicide in Staten Island.

*The world can be a s***y place sometimes.*

He waited in line, glancing over at CNN, streaming headlines of a series of murders on Staten Island. As he drew closer, his stomach sank. He recognized the New Springville homes, where Jeff lived. His eyes slid down to the newspaper in hand, trembling as he peeled it open and turned to the article on the murders.

Sprawled across the top in imposing bold print, read "4 Families Slain by Serial Burglar."

The NYPD is searching for an unknown number of assailants after a killing spree left 12 people dead on Saturday night. Police say invaders, searching for valuables, killed all residents in each of the three townhouses. The assailants targeted homes on Klondike Avenue, south of Willowbrook Park. Police are still investigating possible motives. A spokesperson with the 120th precinct said while police have no suspects or eyewitnesses, they are pursuing every clue and source. The victims' identities are being withheld as authorities notify next of kin. Among the dead were a young couple, two teenagers, and a seven-year-old girl.

Steven's numb fingers dropped the newspaper. *There's no way this is a coincidence.* They witness the first possible contact with the Soulstealer in almost a thousand years, and now Jeff and his entire family were dead?

Calm down. You're not even sure it was them.

Yet his mind raced. They witnessed the new Soulstealer on Friday night. The Raptors didn't want it getting out, so they eliminated everyone involved.

Steven bolted outside and jumped on his motorcycle, freezing as he inserted the key.

They're not amateurs. If they got Jeff, then a day later is too long not to nab Raeleigh. There's no reason she should still be there.

Steven grimaced.

Unless...it wasn't really Jeff's family who was targeted. Or some burglars randomly selected them.

Still, the description of the family with a young girl on Klondike Avenue remained a coincidence at best.

What do I do...what do I do? Should I ride to Raeleigh's? Jeff's?

Steven's hand went to his pocket, tracing the edge of the backup thumb drive containing the only sure footage of the new Soulstealer. He could *not* let it fall into the hands of the Raptors, who'd make sure it never saw the light of day.

Steven interrupted his own train of thought and smacked his forehead. *Call them both, duh.*

He whipped out his cell phone but fumbled through the app screen to access his recording app, then dialed Jeff's number. It rang until he heard Jeff's voice telling him to leave a message. He dialed Sara's number, which went to straight voicemail. He texted Jeff and Sara: *Saw the news, call me NOW!!!!!*

He scrolled to Raeleigh's number and hovered over the call button.

He finally pressed "call." It rang several times until Raeleigh's soft voice answered.

"Steven."

"Raeleigh! Did you see the news?"

"Yes." She sniffled.

"Was it them?"

"I don't know. I haven't been able to reach them."

"Raeleigh, if it was them, then you're in trouble. They'll come for you next. You need to get out of there."

"Garrett said we'll be fine. He said he chose our location carefully and—"

"Garrett is a grade-A idiot if he thinks the Raptors don't know where you are! These guys aren't going to allow that video to remain intact. They'll come after it and whoever has it. Forget about Garrett's *dumb a*** sense of safety; the Raptors aren't playing around." He lowered his voice. "Raeleigh…please."

"I…Garrett said if you called, he wanted to speak to you."

"What? Why the hell does he—"

Garrett's annoying voice came through. "Steven."

"What."

"When are you coming back to the house?"

"I'm not sure, nor do I plan on saying over this unsecure line. I'll get there when I get there."

"This isn't the time to be wandering on your own."

"Oh, so now you believe in all the 'make-believe' stuff."

"When people start dying, yes, I take it seriously."

"If you take it so seriously, why would you tell Raeleigh you're safe in that house? You can't believe the Raptors don't know where you are."

"I told her that to make her feel safe. Besides, the murders happened last night. Don't you think they'd have come after us by now?"

What the hell is wrong with this guy? But he has a point. Do they really not know?

Steven contemplated a few explanations, none of which comforted him, nor led him to think Garrett was anything but an idiot.

"Tell you what," Garrett continued. "Come by the house. Raeleigh has her transcript ready. You'll get here, she'll give it to you, you can see everyone's fine, and then you can be on your way."

Why're you trying so hard to get me to come to you? Steven wondered. *Let's test the waters.*

"Thanks, but I'm going far away. I recommend you and Raeleigh do the same."

"C'mon, Steven, don't you want to know what the exchange was all about? And I thought you cared about Raeleigh?"

"Of course I do, but she's in your very capable hands. Besides, I can get anyone to transcribe the words off the video."

"I thought you said Jeff and Raeleigh had the only copies?"

*S***! Why'd I say that?* Steven tried to recover. "Yeah, when I get Raeleigh's copy back, I'll find someone who can do it and—"

"Which means you need to come back here first."

Steven shook his head. "No, I'm not coming back. Give Raeleigh my best. Bye, Garrett."

"Steven, don't you care if Raeleigh lives or dies?"

Steven's stomach lurched. He held his breath as his mind reeled. "That's a stupid question, and you already know the answer."

"Then come back."

"What the hell are you saying?"

"I'll put it for you simply." Garrett cleared his throat. "We rise further."

A sharp click followed, then a dial tone. He gaped at his phone in disbelief. Rage coursed through him, but he clung to the logical side of his brain and accessed the voice recorder app still running, sending the sound bite to his email. Zero doubt remained about the Raptors removing all trace of the Soulstealer's return.

Now he faced a tough decision. Save Raeleigh, or warn the world?

CHAPTER 10

WITH OR WITHOUT

Tell the world the Soulstealer made its return…or save Raeleigh from murdering fanatics. Steven only felt enough courage to choose one. The Raptors likely set up an ambush for Steven as soon as he arrived at Raeleigh's house, and counted himself fortunate he had called ahead.

Steven rode his motorcycle south on Interstate 87, toward Albany. The road continued for another ten miles before he either took a left to Raeleigh's or merged right to New York.

His head reasoned that he should warn the world, but his heart demanded he rescue Raeleigh. The longer he thought about it, the more his head prevailed, though he hated himself for even considering abandoning the only woman he could ever say he loved.

There won't be anyone left on Earth to love if you make the wrong decision. Okay then, onward to the Templars.

Steven harbored no illusion; he faced an uphill battle. This wouldn't be the first time Solis America thought the Soulstealer had returned. Several years before, a Raptor ploy convinced Solis America to implore the Templars to sound the alarm, and they did. After the hoax became obvious, journalists worldwide ate them for breakfast. Steven's only saving grace was the millennium-old oath sworn to kill the Soulstealer by the survivors of King Philip's Friday the 13th; now the modern-day Knights Templar of the Freemasons.

He hoped the Gatekeeper video, the news clippings about Jeff's murder, and Garrett's unwitting corroboration proved enough to cause them to take him seriously once more.

One could hope.

CHAPTER 11

CRY WOLF

A few days later, Steven stepped inside an old elevator inside a nondescript brown office building off highway 610 in Bellaire, Texas, and pushed the number four. After what felt like an eternity, the rickety elevator came to a bouncing stop and opened its doors. He stepped out and walked toward one of the suite doors and knocked. An elderly gentleman opened the door, wearing dark blue trousers and a crisp white collared shirt under a grey sweater. A look of irritation swept his clean-shaven face. His bald head had a thin layer of sweat, making it shine under the fluorescent lights. Small oval glasses balanced on his thin pointed nose.

"Mr. Carpenter," he deadpanned.

"Hello again, Mr. Tucker." Steven waved.

"What can I help you with?" Mr. Tucker replied, though he didn't seem keen on helping Steven with anything.

"I've something for you to see."

Mr. Tucker pursed his lips. "I'm hesitant to look at anything you give me, Steven. My predecessor did, and it was the poorest decision he made while holding this office. We were made a mockery."

Steven nodded. "I understand that, Mr. Tucker. But if there's *any* part of you that believes the Soulstealer...I mean, the Bane, has a chance of returning, *this* is the time to listen...please."

Mr. Tucker exhaled a prolonged sigh and walked back inside, leaving the door open. Steven entered and locked the door behind him. They went back into an inner office. Faded pictures of past prominent members hung in inconsistent places throughout the office, and a white feathered cavalry hat rested on the edge of his desk.

"You realize," Mr. Tucker began, "that many, even in the Templars, no longer believe the Bane was ever real."

"Yes, I realize that."

"Please sit." Mr. Tucker motioned to a chair across his desk. Steven sat as Mr. Tucker took his time seating himself in the creaky timeworn chair. "What do you have this time?"

Steven reached in his pocket and withdrew the backup thumb drive, printed transcript, and torn-out *New York Times* article about the Staten Island murders. He slid them across the maple desk. Mr. Tucker glanced down at the thumb drive, then back to Steven. He skimmed over the transcript and read the news article as he inserted the device into his laptop.

On the long road to Texas, Steven had stopped at a dozen or so places until he found someone to transcribe the silent exchange in the video. He tried his best not to think about Raeleigh, going so far as to turn his phone off at the beginning of the trip. He still hated himself for abandoning her to the Raptors.

Mr. Tucker set the paper back down on the desk and turned his attention to the laptop. He clicked a few keys, and Raeleigh's hesitant voice came through the speakers. Mr. Tucker considered the conversation without a change in expression. He glanced at Steven when Garrett made his comment about taking things seriously when people die.

When the clip ended, Mr. Tucker studied Steven a few moments before responding. "I assume the murders described in the article are what the other gentleman was referring to?"

"Jeff," Steven tried to say, his voice cracking.

"Ahhh," Mr. Tucker said. "The family with the small girl." Steven nodded. Mr. Tucker's expression softened. "I am truly sorry to hear that." He cleared his throat. "But I must ask—and forgive me if I'm insulting Jeff's memory—but how do you know the two events are related?"

"There's no way they aren't. We see a verifiable exchange between the

Gatekeeper and an unknown person, then suddenly the Raptors kill Jeff and his family."

"The article says his family was murdered by burglars, as were three other families—"

"Yes, but…I was thinking about that on the ride here. The Raptors do *not* want to draw attention to themselves, nor make investigators curious about Jeff's role as a member of the Ordo Solis. Nor could they let Jeff keep his surveillance footage, which clearly shows who the new Soulstealer is. So they disguised the assassination as criminal activity."

"I see. And for my sanity, the Soulstealer is your word for the Bane?"

"Yeah. It describes its purpose perfectly." Steven felt himself growing frustrated. "Now Jeff is dead, they tried to bait me back into their grasp, and I've no idea what the Raptors have done with Raeleigh. But what I *do* know, Lawrence, is they've gone to extreme measures to keep this secret. It goes far beyond a trick. They tried to *cover this up*." Steven thudded his finger onto the furnished table.

Mr. Tucker raised his hand. "Please, calm yourself, Steven. I understand this is a highly charged time for you, but maintain your focus. We must continue our frank discussion."

Steven breathed deeply, trying to settle his emotions.

"This has happened before, Steven. It's not the first time the Raptors have pretended their leader has returned."

"I realize that, but the last time there was no verifiable evidence that an exchange occurred, and I have a bit more than hearsay to show the Raptors are seriously reacting to this."

"Yes. This is true. But as heartless as this may sound, what makes you believe this isn't another attempt? No matter how convincing or low they stoop, it could be another ruse."

"It could be, but the dots don't connect any other way. The Raptors, they're smart. *Seriously* smart. They dealt us a mortal blow several years back when they convinced us all to go public with the fake return." Steven sighed in embarrassment. "The truth is, we were…are, literally months— at maximum a year—away from collapsing on our own. There's no way the Raptors don't know that, especially with Garrett being a traitor. All they had to do was wait, something they've proven time and time again."

Steven folded his hands on the desk. "Look, Mr. Tucker. I know we embarrassed the Masons. You all put your faith in us, and we let you down. I let my emotions cloud my judgment the last time. This time, I haven't. I left someone I deeply care about because I know that this—this is it! I've watched the Raptors for most of my life, and I've *never* seen them act this way. If I wasn't sure before, I became sure when Garrett felt he needed to reveal himself to bait me back. It was a desperate attempt to contain the situation."

Mr. Tucker removed his glasses and set them down. "If what you say is true, Steven, why haven't they arrived here?"

"I'm not sure. Maybe they're on their way, or maybe they didn't think to look at—"

A loud knock sounded from the outer office door. Both men looked toward it.

"Orrrrrrrrr…" Steven drew the word out, "maybe they're already here."

CHAPTER 12

AND BLOW YOUR HOUSE DOWN

The banging increased the longer it went unanswered. Mr. Tucker rose from his chair.

Steven sprang to his feet. "Don't!" He yanked his phone out of his jacket pocket, fumbling to turn it on. The service meter displayed a "searching" animation.

Mr. Tucker faced Steven, raising an eyebrow.

"It could be nobody," Steven said, "but if I'm right, you do *not* want to answer that."

"What do you propose?"

"Isn't there a phone call you can make? Get some of those Templar knights over here?"

Mr. Tucker chuckled. "Lad, you sorely overestimate us. Most in the Commandery are old men. Our fighting days are long behind us."

"But…" Steven stammered, his phone still hunting for a signal. "Is there another way out?"

"Afraid not. We're on the fourth floor."

The thumping on the door intensified. "We could call the police."

"And tell them what? That there are fanatics here to kill us?"

Steven's phone dinged to half a bar. He thumbed the emergency key, dialing 911, and waited for the pickup. "I'm sure they've heard worse," Steven muttered.

The banging stopped, replaced by an eerie silence.

"911 emergency," the operator said.

"Hi, my name is Steve. Someone's trying to force entry into our office."

"What's your location?"

"I'm at…" Steven trailed, looking at Mr. Tucker, who told him. He repeated the address into the phone.

"Police are on their way," the operator said. The banging resumed.

Mr. Tucker grunted. "I'm going to answer the door."

"Hold on! The police are coming. Just wait," Steven hissed.

"Sir, what's happening?" the operator asked.

Mr. Tucker strode toward the door. "If it isn't the Raptors, then someone could get injured. If it *is* them, then the police should arrive momentarily."

Steven cut the call and dashed in front of Mr. Tucker. "Just hold on, at least wait until we can hear the sirens."

Mr. Tucker folded his arms against his chest. "Fine, until we hear the sirens."

Before Mr. Tucker finished the sentence, Steven had yanked the thumb drive out of the laptop and stuffed it, the transcript, and newspaper clipping, into the pocket of his leather jacket. He turned around and bolted through the office. He looked around frantically and caught sight of a small break room.

"If I'm right," Steven muttered, "nothing but death'll follow." He heard the faint sound of a siren approaching and ran back to Mr. Tucker in the main reception room.

"Give me two minutes, please!" Steven hissed. Mr. Tucker crossed his arms. The banging turned into a rhythmic boom, shaking the door hinges.

Steven ran back into Mr. Tucker's office and finagled the window, then dashed back into the break room. There he opened one of the smaller two-door cupboards at knee level. He rotated his oversized frame through the undersized gap until his back rested against the rear wall. If anyone opened the right-side door and even glanced in his direction, he'd be finished, but he couldn't think of a better option. He heard the police car screech to a halt outside the building.

Right on cue, Mr. Tucker called out, "I'm coming!"

The banging ceased, followed by a muffled "Stop!" and a metallic *puff* from a silencer. Then a crash and a loud thud. Steven held his breath, refusing to make the slightest peep.

"The window!" someone shouted. A few seconds later, "Look everywhere!"

The moment stretched into eternity as Steven prayed he wouldn't be discovered. When someone flung open the adjacent panel with a *slap*, Steven's heart sank.

"Police!" someone yelled, followed by a barrage of gunfire alternating with metallic *puffs*. Steven clamped his hands over his ears.

The battle lasted a full minute before stopping. Steven heard a gasp of breath on the other side of his cupboard door. Someone coughed, followed by a thick *splat* on the ground.

"Ahgo, you alive?" someone distant shouted.

"YEAH!" the unseen person near Steven replied, then whispered, "Barely."

"They're dead. Hurry up and help me get our people out of here before their backup arrives!" the other guy said.

"ALRIGHT!" The person near him added in a lower voice, "F***ing worms, damned f***ing worms, they can't just give up and die." He groaned while standing. "Gotta make s*** hard for us when *alllll* you gotta do is sit still and let us kill you. You and the rest of your f***ing do-gooder worms."

Steven listened to the guy stumble out of the kitchen and realized he'd been holding his breath the entire time. He let out a subtle hiss of air. Sweat trickled down his neck as the footsteps continued.

Another crash resounded outside. "What happened?" a third voice called out.

"What does it look like, *dumba**.* The cops got the drop on us. *You all* were supposed to have taken care of them! Hurry up and grab our guys— two are here, another dead around the corner. Make sure to spray them! Ahgo, help me carry G. If we hurry, we might catch the worm before he gets away. His fat a** went out the window and ran toward the highway."

"That's a loooong fall. Let's hope he snapped his leg on the way down."

More sirens grew closer. Steven said a quick prayer for the police to arrive and kill the rest of the Raptors. When silence came, he still refused to move. It took ten minutes until the sound of boots flooded the office. "Bellaire Police!"

"Yes!" Steven cried out. "I'm in here. Please, for the love of God, don't shoot me! Please don't shoot me..."

The cupboard door opened and someone wrenched Steven out, shoving his face into a puddle of blood on the ground. "You're under arrest! You have the right to remain silent..." the words faded out as Steven fainted.

CHAPTER 13

THE 5-O

It didn't take long for the investigators to categorize Steven as a kook. He told them the truth from start to finish, but they repeatedly expressed their disbelief.

"So, you're trying to save the world from a demon thing," one investigator questioned. The other shook his head.

Steven chose not to answer. *This is wasting my time.* Instead, he glanced around the dimly lit interrogation room. Boring white walls trapped him on all four sides. The coffee they had given him had already gone cold and sat lifeless in the small red mug.

The investigator pursed his lips. "No? Not save the world? What then?"

Steven considered the question in silence.

"Aren't you going to give him the decency of an answer?" the other investigator goaded. Steven didn't take the bait.

"Steven, just tell us what you were really doing there, and then we can all be done here."

Steven remained silent.

I need to get outta here and find the other Templars.

Investigator number two sighed. "We can do this all day, go home, relax, then come back and do it again. You, on the other hand, will stay here until you tell us what we want to know."

Now it was Steven's turn to sigh. "Really, Mr. Investigator. You tell me what you want me to tell you because this beating around the bush is doing nothing for either of us."

"Tell me again," the first investigator suggested.

"No, ask me in some other way." Steven reprimanded, perking up.

"What," the second investigator glowered, "do you know, about the masked gunmen?"

Steven replied, matching the investigator's rate of speech. "They're called the Raptors, and they want the information I possess."

"Do you know any of their names?"

"You asked that already."

"We need to know."

"You already know my answer; me telling you again isn't going to change that. It is, however, putting Raeleigh in more danger and allowing the Soulstealer to grow stronger by the second."

"The thing that's going to destroy the world."

"That's the general idea, yeah. Anyone with Google can figure that out. You're talking to the one group that exists to defend humanity against it. We say he's back. You've a quadruple family homicide that covered up the ransacking of Jeff's surveillance equipment. I don't know what Garrett has done to Raeleigh, but now you have a Mason guy dead by the same people. Only this time, you've seen what they wear and two of your officers were killed in the crossfire. What else do you need to see? They're here, they're active, and they're obviously showing themselves over something they think is very, very important."

Steven paused for a moment, then added, "Find that guy in the video, and you'll have found what they were willing to kill for. In the meantime, I need to phone my attorney. We're done here."

His lawyer took longer than Steven wanted to get him released. Even with his attorney raising all sorts of hell over amendment violations and lawsuits, the police took their time out-processing Steven. They kept all the information related to the Soulstealer as evidence; Steven only secured copies after relentless hassling. At least they honored his request to be released early morning.

Steven peered through the window and scrutinized everything within eyesight. As soon as he got his bike out of the impound, Steven thumbed the ignition, cranking the handlebar. His Victory Hammer S roared to life. Steven wasted no time gunning it out of the station. He took a hard right and scanned his surroundings for any sign of Raptor presence.

He needed to regroup, gather his thoughts, and figure out where to find the rest of the Templars.

CHAPTER 14

IN HONOR OF...

A quick search told Steven where he needed to meet up with the rest of the Templars. For all their supposed secrets, they didn't make much of an effort to hide. He waited almost a week for one of their meetings. Sometimes he slept in a cheap motel, other times in the woods, a bar cot, or under an overpass. All to evade the Raptors and avoid unwanted attention.

When the time came, he arrived two hours early. His surveillance skills ranked as amateur, but he figured it was his best hope at avoiding capture.

The spacious auditorium contained multiple exits, allowing for a speedy getaway. Steven hid his bike about two blocks from the venue behind a rusty dumpster next to a red-brick office building.

The Templars arrived one by one, and no one took notice of him sitting in the outside lobby. None appeared under 60 years old. He guessed they assumed he was one of them, though he sported none of their extravagant attire; they topped their ornamented Army officer uniforms with that white-feathered cavalry hat Mr. Tucker had in his office.

One such elderly gentleman sat next to him with a toothy grin. Everything about him was papery white, from his skin to his thin voluminous white hair. The only other color about the man came from his uniform and bright blue eyes. "Hello, chap!"

"Good evening." Steven felt a rush of encouragement. He noticed a faint smell of tobacco lingering around the old man.

"Are you the initiate?"

"No sir," Steven replied. "I'm here to discuss a sensitive matter."

"Ahhh." The gentleman pulled his head down and narrowed his eyes. "You may, or may not, be in the right place. Such matters are only selectively discussed," he said in an eerie tone before reverting to his chipper demeanor.

"This will definitely be one of those *selective* topics. And I'd like to spend as little time as possible here. My life is in danger."

His fluffy white eyebrows rose. "Danger, you say? What an odd choice of words. We don't hear that very often. Which matter are we discussing?"

"Our mutual adversary, the Bane."

The elderly gentleman chuckled. "You're one of those, are you? I haven't heard that name in a long time, my boy. Such tidings haven't been given serious consideration since the Crusades."

"They're serious once more."

"And you are?" he asked, rising from his seat.

"Steven Carpenter."

"Delighted." He grinned, then ambled over to a group of aged Templars. He spoke to them, and a few peeked over their shoulders at Steven. After some time, the group made their way over. A few sat on the couches in and around him, but the rest stood.

"Mr. Carpenter," one of them said with a tolerant frown.

"Good evening," Steven replied.

"Guthrie here says you want to talk about the Bane."

"Not so much talk about, sir, as to tell you it's returned."

An audible groan rumbled throughout the group. Some of the Masons grimaced.

"Mr. Carpenter, I'm afraid some of us more experienced Knights have heard that one before. We have a meeting in a few moments that requires our presence. Can you finish your discussion before then?"

"Probably. Let me start off with this. I assume you all know about Lawrence?"

"Of course, this meeting was called in honor of him."

"I was with him when he was murdered by the Raptors. They came for these." Steven held up the transcripts in one hand and a thumb drive in the other. "They got to him first, and they would've gotten me if it hadn't been for the police."

"You...you were there when he died?" one of them choked out, his face wrinkling.

"I was there, yes. I showed him what I'm about to show you. Believe me when I say that this is what the Ordo Solis and the Knights Templar have been preparing for. I understand you're here to honor Lawrence's memory. Please, do him a greater honor by doing what he can no longer do: warn the world of what's happening."

CHAPTER 15

A FEW GOOD MEN

"You can understand our skepticism, Mr. Carpenter," the elder Templar continued. They all retired to a separate chamber inside the Auditorium. A small projector showed the exchange with the Gatekeeper, paused on the Soulstealer's young face. They met in a large, plain white room with a long white table down the center. Tan carpet covered the floor. A large water jug gurgled in the corner whenever someone filled their glass.

"Yes, I understand. We were duped before. But it could've been to downplay something like this; the signs are undeniable."

"Ahhh," another Templar spoke. "The facts are compelling, certainly, but never undeniable."

"There're lots of dead people over this kid." Steven crossed his arms. "This is it. It's back. And the Raptors are doing everything they can to extinguish all traces."

"Why haven't you put this on the YouTube yet? Cement its existence there."

Steven bit his lip to keep from laughing. "Because as soon as I do that, the trolls will attack and tear it apart. By the time anyone with influence gets to it, it'll be nothing more than 'fake news.'"

"I see the pieces, Mr. Carpenter; I clearly see the dots. But I fear you have not done a good enough job connecting them together. How do you truly know this is the Bane? Why, after all these years, has it returned? These unanswered questions will dissuade anyone with substantial influence from taking up your cause."

"The connection is there!" Steven exclaimed, shaking the transcript. "People are dying! The exchange is clearly readable! And for the record, it's *our* cause."

"I did not say you were lying, Mr. Carpenter. I said you haven't reasonably shown the Bane's return. At the very least, you've shown a compelling case to find this boy, but not much else."

"For Lawrence," one of the Templars grunted.

Steven sighed. *It's a start.* "Okay, I'll take it at this point. What can we do now?"

"Well, lad," the gentlemen he spoke to earlier said. "Our public standing has…diminished…after we exercised our influence to warn the world of the fake Bane. I do not believe it will work a second time. We will need to find a new way to convince them." His expression turned into a wild grin. "I, for one, am looking forward to the challenge. Give an ole codger like me one last bit of excitement before the good Lord takes me home. At any rate, it's the least I can do for Lawrence."

"Mr. Carpenter," another Templar said. "I believe we've taken in your whole presentation. If you could please wait outside while I confer with our brethren, we will deliver our answer to you shortly."

Steven nodded, retrieved the transcript and thumb drive, and left the room.

He waited about 20 minutes in the lobby before being ushered back inside the conference room. The old gentleman he spoke to at length kept smiling.

"Mr. Carpenter, we believe this to be a threat worth serious consideration. We will aid you in what must come next. We have one condition, however." He cleared his throat. "We shall do this under our terms this time. It may take longer, and it may be only a gradual sense of awareness."

"Okaaaaaaaay. If that's the price of your help, I'm fine with it. As long as you're all fully aware that the longer we take, the more powerful the Soulstealer gets. Also, the Raptors won't just stop with Lawrence. Once they figure out you're all involved, they'll come after you as well, especially if the only ones who know about the Soulstealer are in this room."

The head Templar nodded. "It is understood. We believe it to be a necessary risk."

"Alright." Steven sighed. "I'm all in. What do we do next?"

The old gentleman with the wild grin chimed in. "Ohhh, I think you'll like what we're thinking of doing next. I came up with the idea myself." The rest of the Templars chuckled. "It's an old Masonic technique. We call it 'the Sparrow's Roar.'"

CHAPTER 16

CAUSE

Steven stared at the ancient chalkboard before him, trying not to jump up and down. The week the Templars accepted his request for help, he and a group of six met every other day to review and discuss the way ahead. On the left-hand side were lists of names, a pro-con Venn diagram, and tables of to-dos upon which to formulate the plan. On the right, a rough outline of Guthrie's famed "Sparrow's Roar."

Steven scratched his chin. "Sooo…this is kind of a bumpy road to getting the public on our side."

"And yet," Guthrie replied, "it produces the same result. Everyone understands that the Soulstealer isn't a myth, and it instantly reopens our organizations up for backing by the world powers."

Steven grinned. "Has this ever worked before?"

"Sure, sure. But not by any of us. Some very ancient figures did the same thing with great success. We're just taking that idea and tweaking it somewhat." He matched Steven's smile.

"It's bold."

"And dangerous," a Templar grunted from Steven's right. This Templar voiced his criticism each time they met. He'd yet to offer anything of value, which led Steven to wonder why he kept attending the meetings. All he did was disagree and stomp his black cane into the ground.

"Do you have another suggestion?" a third Templar asked.

"Of course! Steer clear of this and let the man figure it out himself," the naysayer replied, gesturing to Steven. "We already lost one honorable member due to these people; we need not lose another." He folded his arms, a heavy wrinkle forming between his snowy eyebrows.

"It is our obligation to assist those who fight the Bane," Guthrie said. His blue eyes filled with pride.

"It's one short sentence in a *very* long oath."

"Then you should have no issue satisfying such a menial part of your vow." Guthrie winked at Steven. "Besides, big things have such small beginnings. I, for one, did not come all this way through life just to abandon our values when it becomes hard."

"The world thinks us some damnable bunch of conspiracy nuts," the naysayer continued.

"Elmer, there was never a time when the world thought us anything else. Our secrecy will always make the public suspicious of our motives. You can tell them a thousand times that the knowledge we withhold is almost exclusively used to prove who we are to one another, and they will *still* think we're the ancient Illuminati evil wanting to create a one-world order. People fear what they do not understand."

"And you think *this* plan is going to help them understand us better?" Elmer, the naysayer, asked.

Another Templar regarded Steven. "Don't worry. Elmer may voice some harsh misgivings, but there is no one more resilient. He continues a fight long after it should've ended. It's both his most admirable and more annoying personality trait."

Elmer grunted. "I stand with my brothers, of course. But I have a duty to tell you this is a mistake. Those sinners will come for us if they find out we're helping."

"Uh, actually," Steven murmured, "they probably already know you're involved."

All heads turned toward him.

"How do you figure, young man?" Guthrie asked, his eyebrows drawing together.

"Well, they knew to come to your office in Bellaire. I'm almost certain they didn't follow me. So it follows that they have an idea that you, or at least the Masons, are helping the Order. Also, as you're aware, I recently discovered one of our own to be a Raptor, so they definitely know how much you assisted us several years ago."

Guthrie looked at the Templar at the head of the conference table, who seemed to carry the most influence. The man merely nodded.

"So, it's settled then," Guthrie said.

Steven looked between them in confusion. "What's settled?"

"We will move forward with the plan immediately."

"Uh…how?" Steven continued. "I thought you said this sort of thing takes time?"

The Templar at the head of the table held up his hand. "Steven, please trust us. If what you say is true, then it is only a matter of time before the rest of us are targeted. We will need to move quickly to stay ahead of the danger."

"Those little devils," Elmer growled. "Some of us have been in more actual wars longer than they've been alive. If they want a fight, we'll give 'em one the likes of which they've never seen."

The head Templar set both hands on the table. "Very well. We stay here until we finish our preparations."

A few hours later, Steven stood, arms crossed, in front of the dusty chalkboard with a timeline of events sprawled across the board. The cherry-oak table in the middle of the room seated most of the other Templars; now numbering eight in all, including Steven.

Steven reviewed the timeline, laughing aloud. "I like it. I really, really like it."

Guthrie stood beside Steven. "And they say us ole codgers have no imagination!"

"It'll take some doing on our part, but this is so unexpected that there's no way the Raptors will be able to contain this," another Templar chimed in.

"Pah!" Elmer huffed, hunching over his black cane. "There is also no way the Raptors *won't* react to this. Don't be fooled—this plan may take them by surprise, but they *will* respond. We just need to have a way to deal with the likeliest of their reactions."

"Well then, let's take care of that next," Steven said.

"Tomorrow," Elmer said. "I've had enough excitement for one day."

"Agreed," the head Templar said. "We've made significant progress today; let's all go home and allow this to stew. We'll finish tomorrow, same time."

"But we still haven't decided on anyone."

"I understand, but I still wish for us to rest on this—we're not all as young as you, Mr. Carpenter. We'll decide tomorrow."

Steven pursed his lower lip. *So close.*

Guthrie patted him on the back, his light blue eyes gleaming. "Come, my boy. You may stay at my place again tonight."

Steven triple-checked the deserted parking lot before stepping outside; a few cars passed by on the side highway. Guthrie and Steven ventured the 15 minutes back to the old gentleman's residence; Steven was on his bike and Guthrie in an old Mercedes. At the behest of the Templars, he tucked his beloved Anvil away in Guthrie's tiny garage.

Chapter 17

Precipice

Dust particles floated everywhere around Guthrie's home. Within a few minutes of entering, Steven began sneezing. Guthrie invited him to sit in an old creaky leather chair next to a smoldering fireplace. They sat opposite each other in identical armchairs. Guthrie lit a long tobacco pipe resting on the stand beside him and took a deep draw. His papery skin looked like it would collapse into a powder at any moment. His blue eyes, however, remained vibrant and full of life.

"Sooo," Steven began, "Is this what you do with your evenings?"

Guthrie grinned, tilting his head, and bringing his index finger up to his ear. "Hear that?"

Steven jolted upright, eyes darting about. "What?"

"Exactly. Magnificent, isn't it?"

Steven sunk back into the leather chair. His body relaxed and solace enveloped him. His instinct to run subsided and he forgot his paranoia.

"Tell me, lad," Guthrie began, "what made you join the Order of the Sun?"

"Curiosity and mystery, mostly. I was infatuated with the Soulstealer as a kid. I pretended I was the Inquisition finding a nest of Unas, or the knight who slew King Alexios. One day I struck up the nerve to find the nearest Order member. His name was Billy; you remind me a little bit of him. Anyways, Billy really sold me on becoming a volunteer. I wouldn't have joined, if not for him."

"And where is this fine gentleman now?" Guthrie took another long draw of smoke.

"He passed several years ago from heart failure. His wife, Helen, passed away months later. They were the coolest couple ever. I owe them a great deal."

"Life is ever-changing, my friend. The hand of time writes, and having writ, moves on. It is both the source of great joy and terrible sorrow. I have lost many friends since my time on this earth. In a few short years, all the loves we loved, fights we've had, shouts, cries, whoops and hollers will have faded from time forever. Such wonderful history I wish I could visit once more, but now survives only in here." Guthrie tapped his forehead.

The two of them sat in silence for a time, each lost in thought.

"Tell me something," Steven said.

"Hmm?" Guthrie puffed on his pipe.

"Aren't you afraid of dying?" Steven glanced around the room while Guthrie exhaled a cloud of smoke. Tall bookshelves covered the walls, stacked with books and faded family photos.

"At this stage of my life, it isn't that I'm afraid to die, it's that I do not cling to life. All death is certain, and I can only be so fortunate as to have experienced life this long."

"This is a big deal to the Raptors. They're going to come after us, and they won't care who they kill."

"I once got into a tussle with a boy on the other baseball team. He taunted from first base, and I tripped him as he ran by. It was the silliest of fights, but so important to us at the time."

Steven stood. "Well, the stakes of losing *this* fight is the extinction of humanity." He noticed a small gold bar to his right that held a crystal bourbon set. Dark liquid filled the rectangular-shaped pitcher, and two round glasses sat in front of it.

"Just another fight that's important to us at the time." Guthrie winked. "You look like you could use that drink."

Steven gave the old man a quick smile and walked toward the bourbon.

"Here's something I don't understand. Why do it? Why do the Raptors follow him? It exists to feed off them and everyone else."

"Some will do anything to belong; others believe in more than physical well-being."

"But it's *evil*. Like, the very definition of evil," Steven continued. He poured himself a glass and drained the dark liquid down faster than planned.

"People have committed far greater wrongs over far less. Besides, you happen to be involved in only one of a handful of causes where the followers can actually see what they're fighting for. That makes them all the more fervent and treacherous."

"So many lives ruined," Steven muttered. "And for what? To enable some despicable thing to continue its destructive path of misery and suffering." Steven poured himself one last drink and sat back down.

Guthrie said nothing, still puffing on his pipe.

Steven crossed his arms. "It blows my mind how there're actual people who serve that monstrosity, committing such horrendous acts of evil. Why can't they see that? Why couldn't we all just live peacefully together; there's enough room on this earth for all of us."

Guthrie pursed his lips. "The hand of time writes, and having writ, moves on."

CHAPTER 18

KNIGHT HUNTERS

Steven labored over the conference room with the Templars for what he hoped would be for the last time. They finalized the plan, fine-tuning the last detail after talking through potential obstacles. A blank illuminated display overlaid the chalkboard, stemming from an old-fashioned overhead projector sitting atop the table.

"And here," the head Templar said, pulling a piece of scratch paper from his briefcase and putting it on the overhead mat, "is the note that would accompany the evidence." The paper magnified onto the chalkboard.

Steven mouthed the words on the draft letter until he reached the last sentence. "'And the longer this miscarriage of evil is allowed to hunt us, we'll hear fewer children laugh, until finally, there won't be any left to laugh,'" he finished, folding his hands. "Nice."

"The only thing we need now," the head Templar continued, "is the influential person to recruit, and the provocative evidence that will leave no doubt in the reader's mind."

"Also," Steven interjected, raising his hand, "you keep referring to it as the 'Bane.' I'd recommend changing it to a more modern name; something that'll connect with today's world."

The head Templar's brow furrowed. "Such as?"

"Soulstealer. It does exactly that—steals people's souls. Call it the Soulstealer, and you won't need to work so hard to explain how evil it is…the name will cause people's imagination to run wild for you."

A murmur of agreement echoed from the group. Even Elmer, the eternal pessimist, nodded.

"Agreed," the head Templar said.

As he marked the paper with the revision, the conference room door flew open with a crash. A dozen figures strode in, wearing what Steven prayed he'd never see again: the Raptor's mask.

A few of the Templars rose from their chairs.

"What sort of hooliganism is this?" Elmer exclaimed.

The masked figures encircled the room, each carrying a silenced pistol, pointing it to the Templar nearest each of them.

"They…they serve the Soulstealer!" Steven cried out.

The door closed behind the last Raptor, who walked straight to Steven and spoke in a metallic voice. "Hello, worm." The Raptor angled his weapon to the Templar beside Steven and fired straight into the man's forehead, flinging his head backward. Blood spattered Steven's face.

Steven dared not move, his mind paralyzed. The Raptor looked toward the overhead projector, scanning the magnified picture. "Seems we arrived just in time." He strode over to the projector and ripped the letter from the mat. The head Templar made a frustrated grunt in protest.

The Raptor pointed his weapon straight into the Templar's face. "Where're the rest of these plans?"

The Templar grinned and tapped his head. "Up here."

The Raptor fired into the Templar's head, and a shell casing clattered onto the conference table. "Good answer." He moved to the next Templar.

"S***," Elmer grumbled, fumbling for his cane. "I've fought two wars, you little brat. I won't be stood here and slaughtered like an animal." He turned toward the nearest Raptor, swinging his cane with surprising speed, and clubbed the nearest Raptor in the head.

The Raptor cursed and fired a few rounds into Elmer's chest. The old man collapsed onto the table, gasping for breath. The Raptor closed the distance between them, firing two more shots into Elmer's face. The old man shuddered still as crimson red pooled beneath him.

"We're wasting time," the Raptor complained. "End this now."

Steven gazed at Guthrie, who smiled his goofy smile back at Steven. Guthrie nodded solemnly and started to sing. "And when the night is gloomy…"

The other Raptors discharged their weapons into whichever Templar sat closest, and Guthrie sang no more.

Tears streamed down Steven's face. He only met these men weeks ago and already considered them close friends. It felt like a part of Steven died with each of them. A couple Raptors on the other side of the room began dousing the bodies with gasoline.

Steven stared at the scene until someone reached around and covered his nose and mouth with a wet rag. He struggled for only a few seconds before his world went dark.

CHAPTER 19

BOUND

Steven awoke as his body tensed from being thrown. He landed as a slam sounded overhead, followed by the vibrations of an engine starting. It took him a few seconds to realize he was in the trunk of a vehicle. Something was stretched over both his eyes and face, and earmuffs muted all sounds. He wriggled his hands and feet in vain against his bindings.

After about an hour, they stopped. Fresh air struck his cheeks when the trunk opened, and hands yanked him out. He was dragged across grass, then concrete, up wooden steps, and thrust into a creaky chair. A residual numbness held him after what happened to his Templar friends.

Hands pulled off the blindfold, gag, and earmuffs. The sun's glare shining through the windows blinded him, and he squinted to make out his surroundings. Blurred darkness turned into blurred figures, which evolved into a room full of Raptors. They surrounded him; some sitting, others standing. All carried a weapon of some sort. A few held silenced pistols, while several toted full-on carbine rifles. The Raptor to his immediate right wielded a machete.

Steven's gaze rested on a woman in a chair opposite him with a burlap sack over her head, whose long hair extended past the edges. One of the Raptors approached Steven, its mask inches from his face, clutching a Bowie knife in one hand and brass knuckles in the other.

The Raptor turned to the other bound figure and traced the edge of the dagger along the woman's shoulder. She shuddered, whimpering. The Raptor grabbed the bag on her head and tore it off.

Steven breathed a sigh of relief at not seeing Raeleigh.

"So," the metallic male voice said. He bent down next to the frightened woman and loosened the blindfold before taking the earmuffs off and dropping them. "Tell us something." He turned back to Steven while still tracing the blade along the woman's shoulder. She flinched away from the weapon; her tear-stained face wrenched Steven's heart. A desperate groan sounded from behind the woman's gag.

The Raptor held a finger up to the woman's mouth and trailed the blade from her shoulder up to her throat. A poor, innocent bystander caught in a war between the crazies.

"Sh-sure," Steven replied, trying to find his voice.

"What were you going to do with the letter?"

"I was, uh…" Steven hesitated.

The Raptor slashed his knife across the woman's throat and pushed her off the chair. She writhed on the floor against her bindings, gurgling as the life drained from her body.

"I was answering you!" Steven cried out.

The Raptor pointed his bloodied knife at Steven. "When I ask you a question, you answer immediately." The Raptor motioned to the others. They dragged in another woman with a burlap over her head and sat her in the chair opposite Steven.

The Raptor pulled the bag off her head and let down her blindfold. *Not Raeleigh*, Steven thought with relief. The woman cried through her gag as she took in the room, struggling against her bindings.

The Raptor stepped over the dying woman on the floor, who gave a sluggish squirm. He pulled a silenced pistol from a drop-leg holster and placed the barrel against the new woman's head. This woman stopped struggling, opting to close her eyes and mutter something that resembled a prayer.

"This mother of four would very much like to see her children tonight," the Raptor said.

"Okay, okay…just, tell me what you want to know!" Steven pleaded.

"What were you going to do with the letter?"

"We were going to send it to CNN and Fox," Steven blurted. "Convince the public that the Soulstealer has returned."

"Soulstealer?"

Steven paused. *Am I supposed to...*

The Raptor's handgun belched fire. The woman's head lurched sideways, and the Raptor used the momentum to push her off the chair.

Steven stomped wildly and threw his head from side to side. "I didn't know I was supposed to answer that!" he cried, struggling against his bindings.

"*Every* question I ask, you answer immediately!" the Raptor sneered.

Steven stared at the empty chair. The slashed woman twitched ever so slightly. The shot woman didn't move.

The Raptor motioned again, and another woman was dragged in. He stroked the captive's head with the end of his pistol barrel before ripping off the burlap.

Steven's eyes dilated in terror. "Raeleigh," he choked.

"I'm glad we don't have to acquaint the two of you." The Raptor loosened the blindfold and removed the earmuffs. Raeleigh looked at Steven and sobbed, her dark brown eyes filled with agony.

"Now, next question, and you better get this one right." The Raptor placed his gun up against Raeleigh's head. "What were you going to do after you sent the letter to the press?"

"Celebrity. A celebrity would confirm, use influence to start resistance," Steven blubbered.

"Celebrity?"

"The whole plan...the whole plan was to make it *look* like it came from someone famous, with lots of influence. The Templars felt that the right kind of evidence and public demand would make the famous person just go along with it and claim the letter. All we had to do was wait and let it snowball."

The Raptor laughed. "A celebrity...*that* was your grand plan?"

"*Yes*! For God's sake, yes, that was our plan!"

It took the Raptor a few seconds to stop laughing. "A celebrity might have public influence, but he'd *never* have the power to do anything about it."

The machete-wielding Raptor beside Steven let out a subtle cough.

Steven's interrogator held up his hand. "You're right; we're getting off track. Let's refocus. Who was going to be your celebrity?"

"We hadn't gotten that far."

"Hmm," the Raptor said. "I think you're lying." He pushed his barrel against Raeleigh's temple, further tilting her head. Her blonde hair swayed behind her.

"No, not at all, I promi—" Steven tried to say, interrupted as the Raptor pulled the trigger. An empty *click* echoed throughout the room. "*We hadn't chosen anyone!*" Steven screamed. "*We hadn't chosen anyone!*"

His interrogator waited for Steven to stop blubbering. "We know." The Raptor slid the weapon into his holster with a *schoomp*. "Consider that your saving grace."

The Raptor grabbed a handful of Raeleigh's sweaty hair, extending her exposed neck over the bloodstained floor below. The Raptor drew his bloodied silver Bowie and pressed it against her neck. She flinched and closed her eyes.

"Anything! Anything you want, just ask! I'm not lying!"

"I need you to shut up until I ask you a question," his interrogator snarled. After some extended silence, he continued. "How many know of this plan?"

"Just me, and the ones you...you..." Steven stammered.

"Slaughtered?" the Raptor offered.

"Yes."

"No one else?"

"Not unless the Templars told someone else what was happening," Steven blurted, a pang of regret striking him. He hoped he hadn't just put anyone else in danger.

"One more question. Give me the location of all pieces of evidence."

"If I answer that, she and I are both dead," Steven snapped, drawing back in surprise at his own response.

Now it was his interrogator who hesitated. He released Raeleigh's hair, letting her sit back up. "I've been asked to bring *you* back alive." The Raptor pointed his dagger at Steven. "*She*," he continued, pressing the tip of the dagger against Raeleigh's pale temple, "is optional. You've answered my questions to my satisfaction thus far, so I'm inclined to bring you *both* back alive. But if you don't, then I've no more use for her, and *she,* will look like *them*." He gestured at the two motionless women.

Steven gazed out the window, seeing nothing but rolling plains and some forest off in the distance. "There's only one copy left." He lied like his life depended on it, marking the second time he put Raeleigh in danger. "It's in my motorcycle's trap compartment, behind the heat shield, right-hand side."

"Where's your bike?"

"At one of the Templar's houses." He gave the address.

His interrogator nodded; three Raptors left the room. "Anything else I should know?" The Raptor wiggled his knife. A trickle of blood traced a path down Raeleigh's face. She kept her eyes shut.

"No," Steven mumbled. "That's everything I can think of. You win." Sweat ran down his neck as he kept his attention on the dagger against Raeleigh's temple.

"There was no other outcome. We, the Raptor's claw," he recited.

"Rise further," the rest of the Raptors finished. Someone behind Steven reaffixed his blindfold, earmuffs, and gag. The burlap bag was wrapped around his head, setting him in darkness once again.

CHAPTER 20

SQUEEZE

He and Raeleigh were dumped in a car trunk and driven for what seemed an eternity. Finally, the car stopped, and the Raptors hauled him out and led him...somewhere. Although he was glad he could finally straighten his legs, he hated being separated from Raeleigh. With each step, a different part of his body hurt. His stomach growled, his muscles ached, and his head hadn't stopped spinning. He was so lightheaded he kept stumbling, and his captors eventually dragged him, a reaction that no longer surprised him.

Steven considered himself a traitor for giving up all that information. *Eh, what does it matter now? The Order, the Templars, it's all finished. That damn demon finally won.*

His captors pulled him up a flight of stairs, then through a series of twists and turns of what felt like doors, but he couldn't even begin to guess what was happening around him. The Raptors finally dropped him. Raeleigh fell on top of him moments later. The bag over his head flew off, but the blindfold and earmuffs remained. They pulled him back to a standing position, rotated him 360 degrees, then refastened the burlap.

This is so unfair, Steven thought. *My entire life devoted to an empty gesture, only to have all my efforts rewarded in the most brutal of ways.*

As if sensing his despair, Raeleigh's bound hands squeezed his ankle.

Thanks, Raeleigh. My beautiful love. He suspected the end was near, but Guthrie's words suddenly rang in his ears. *He didn't cling to life.*

Steven was led up a flight of stairs, leaving Raeleigh behind. He knew they reached their destination when they threw him to the ground again. Hands untied his bindings, took off the bag, earmuffs, and blindfold.

The searing light stunned his senses. The sound of a door slamming rang out as Steven's eyesight adjusted.

After about ten minutes, he could see more clearly. They had left him in a dimly lit room with no windows. The door proved the only thing of interest, which Steven tried and failed to jiggle open. Someone laughed on the other side, which Steven guessed to be one of his Raptor guards.

Well, at least I'm not dead. Not yet, anyway. A wave of exhaustion hit him. He scanned his new home. The room was bare, not even a pillow. He laid on the floor and curled into a ball, falling asleep much faster than he anticipated.

CHAPTER 21

THE WALK

Two days later, Steven curled up against one of his prison room walls. He tried not to touch his stomach, which was bruised purple from yesterday's introduction to the Soulstealer. A stroll with his nemesis through the topiary garden ended with an overzealous Raptor slugging Steven in the gut for not answering the Soulstealer's questions fast enough.

"F*** this," he muttered, standing. "F*** the Raptors, f*** this f***ing war, and f*** the Ordo Solis." He stormed over to the door and pounded on it. "Do you hear me? F*** you guys!"

No response.

"Are you gonna give me anything to eat, or is your plan to watch me slowly DIE OF STARVATION?"

Still no response.

"F***ers," he spat.

He returned to the wall and slid down against it. The longer he stayed there, the more sorrow ate away his anger. A soft knock vibrated through the wall behind him. Steven swiveled around, eyes narrowing. Another knock echoed through the wall, this time louder. His head shot up.

Could it be Raeleigh?

Steven put his ear against the wall. A few more knocks, then nothing.

"Weird," Steven mumbled.

The door to his prison opened and three Raptors entered, one of them with a burlap bag in his hand.

"What now?" Steven barked.

Two of them stopped next to Steven. They pulled him up, threw the bag over his head, and propelled him forward. Points of light shone through tiny specks in the rough meshing as he tried to regain his footing. The Raptors gripped his shoulders and led him down what felt like a steep platform, sending a fresh breeze through the bag and into his lungs.

As they removed the burlap, his gaze locked on a young man waiting in front of him. Steven's blood again boiled and chilled at the same time.

The Soulstealer. The Bane of Humanity.

"Hi again," the Soulstealer said in a high-pitched tone. His stale buzz-cut and babyface reminded Steven of Ed Norton in American History X.

Steven couldn't tell if he wanted to throw up or strangle the kid, but couldn't do much with Raptor guards pointing their weapons straight at him, most of which were hefty carbine rifles.

"I was going out for a walk again, and I figured…maybe you'd like some sunshine as well."

Steven offered no reply, unsure of what would come out of his mouth if he did.

You can't be a day over 25. And somehow you're responsible for a whole bucket of death and suffering.

"Please, if you'd join me on my walk, I'd feel better about all of this." The Soulstealer gestured toward the garden.

Steven wanted to scoff, but remained stoic. The Soulstealer offered him a choice, but the ones guarding him didn't. Steven put pressure on his stomach, trying to relieve the bruised ache for a few seconds.

They began to walk. Behind him loomed a mansion, overshadowing part of the maze of hedges they now navigated. The hedges stood only three feet tall, revealing the entire backyard, all the way to the fence line. He spotted several grass figures all scattered throughout the garden.

Steven continued winding left and right, careful to keep as much distance as the Raptor guards would allow. Occasionally they'd nudge him closer to the Soulstealer when Steven veered away.

At last, they arrived at a circular clearing with mammoth bells fashioned from grass, frozen in the act of ringing. The Soulstealer, his Raptor hounds, and Steven stood in front of the display a few moments before moving along the path.

They came upon a second display. This topiary looked like a muscular man with short hair and square glasses. Below him read a placard: "Here stands the first to open the gate."

Odd, Steven thought at first. But the more he considered the phrase, the more it made sense. *The Gatekeeper,* he guessed.

"I think about…" the Soulstealer began, "what sort of struggles our different sides went through all these years, and how it could've been avoided."

Steven pondered the question without looking at the Soulstealer. He resisted the urge to ask the Soulstealer how he didn't already know the answer. The question raised some interesting implications in the Soulstealer's involvement with the Raptors. He filed the thought away for when they returned him to his dungeon.

The Soulstealer continued down the path, glancing behind him as he grazed the side of the hedges. A few feet behind, a Raptor followed Steven, a carbine rifle pointed at his back. He thought this was a bit overkill, seeing as how six Raptors could seize him at any given moment. Steven's eye caught the reflective light off a Raptor's black onyx mask, sculpted in frozen rage.

They approached another topiary figure; a short man with thick, horn-rimmed glasses. Steven searched for a descriptive placard, but like the bells, nothing revealed its inspiration. Out of the corner of Steven's eye, the Soulstealer smirked at the leafy character before moving on.

Up ahead, Steven spotted the extravagant display long before they rounded the hedge. He slowed his approach as he reached the last, and final exhibit, where all the other garden trails led.

There rested three polished statues of hardened metals and crystals. The two outside figures wore Raptor masks; one featured a face in frozen agony, the other displayed rage. The dark metal glimmered as light reflected off the various textures that gave them shape. Both characters gazed up in admiration of the oversized statue in the middle.

At first, Steven didn't know what to make of the monumental character between them. Then it dawned on him that he gazed at a depiction of the Soulstealer. Unlike the two flanking figures, the Soulstealer's form consisted of bright, vibrant materials: emerald, topaz, gold, silver, diamond, and ruby.

The figured outstretched one palm in invitation. The other hand raised a closed fist toward the sun as if challenging it to a duel.

By far, its most unusual characteristic belonged to the head—or rather—heads. The left head had features not unlike the short guy with horn-rimmed glasses, but it was smiling at him. The second head embraced a more wraithlike appearance. Its less defined features observed the high sun with an obscure sneer.

The sight unsettled Steven, although he couldn't help but be entranced. He stole a glance at the Soulstealer, who stared at the defiant abomination. Steven would sell his beloved Anvil to know what went through the Soulstealer's mind at that *exact* moment. Was the Soulstealer proud of how far he'd come? Did he understand the statue any better than Steven?

Steven's lips parted to form words, but he resisted the temptation and clamped his mouth shut.

The Soulstealer inhaled and held his breath, closing his eyes for a few seconds. "Thank you for walking with me. I know it can't be easy for you right now."

Steven's eyes bulged and he ground his teeth. *The gall of this f***ing kid!*

The Soulstealer nodded to the surrounding Raptors and turned onto another path. Four Raptors went with Bane; the other two grasped Steven and led him back to his prison. He seethed with rage as they parted ways.

"One day, I'm gonna say those words over your dead corpse," Steven whispered to no one.

That is, if he remained alive long enough to pull it off.

CHAPTER 22

SOUTH BY SOUTHKNOCK

Steven leaned against one of the walls when the same *tit tit, tit tit tit,* sound vibrated against it. He turned around, putting his hand against the wood-reinforced plaster wall.

Tit tit, tit tit tit.

Steven scrunched his dark eyebrows, deciding to risk what he pegged as another Raptor trick. He thumped the sequence back to the other side, casting a fretful glance at the door. He heard nothing in response, and drew closer to the wall.

"Are you there?" he whispered as loud as he dared. No answer. *Maybe the wall's too thick.* He repeated the original sequence back to his wall-buddy.

Tit tit, tit tit tit, came the reply.

Steven tensed in excitement, mind racing with possibilities. *Well, it's a start.*

A clamor sounded at the door; Steven whipped around and leaned against the wall. In walked four Raptors. Two of them guided him out as they fastened the bag over his head. He once again was led through the halls in complete darkness. Everything was silent, apart from the clamoring of the Raptor's boots against the ground. When his feet touched the stone patio, he steeled himself for the next encounter with his hated foe. The thing trying to end the world.

"Hey Steven," the Soulstealer said as the burlap bag came off. "Just another walk."

His enemy began to walk along the path, marking the third day the Soulstealer "just wanted to walk." Steven couldn't find a motive behind it. A rifle barrel prodded him forward when Steven didn't make to follow.

The Soulstealer crossed his arms as they walked through a new section of the hedge maze, coming across a grass figure warrior donning Asian-looking armor. Its hands juggled a combination of airwaves and water drops. A double-bladed melee staff leaned against his chest; his face tight in concentration.

The Soulstealer made no comment and moved on after a few minutes. The second display featured a group of characters, each unique. The placard on the ground read: "To those who made it possible." Another cryptic expression of gratitude toward anonymous persons. The Soulstealer continued, his face pensive.

Maybe now is the time to say something. Whatever he's thinking, it can't be to my benefit. But again, Steven resisted the urge; he'd not give the Soulstealer the satisfaction of polite company. If it took the Soulstealer walking with his enemy to make him feel at peace, then he'd do it by himself.

They neared the glittering trio-statue when the Soulstealer abruptly said, "I will."

Steven glanced about, not seeing any reason for the statement. *Why's he talking to himself?* Yet another interesting thought he'd consider once he returned to his cell.

With their walk concluded, the Raptors bound and bagged Steven and led him back toward his room. He knew they went someplace different when they pulled him up a flight of stairs. They handled him through a doorway and pushed him into a chair.

When the bag came off, he found Raeleigh sitting there, bound and gagged. Fear and panic set in. "I—I—I—" Steven stammered. "Whatever you—"

The nearby Raptor stuffed his mouth with a cloth.

He surveyed the small dining hall. Six Raptors lined the wall behind Raeleigh; only one held a weapon. Steven met Raeleigh's soft brown eyes once again. His chest heaved as he bit against the gag in his mouth. Small lines around her eyes crinkled with a smile.

"She's breathes," the Raptor's metallic voice said. "And I know you want her that way." Steven recognized the high voice as female. She spoke with an accent, but Steven couldn't tell what kind with the digitized voice.

Steven's body wobbled in agreement. The horrific events of the past week shook his mind, and he felt dizzy. Raeleigh didn't cry, nor look sad. Steven refused to look away from Raeleigh's calm face. His mind's eye memorized the way her blonde hair fell past her shoulders and gold flakes flit about her brown eyes.

"How many Ordo Solis members in America?" the female Raptor asked, pulling the gag from Steven's mouth.

"None."

"You are sure?"

"Yes," Steven said, not breaking eye contact with Raeleigh.

"How do you make connection Solis Europe?"

"Through email, sometimes a phone call."

"Who is contact?"

"Enzo. That's the only name I know."

Raeleigh kept her cool, but Steven saw fear growing in her dark eyes.

"Is the person in your mobile?"

"Yes."

"What is the password?"

"Four eight two eight."

"E-n-z-o?"

"What?"

She pulled out his phone from her pocket and wiggled it in the air.

"Oh…yes, E-n-z-o."

"What is the count of Solis Asia?"

Steven shook his head. "None. They haven't been active for years."

"Goooodddddddd," she said. "Good. Good cooperation. *Gracias.*"

The Raptor returned the gag to his mouth.

"That is what we require for now," she added.

Out of the corner of his eye, Steven saw one of the Raptors from the wall approach him with the blindfold bag. Steven's heart pounded as he brought his bound hands to the surface of the table. He turned his wrists and used his knuckle to knock the *tit tit, tit tit tit* sequence on the table.

Raeleigh's eyes widened, eyebrows jumping as she flashed him a quick smile. Steven's spirit soared.

The female Raptor's voice sounded from behind him. "Out," she commanded, as the bag covered Steven's head.

Little did she know, they led away a much different man than the one they brought in.

So it was *Raeleigh*. Steven clutched his heart as his shattered hope surged once again.

He didn't care if they *were* the only ones left in Solis America. The two of them would be the end of the Soulstealer.

Somehow. Someway.

CHAPTER 23

ERSATZ

The boredom set in so deep, Steven found himself struggling through a series of push-ups. He lifted himself on his fifth push-up, but his weight pulled him back to the ground. He settled his body on the floor.

"What in the world am I doing?" Steven panted, wiping his sweaty forehead.

The wall beside him echoed a familiar sequence. *Tit tit, tit tit tit.* Steven leaped to it, having waited for it all day. His knuckles met the plaster, imitating the pattern back to Raeleigh. He counted the days by the long stretches of time between the Soulstealer's leisurely strolls and Raeleigh's secret communication.

The door lock clicked, prompting Steven to turn around and set himself against the wall. In walked two masked Raptors, one so muscular he resembled a balloon animal. The other was more slender, with contours around her chest revealing her natural curves.

"Out," she commanded. She sounded like the woman who had interrogated him days before.

Steven took his time moving toward them. The larger Raptor put the burlap over his head and thrust him down the corridors, up a flight of stairs, through a doorway, and into a chair.

"Can't you guys be a little more gentle?" Steven said as he fell into the chair. "I'm not going anywhere."

They removed the burlap. It was the same room where he had been interrogated with Raeleigh. He strained to think how recent it was; his concept of time was all but nonexistent.

The female Raptor peeled back her mask. The gesture surprised Steven, and he gawked at a gorgeous woman with sun-kissed skin and brownish eyes. Her lethal stare bored a hole straight through him. She took the seat next to him.

"We have not much time," she whispered, stealing a glance at the door. Her accent sounded Spanish. "This no trick of ours. I am not Raptor. But I must know, are you sincerely Ordo Solis?"

Steven peeked at the male Raptor standing a little too close for comfort.

"He is okay; we are both undercover," she said. "Please answer, I must know."

Steven crossed his arms, not knowing what to make of the new development. As much as he craved an answer, he didn't trust a thing happening within these walls. When he didn't respond, she took a few steps back and rapped her hand on the table behind her.

Tit tit, tit tit tit. "It was me, to communicate to you both to know each other is okay."

Steven tried not to flinch, but the bridge of his nose crinkled.

"Please," the woman pleaded. "We are desperate to finding a someone who can do what we cannot."

The hell with it. "What do you want?" Steven demanded.

The woman breathed a sigh of relief. "Your garden walks with Nythan supply you opportunity to receive information without drawing a suspect. We require to know everything we can. Schedule, location, history, anything you can tell. Also, to tell Raeleigh of this for help as well."

Steven narrowed his eyes. "Nythan?"

The woman hesitated. "Yes, *el Diablo*. His name."

So, the Soulstealer's name is Nythan.

"We must know. Can you do this?" She stole a glance at the door.

"Who is *we*?"

"We have no time for these questions."

"If you want my help, looking like *that*," Steven said, pointing to the burley Raptor's mask, "I'm going to need to know *exactly* who I'm working with." He folded his arms.

The woman sighed. "I'm CIA."

Steven sniffed. "Well I wasn't expecting that, but okay. Prove it." He turned to the Raptor beside him. "Him too?"

"*Sí*," she answered. "We cannot prove anything, but we can work together. I will not ask you any question about anything important. Just help, that is all."

As if there was anything important left for me to give. Well, other than the fact that there's still a hidden duplicate of all the evidence making its way across North America.

"Why do you need my help?" Steven asked. "If you're CIA, you don't *need* my help."

"We have zero proof of what he is. Video of him in the bar, and much news on the Mason deaths, but no video showing him…do what he does."

Ahhh. Now I get it. These agents haven't been able to convince the CIA that the Soulstealer is real. "How's the CIA involved in any of this?"

"Long story, much longer than I have to tell. Will you?"

Steven shrugged. "I'll see what I can do."

Before anything else could be said, the doorknob turned. The brawny Raptor swung his fist into Steven's stomach, causing Steven to double over as the door opened and in walked two Raptors.

"Bring the woman," the female Raptor said, her mask already back in place. "She will make him reply to me." One Raptor left the room, presumably to get Raeleigh.

Here we go again. Steven fought through the pain to stand. Although this new development piqued his interest, he couldn't overcome the suspicion of yet another Raptor ploy.

Part of that didn't make sense, but did it need to? The Raptors loved playing mind games; he wouldn't put it past them to give him hope, only to crush it later. Still, what she asked is something he'd do anyway if given the chance. Best case scenario, he'd be helping the CIA. Worst case, he'd be embarrassed yet again before he died.

Moments later, the Raptor brought Raeleigh. Her dark brown eyes lit up when she saw him.

"You two," the female Raptor said, pointing to the Raptors. "Wait outside." They left, leaving Raeleigh.

"*Por favor*," the female Raptor said, gesturing to Raeleigh. "Tell her."

"They say they're CIA and want us to get information out of the Soul-stealer during our walks."

Raeleigh nodded. "Okay."

Steven shot Raeleigh an uneasy glance. "How do we know this isn't a trick?"

Her sad eyes said everything. "Would it matter if it was?"

"I guess not. Best case scenario, these two really are CIA. Worst case, they're toying with us…for the umpteenth time."

"A bit redundant, if you ask me," Raeleigh said.

Steven's body shook in a silent chuckle. "Alright, let's do it."

He couldn't stop himself from feeling a *little* energized at the prospect of fighting back, and just when he had gotten comfortable with the idea of giving up.

CHAPTER 24

TRUTH IN LOVE

They strolled past the grass figurines at a leisure pace; him and Raeleigh… with Nythan in-between. He was desensitized to the eight Raptors with rifles, but the sight of one of them pointed at Raeleigh got his blood boiling. He ground his teeth, knowing there was nothing he could do. Not yet anyway.

Steven thought the Soulstealer's host, Nythan, was either completely naive or excessively toying with them. Neither truly mattered to him. His newfound mission with the two undercover CIA agents brought him back up to fighting strength.

Time to turn the tables. He steeled his face and put on a bored expression. "So, you've all these people do your bidding. Do you have an army or something?"

"These hedges were recently trimmed," Nythan said, smiling.

Steven ate the things he really wanted to say and instead cocked his head at Nythan. "What?"

Raeleigh spoke next. "Were you always…like this?"

Nythan drew in, one eye scrunching slightly. "I'd prefer not to answer that. I'm not offended or mad you asked. It's just, you know, we're not on the same side."

They turned the corner and started down the short path to the disgusting two-headed statue of the Soulstealer. Steven found himself unable to contain his kindling rage. "Right, 'cuz telling us might impede your quest for world domination." The Raptor to Steven's right took a step closer, but Steven felt undeterred.

"It's not *like* that." Nythan stopped in front of the statue.

"Oh really, what's it like then? Because *that*.." Steven's hand shot out, finger pointing at the middle statue, "shouts 'I want to engulf the world in fire and brimstone.'"

"Steven!" Raeleigh hissed.

"No, no, it's okay." Nythan raised his hands. "You have a right to be angry. It's about time we acknowledge the elephant in the room. My people hurt you."

Steven's fingernails cut into the palms of his shaking hands. "No," his voice rose. "Hurting someone usually involves a small or moderate amount of pain. Hurting implies they can recover." His chest heaved, face trembling as the rage inside fought to burst out. "Your people *slaughtered* us." A single tear fought its way down the side of his face.

Nythan again waved his hand at the Raptor inching closer to Steven. "I under—"

"Women," Steven talked louder. "Children. Old men. Entire families. *You* are responsible for their gruesome deaths. *You* could've stopped it." Steven pointed straight at Nythan's face. "*That's* what you represent. Death. For God's sake man, you people killed three families just to hide the fact that you pillaged our headquarters for that video of you and the Gatekeeper. Jeff, his wife Sara, and his daughter Trista were in that house. All of them gone. And to make things worse, you *raped* Sara before killing her, just to make it look like a convincing burglary!"

Steven inhaled deeply, trying to regain his breath. When he saw Raeleigh's distraught face, the hot steam poured out of him like a release valve. His shoulders slumped and his arms fell. "But oh, I forgot, you want to take over the world...and you'll stop at nothing to get what you want."

"Damn it, Steven, I keep telling you it isn't like that!"

The rage surged back before Steven even realized. "WELL, WHAT IS IT THEN?" He shook his fist at Nythan. "Cuz these Raptors sure as hell aren't here to throw you a birthday party for world's oldest demon!"

The Soulstealer's attention suddenly diverted and he pointed at a Raptor behind Steven. "Don't you dare!" Nythan bellowed, then winced. His face transitioned across a full range of emotions; confusion, anger, contempt, revulsion, and grief. He turned to Steven, holding his gaze. "Just hold on a second."

Steven narrowed his eyes. "I've held on for a long time, Nythan, a long-a** time. I've heard the stories from other Solis members. I've seen the century-old still shots. I've held onto the hope that if you were to even return, we could do our part in putting you down like the dog you are." Steven crossed his arms.

Nythan sniffed and continued staring at Steven. "How did you know my name?"

Raeleigh's eyes widened in terror. Steven felt the floor disappear beneath him. *Well s****, he thought. "Uh," was all he could get out.

"Steven," Nythan started, turning to Raeleigh, "Raeleigh, please just listen for a second. I had no idea the Raptors would do all these things. I told them *not* to harm innocent people. Now, granted, Bane..." Nythan froze. His jaw clamped shut as if it were switched off.

Steven frowned. *Why is he talking about Bane from the third person?*

"Look, they got overzealous," Nythan said. "They *really* wanted to keep me safe. And I get it...it makes sense—" Nythan's eye twitched and his nose crinkled. "...but I—I didn't know they'd do that to the Masons, or those families—" He winced again. "I'm really, really, sorry about that. They didn't give me a chance to—" Nythan's mouth jerked. "...make it clear to them that I did *not* want a bloodbath. It all happened so quickly."

Nythan shut his eyes with a huff. "Hold on."

Steven eyed Nythan, trying to figure out if he had Tourette's Syndrome or if something more confusing was happening. Steven stole a glance at Raeleigh, whose mouth was slightly agape. He looked back at Nythan in time to see him smack his lips as if tasting something rotten.

"In any case," Nythan started again. "I'm telling you all of this because I want to do something different this time. *I* want to be different. My goal doesn't have to come at the expense of you or whatever else you think I'm trying to destroy."

Steven stared at him, his confusion overtaken by suspicion. "What exactly are you playing at here?"

Nythan extended his hands up at the sky. "I'm not playing at anything!"

"Just…Steven," Raeleigh cut in. Steven shut his mouth as she focused on Nythan. "What *is* your goal?"

Nythan suddenly burst out laughing. Steven went wide-eyed for a split second, then regained his composure. *What in the* hell *is going on here?*

"Sorry," Nythan said to Raeleigh. "I promise I'm not laughing at you." He then stared at Steven.

This kid's f***ing crazy, Steven thought.

"My goal…" Nythan continued, "Is to transcend."

Raeleigh pursed her lips. "Transcend into what?"

Nythan shrugged.

Steven narrowed his eyes. *What* is *this kid doing?* "And when you transcend," he interjected, "you become a god and destroy the world with a meteor or something?"

"No, I'm not trying to do anything like that."

Steven resisted the urge to laugh. "Says the guy who wants to become all-powerful."

Nythan huffed. "I wish I could tell you everything. I *want* to tell you everything. But as soon as I do…ugggh! I can't even tell you why I can't tell you!"

"Nythan," Raeleigh said. "Why can't you tell us?"

"Because you guys want to destroy me. I don't want to hurt you, so I don't want to tell you too much that the Raptors have to…ya know," he said, jutting his head to the Raptor beside him.

"But the Raptors answer to you. Tell them not to hurt us."

Nythan gave her a boyish grin that sent a chill down Steven's spine. "I did. That's why you guys are still standing here."

"Oh," she said, frowning. "Well, what *can* you tell us? You don't seem to be as bad as we were led to believe. Even me talking to you this week… you can't be more than twenty-one years old. You're just a baby."

Steven compressed his lips. "Except that he's been alive since before Christ, and we've been fighting him, and the world's been fighting him, and millions of lives have been lost in the process. Now we're all here chatting like old friends."

Raeleigh let out a giggle. Steven jerked his head back, raising both eyebrows. Nythan went bug-eyed, looking between the two.

"Yeah, but I feel like something's missing," Raeleigh said, looking at the Soulstealer. "Unless he's just completely misleading us, this is *not* the bringer of death you and Jeff have been warning about all these years."

Steven crossed his arms, looking at Raeleigh. *Please tell me this is part of your ploy.* "Well, I wouldn't expect him to come right out and say it."

"Yeah, but…Steven, just look at him."

"I am, and I'm not fooled." Steven pointed at Nythan. "This face right here has destroyed a lot of lives."

"No," Raeleigh said. "What I mean is, it's obvious to me that there's something about all this that doesn't make sense. We're missing *something*, and he obviously doesn't want to tell us for fear we'd know too much."

Nythan didn't respond.

Raeleigh gestured toward him. "Just nod if I'm on the right track."

Nythan bobbed his head up and down.

Just what are *you hiding,* Steven thought, suppressing the urge to roll his eyes. "What does any of this matter? He's the Soulstealer. He eats people's souls like it's a damn four-course meal. And he wants to do that to everyone."

"Soulstealer?" they both said in unison.

Steven scratched at a nonexistent itch on his head. "Uh…yeah. It's… kind of my nickname…for you."

Nythan raised an eyebrow, looking at the Raptors. "Soulstealer…as in, I steal souls?"

"Yup, that's…that's where I was going with it."

"Catchy," Nythan said, his eye twitching and nose crinkling at the same time yet again.

Raeleigh pounced. "See? See! That right there." She pointed at Nythan. "What's going on with that? I feel like, *that's* what it is."

There is *something going on,* Steven thought, then shook his head. "Raeleigh…"

"Oh, c'mon Steven. I gave up after I found out Gar—my *traitor* fiance—was a Raptor. They *have* us. The only way we're realistically getting out of here is through a funeral. But even that isn't likely, because no one will ever be able to find our bodies."

Steven smirked. *She's got a point.*

"...I've had enough time to think," she continued. "To come to terms with it all. We have here in front of us the *whole* damn reason we've been devoting all this time and energy. He's standing, right here! So, before we die, I really, *really*, want to find out what this horses*** is all about."

Steven exhaled a shaky breath, trying to tamp down the swelling in his chest. "I don't think I've ever heard you curse before in your life. It's actually quite attractive."

Raeleigh scowled. "Yeah, well, being betrayed by the one you love and facing oblivion will do that to you."

"Not everyone who loves you betrayed you, Raeleigh." His heart screamed for him to reach out to touch her.

*F*** it,* he thought.

"I mean...you're right. Since we're both going to die here, I might as well come out and say it. Sorry if this's getting a bit mushy for you, Mr. Soulstealer, but I don't know how much longer I have with her."

To Steven's surprise, Nythan took a step backward and swept his hand towards Raeleigh.

Steven didn't hesitate to fill the void the Soulstealer created, drawing close to Raeleigh. "I know you've heard me say this, but I need to say it again. I love you with every fiber of my being."

He stared straight into her eyes, and the rest of the world fell away. "I love everything about you. Your eyes, your ears, your heart, from the top of your head to the bottom of your feet...you're all I ever wanted. The scorching sun, the icy moon, the worst monster imaginable—which, when I think about it, is standing just a couple feet away from us—all that won't stop me from wanting to spend the rest of my life with you. I may not have all the eloquent words that Garrett, that tiny little insecure *bastard*, may have been able to conjure up, but I'm a billion times more sincere about it."

Raeleigh gazed moonstruck into his eyes. Steven's right hand shook so violently against his body he felt it in his cheeks.

"Will you just…shut up," she blurted. She threw herself up on her tippy toes and kissed him. The world came back into view a few seconds later, and he pulled away, looking around.

Nythan let out a sly grin. "Don't mind me. You may think I'm Satan and all, but I've no intention of interrupting what you've got going on here."

Raeleigh's musical laugh filled the awkward silence around them as she wiped tears on her sleeve. "I can't believe we're in this situation. This is so unreal."

Steven blinked, his mind consumed by the kiss Raeleigh just planted on him.

Nythan nodded. "Yeah, my thoughts exactly." He shrugged. "Anyways, yes, there's more to it than just me being your worst nightmare. This whole *evil nemesis of the world* thing these past centuries is just as misrepresented as everything else in history."

The words snapped Steven out of his trance, and he fixated on the Soulstealer.

"I'll admit…*some* of it is as bad as it seems. But the more I learn about it all," Nythan continued, "the more I realize that neither side took the time to try and make it work. I wanna change that. I can't change all the horrible things we've done to each other. If I could, I would. I'm just trying to…make it all stop."

Steven thrust his jaw forward. "You make it sound like you're…not…a part…of the struggles between you and us. I don't get that." His thoughts bogged down when trying to think through what was happening with Nythan. He wanted to figure out what was going on, but he wanted to kiss Raeleigh more.

"In a way, I'm not," Nythan said, "and in another way, I am. It's reallllly complicated. There's more to consider than just what you and I know. That's the best way I can explain it, at least for now." Nythan shrugged, then straightened as his face turned to stone.

"Yes," Raeleigh started, "I think I understand. But answer me this, if you get what you want, what happens to us? Not *us* as in Steven and me, but *us* as in humankind. What happens to the world?"

Steven felt flash anger at what the love of his life was saying. "Raeleigh, he's still the enemy."

Nythan rubbed his chin. He stayed silent for a good ten seconds, then said, "I'll tell you on the way. We're leaving tomorrow."

CHAPTER 25

THE GREAT REVEAL

The kiss from earlier that day kept replaying in Steven's mind. He finally said what he always wanted to say to Raeleigh. Too bad it took the threat of impending death to do it. His heart leaped a beat as he touched a finger to his lips.

What if she thought it was all just an act?

The sound of his room's door being unlocked cut that worry short. In walked the slender woman and balloon animal of a Raptor; the duo who claimed to be CIA.

Balloon Animal unfurled a burlap bag, and Steven smirked. "Yeah, yeah. I know the drill."

They led him through those same corridors, flight of stairs, doorway, and into a now familiar chair. The bag came off, as did the female Raptor's mask.

"Time to tell," she said. "What did you hear?"

Steven swelled with excitement.

"Well," he began, "w—"

Before he could finish, the door flew open. In spilled half a dozen Raptors the size of linemen. They seized Steven, slammed Balloon Animal up against a wall like he was made of paper, and a couple of Raptors stopped on either side of the woman. Behind them walked the Soulstealer.

"Hola, Mia," Nythan said.

"My Lord," Mia said, bowing. "I was just—"

"Yes, I know." Nythan waved her off before looking at Steven.

Steven raised his chin and met the Soulstealer's gaze, which shifted to Balloon Animal, who was covered in Raptors.

"Don't worry," the Soulstealer said. "I'm not going to hurt you, Mia. I'm actually glad that you work for the CIA. I need their help."

Well f*** me sideways, Steven thought.

"I don't—"

Nythan circled a finger around the midsize dining room. "This place has cameras."

Steven felt chills along the back of his neck.

"Bring them," Nythan commanded.

The Soulstealer's guardians hustled Mia and Steven out of the room. As Steven was thrust into the corridor, he was blindfolded, earplugged, burlapped, and his bindings were refastened. They led him outside and into the backseat of a truck, where a soft set of hands behind him grasped his.

Steven smiled. *Raeleigh.*

He clung to her throughout the bumpy two-day journey. At the end of the drive, a firm set of hands brought them out of the SUV and up a flight of clanging aluminum stairs. Even with the earplugs, the roaring of aircraft propellers reverberated in his eardrums.

The hell are we going? Steven thought.

On the plane, the Raptors pulled him and Raeleigh apart and pushed him into a stiff cushioned seat. At some point, Steven fell asleep, only to be jarred awake as they struck the ground and came to a rapid halt.

His captors again wrangled him out of his seat. A wave of intense heat blasted his face as he stood in the door. The familiar scent of water reached his nostrils. Steven descended the plane's stairs and was led about ten yards forward until he ascended another flight of aluminum stairs, then seated once again in another stiff cushioned seat.

I don't even think we're on the same continent anymore, Steven thought.

A cool breeze hit his face as he was led down the plane's steps. He sucked in a breath of fresh air before being shoved into the back of a large vehicle. His lower back ached from the constant seated position, but he felt comforted knowing Raeleigh couldn't be far. Moments later, someone was forced into the seat next to him and collapsed against his shoulder. The person's hand grazed his. Steven grabbed it, slowly realizing the hand felt too slender and calloused to be Raeleigh's. He disengaged himself from the stranger, but the hand clenched his.

Oookay, Steven thought as he stopped struggling. *God, please let her still be close by.*

They dragged Steven out, veering him through a series of twists and turns. He was handled into a large wooden bucket before descending downward. Fear pricked at his skin as he bobbed into darkness. The bucket plunked on the floor, splashing him with water. Rough hands jerked him forward. He caught his balance and was led through a hall that echoed with an overwhelming commotion. Hands reached out and touched him; his face, hair, arms, everywhere.

In the span of a few seconds, his bag, blindfold, and earplugs came off. Steven clamped his eyes shut as they attuned to the light.

"No more needed," a raspy voice said. Steven's bindings were cut, freeing his hands. As his eyes adjusted, Steven became aware he was in a cement cavern. He swiveled left, happy to see Raeleigh shielding her eyes from the light. To his right, Mia, the CIA agent, rubbed her wrists as a rough-looking captor cut her zip ties away.

Steven started to feel uneasy. They were standing on a smooth stone stage, surrounded by a horde of people crowding the area who grunted, growled, and howled. Some wore masks of animal bone or human skull. Many of them carried melee weapons. Their dark baggy clothing was adorned with chains and spikes, and their bodies were covered with tattoos and brands.

Steven's gaze settled on a tall naked man standing in front of them, whose entire body was covered in brands and intricate tattoo designs. He wore a fencing mask made of tiny rib bones with no mouth opening or eye sockets.

"Last American rats, I hear," his grizzly voice snarled through the rib-cage mask.

"Where's here, exactly?" Steven asked, checking his surroundings. The cold, dreary cavern of stone showed nothing to reveal their whereabouts.

"Not the USA, cuz I'm pretty sure you're Unas, which puts us in Europe. How about France? Final answer!"

The naked man cocked his head to the side before getting up into Steven's face. His long fingernails clenched Steven's jaw.

"Pretty words. I want tongue," he hissed, wiggling his sharp fingernails.

Steven scrunched his face in disgust. "No, thank you."

"Fortunate one," the naked man continued, "Must wait. Maker come soon. You bleed before Widowmaker."

"Sorry," Steven said, "I'm afraid I'm not much of a widow, see, you need to have lady parts for that to—"

Steven yelped as the guy's sharp nails sliced down his cheek. His face stung with the might of a thousand tiny scorpions.

Naked Man grunted through his mask. "Gravity pulls hand."

Steven figured it best not to correct the guy again. Naked Man turned toward Raeleigh, and a jolt of terror shot through Steven. But the guy turned and strode away, flicking his hand outwards.

A gang of Unas jumped onto the stage, grabbing Steven and the two women and pulling them through a series of tunnels. Their journey ended when they were thrown into a makeshift cell with pasty white bars. Steven gave their new prison a vicious shake, but the rebar-reinforced bars held firm.

Well, at least we're still together. He grabbed Raeleigh's hands.

The CIA agent's trembling hand clasped his exposed forearm; the same slender calloused hands that had reached for him on the ride here. Her eyes widened as she digested her new surroundings. Steven surveyed the area around his cell. Four guards with bone masks stared back at them.

Steven stared them down. *They've killed your friends. They're killing them now,* he reminded himself over and over. He had fun imagining different ways to kill a Raptor and an Unas. The thought made him smirk at the guards. *You gotta keep it together to do that. Just keep it together.*

CHAPTER 26

DO OR DO NOT

Steven paced his cell. He had heard of Unas' brutality, but this brought things to a whole new level. *Were these really made from our Ordo Europe brothers and sisters?* His body shuddered.

The Soulstealer came and took Raeleigh, Mia, and someone from Ordo Europe that the Unas captured. They were to help with some damnable Ordo Solis peace treaty. Steven felt confident the bad blood between the two sides would prove too tricky for common ground to be found. Someone would make the wrong move.

The thought produced as much fear as it did satisfaction. Raeleigh was at that meeting. He prayed she stayed out of the crossfire should things go south. The Unas cleared out as well. One thug guarded his cell, a few Unas walked the tunnels.

If ever he should devise a plan to escape, he couldn't pick a better time. His current confinement, however, wouldn't give him an inch to work with. No one would claim Steven to be a small man, but he made minimal impact trying to shake loose, kick open, or shoulder bash the structure. *No way out.*

Occasionally, some wannabe masked barbarian trotted past. One passed by when a sharp shout came from Steven's right. His guard and the patrolling Unas turned around. They made to bring their weapons up but were riddled with bullet holes; red spattered in every direction. One fell against the wall, the other face-first into the sandy floor.

Steven blinked at their newly minted corpses. He snapped into action, rattling the bone bars and pressing his face against them to peer down the tunnel, but couldn't see more than ten feet. He heard hushed whispers before three figures appeared. They each wore long-sleeved bodysuits and balaclavas. The first pointed its weapon at Steven; the other two switched back and forth between Steven and further down the hallway. Their twitchy movements made Steven wonder if they had ever held a weapon before.

More masks, always more masks.

"Uh, hi," one said, looking Steven's prison up and down.

Steven blinked, then waved. "Who're you guys?"

"Doesn't matter who we are, chap, who are you?"

These guys didn't know I was here. "I'm Steven. Proud Ordo Solis, American branch."

The men glanced at one another, then back at Steven. "We heard you were bagged," one said.

"We don't have time for this," another hissed.

"And you propose to leave this chap here? He's obviously not Unas," the second man replied.

"There're two Solis Americans left," Steven said. "I'm one, and the other, Raeleigh, is currently being held by the Soulstealer as some sort of liaison for the meeting with Solis Europe."

"J, we have to finish clearing this section before they come back," the first man said.

Steven motioned down the hallway. "No problem, please feel free to take 'em all out. But make sure you come back. I'd rather not continue to be a prisoner." He pointed at the long scratch marks on his face. "Not sure how much longer they'll restrain themselves."

"Good idea. Alright. Let's go," the second man said. They hurried away.

Those buffoons have got *to be Solis Europe.* Steven pumped his fist. "Yessssss!"

He paced the length of his cell. At last, he heard heavy footsteps coming toward him. The gaggle of colored balaclavas found Steven smirking as they came to a stop in front of him.

"Here he is," one of them gestured toward Steven.

A slender figure stepped forward and peered through the bone bars. "You're Ordo Solis?" a woman's voice demanded.

Steven winked. "Wouldn't dream of being otherwise."

"Who vas the first of our Order?" she questioned in a thick German accent.

"Jedidiah, the wisest of us all," Steven recited. He imagined the many afternoons he and Jeff spent as Ordo Solis initiates in frigid New England. Their mentor made them memorize whole paragraphs of information to pass their oral examinations.

"And who is ze Lionheart?" she asked.

Steven clenched his fists, shaking them. "We're *all* the Lionheart!"

The woman looked at the bolted lock. "Destroy zese doors, break him out." Two of the men broke the bones from the rebar and pried a few of them apart. Steven wasted no time stepping through to freedom.

"Out, *schnéll!*" she barked. The gang sped down the hallway. Steven ran a few steps before skidding to a halt and turning back.

"What are you doing!" someone yelled back.

"Just a second!" Steven bent down over one of the deceased Unas and ripped off a piece of the tattered clothing. He dabbed the almost dried blood oozing from the corpse and started writing on the wall. After he finished, Steven stepped back to soak in his handiwork before rejoining the Solis party.

I'm coming for her, Bane, Steven affirmed as he sprinted to catch up with his rescuers.

"Hey! Hey you guys!" Steven said when once he caught up to them. "There's a meeting taking place right now. The other Solis American is there."

"We know!" someone remarked. "That's why we're here. Clear out what we can while they're gone. We have the meeting taken care of."

Steven hopped in the air. "Hell yeah! Bout damn time!"

CHAPTER 27

FIRELIT

They guided Steven to a Solis Europe safehouse where he intended to stay until Solis Europe extracted Raeleigh from the meeting.

"Sorry for all the secrecy, chap. I'm George," one of his rescuers said. He took off his mask, revealing a round, pudgy face, green eyes, and short brown hair with a receding hairline.

"I get it," Steven replied. "Where's Raeleigh?"

"Soon. Our folks at the meeting will extract her when they leave."

"Great." Steven took a good look around. The living room looked like it had been decorated in the 1970s. Wood fireplace, plank walls, temple-like ceilings, felt furniture with bright colors, and TV dinner trays scattered about. He peered out the window, noting a tram chug down the street and a wall of orange, pink, white, and brown apartment buildings on the other side.

"Where am I?"

"Prague," George said.

Steven cocked an eyebrow.

"Czechia. Used to be called the Czech Republic. Eastern Europe."

Steven scrunched his lips and raised his eyebrows. "Hmmph. The way these guys work amazes me. I had no idea I was even on another continent until they unfurled me."

George and Steven made small talk until two more Solis Europe arrived. A blonde with the look of a supermodel reached him first. The second, a much taller albino guy, hunched over beside her.

"You," she commanded, looking straight at Steven. The narrowed slits of her icy blue eyes matched her sharp tone, and Steven felt like exposed prey under her stare. He instantly recalled Mia's lethal eyes the first time she revealed herself.

Steven coughed, placing a hand on his chest. "Me?"

"*Ja*, you."

"Me what?"

"Vhat are you doing here?"

"You brought me here."

"*Nein*. Vhat are you doing so far away?"

"It wasn't by choice, that's what. We were kidnapped back in America. The Soulstealer took us here to be pawns in his little game."

"Vhat game?"

"Whatever game he's playing."

"Vhich is vhat?"

Steven felt like they were reenacting a bad 80s detective film. "Whatever the hell game he's playing, is what. I've no idea what it is. He *says* he's after a peaceful resolution to end the last thousand years of rampaging violence."

"You don't know vhat he has planned?" she accused, giving him a long look. Steven didn't know how he became the subject of interrogation, but his patience dropped to zero.

"Look, lady. *It* brought me *there, you* brought me *here*. If you're so interested in my itinerary, how about you go ask the Soulstealer? He's a pretty snooty little bastard; he'll probably take you up on the offer, smirking that stupid little smirk of his."

The woman crossed her arms. Steven squirmed under her unyielding death stare, subduing any urge to ogle. Without a word, she whipped around and left the room.

Her companion alternated between Steven and the doorway. "I uh… I'll be right back," he muttered before following her out.

Steven's gaze slowly slid to George; amusement etched across his face.

"That was Adeline," George said. "She led the team that broke you out. A fireball. We like to point her in the direction of our problems. She makes them go away posthaste."

"I see. Quite the looker."

"Oh yeah, but uh, in this case chap, what you see is what you get. Quite literally, in fact. We leave the deeper problems to those with the uh, appropriate mental faculties."

Steven frowned. "Did you just call her a bimbo?"

George shrugged with a sly grin. "Her ideas are a bit more short-sighted than some of the other more…thorough solutions. She's quite good at doing the job that needs doing, though."

"I'll bet," Steven said, lifting an eyebrow.

"In any case, what she was trying to ask you in her own way was: what happened?"

Steven let out a slow sigh, taking a seat in one of the armchairs facing a fireplace where logs smoldered. Above the brick layered chimney base hung a mirror, letting him spy on anyone who came through the door. "It's a long…super long story. The kind of story that gets worse the longer it goes on."

"Well, chap, insufferably long stories are our specialty. We Solis Euro enjoy a good story."

Steven gave a sad smile. "Believe me, George, there's nothing good about this one. It starts off s***y and becomes downright heinous." He shook his head at the memories of death, sorrow, and suffering. "These guys we're facing…they're monsters. Evil in the purest sense."

"Steven, you're one of the few people who has seen Satan in the flesh. You've talked to him, I've heard. We have *got* to understand our adversary. He has caused quite a stir in the Americas; his fanatics have begun sacrificing themselves to him by the score. It's a worrisome discovery."

Steven stared into the bright fire, listening to the crackling of the wood. He at last nodded his head.

"Okay, let's start at the beginning."

CHAPTER 28

REGAL

Steven's eyes fluttered open amid a series of subtle pokes. He found himself slouched in an armrest chair, propped up by a pillow, still in front of a lit fireplace.

An agreeable-looking man teetered over him. He wore an oval pincenez; the kind that only hung by gripping the upper bridge of his nose. After everything the Soulstealer put him through, Steven felt desensitized to what he once considered ordinary. But even violent desensitization couldn't convince him this guy looked normal.

No more than five feet, the man sported a long brown tailored coat with a billowing white shirt underneath. A dark green vest buttoned up his torso with a golden chain hanging from the front pocket.

Is that a pocket watch? Steven wondered in amusement.

The small man shifted his weight, adjusting his stance and drawing attention to his tan plaid pants.

Steven trembled in silent laughter, wondering how far back in time he traveled for this bloke to be real. The man scrutinized Steven as if expecting something. Steven stood, hunching over as he worked out the kinks of his comfortable snooze. When Steven stopped moving, only then did the little man speak.

"Steven." He addressed him in a British accent, face as bland as his words.

Steven tilted his head in exaggeration. "Mr. Well-Dressed-Gentleman-of-the-Court."

The man's face flushed as he glanced down at his outfit before assuming a rigid posture and pushing his shoulders back. "We have pressing matters to discuss."

"I'm still talking to Solis Europe, right? Not British royalty I assume." Steven grinned.

"Don't be absurd," the man protested, straightening his huge tie.

Steven gestured to the man. "Let's just get this part out of the way. You look like you're dressed to go see Queen Elizabeth. No one dresses like that, not even my great-grandfather. I can't tell if that's how you normally are, or you just came from a Renaissance reenactment."

"Yes, yes, I understand my attire is rather unusual. But we live in unusual times." The gentleman winked.

"That doesn't...that doesn't even make sens—"

"Now!" the man interrupted. "I'm told that Solis America was working on a plan to oust the Satan in the most public of ways. Could you please illustrate your intentions?"

Steven pointed in the direction the man came from. "Sure, right after you walk Raeleigh through that door."

The man huffed with frustration. "We're working that out, Steven, but for now—"

"I've been told what I should do 'for now' since the Soulstealer's return. Bring me Raeleigh, *now*."

"We can't just make her magically appear."

"I don't care how you do it. Just do it."

"Steven, please. We need your help. Our world is under siege once more from the Satan himself. We must stop him."

"And I've every intention of doing just that. *After* Raeleigh and I see each other."

The man stared at Steven for several seconds before turning around and walking out of the room. He returned a few minutes later, crossing his arms.

"There has been a complication with the recovery of your friend."

Steven narrowed his eyes. "Complication, *how*, precisely? And she's not just *my* friend. She's Ordo Solis."

"There was an engagement with the Satan's forces; we have not reinitiated contact with our away team just yet."

"Then I'll be waiting here till you do."

"Well, that just won't do."

"Listen, Winston Churchill. Raeleigh and I are all that's left of Solis America. The rest are either dead, moved on with their lives, or traitors. We've been carted halfway across the world. I've watched innocent people murdered. I've been shot at. Tortured. And had to have stupid conversations like these for months." Steven paused to catch his breath. "Give me the *f***ing* love of my life back. Now, b****."

The gentleman grew crimson. Steven couldn't tell whether it was from rage or embarrassment.

"This way," the gentleman said, whipping around and proceeding back out of the room.

Steven trailed the man past several people eating in a kitchen. They trudged up a flight of narrow wooden stairs that groaned with each step and stopped in front of a closed door, knocking four times.

The door opened, and Steven found himself looking at a well-equipped surveillance room. He spied camera feeds, radios, bionic ears, cameras, and motions detector bulbs. Steven spent a lot of time perusing most of these gadgets on Amazon, waiting in vain for Solis America to fund his wish list.

Steven recognized George among several people sitting at a computer station.

George waved. His green eyes lit up with surprise. "Welcome to our listening post, chap." He turned his attention to the well-dressed gentleman. "What can I do for you, Mr. Hoche?"

So that's his name, Steven thought.

"Steven here needs a debriefing on the latest development," Mr. Hoche said.

George gave a sluggish nod. "Right then, come on over here."

Steven complied. His eyes bore holes into the computer screen as

George accessed a body cam video, and Steven willed it to show him what he wanted to see.

"Mate, before I show you this, I must warn you. It's very nasty stuff. Did not go well for us."

A jolt of fear ripped through Steven's spine, striking his heart. He struggled to compose himself, biting his tongue as he took a seat next to George. "Hit it."

CHAPTER 29

BENEATH THE WILLOW TREE

The red-tinted video showed a well-lit barren room at chest level. Steven saw no carpet, just white plaster walls that needed painting and lights hanging from cords. A few circular tables and a dozen chairs rested in the middle. The person wearing the camera directed people carrying Uzis to various spots throughout the area. There were at least a couple of dozen people. The ones furthest from the camera, scattered about, donned white surgical masks and different colored bandannas.

"What's happening?" Steven asked.

"The Solis Commandery is preparing for the meeting with the Satan," Mr. Hoche explained, straightening his jacket.

"All of them?" Steven continued. Mr. Hoche didn't answer.

The individuals next to the cameraperson wore formal Ordo Solis attire, broadcasting their position as being on the high council, the Solis Commandery. They wore black jackets and pants, a white-colored cape, black circular hats with oversized white feathers, and white neckties. The slanted red cross marked each cape and hat. A flat Mohawk of white feathers extended over their hat and behind their neck. Gilt braid, medals, and embroideries adorned their black jackets. The Commandery wore no useful weapons, only a straight sword affixed to each belt.

"Remember the plan," the man with the body camera said.

"Who's speaking?" Steven asked.

"The former Worshipful Master," George answered.

"Ludwig von Maur?"

"Yes."

"Why do you say former?"

"Keep watching."

The man to Ludwig's left approached so closely he covered the camera lens. All Steven could see were shades of dark gray and black.

"That was Oliver, the Grand Historian."

"Is he in place?" the Grand Historian whispered.

"He's ready," Ludwig confirmed.

The next exchange of words were indecipherable, except for something about a beard.

"When should I go out there to receive him?" someone else asked. Steven still couldn't see through the darkened shades.

"That's the Tiler, Freddy," George said.

Oliver moved out of the camera's way.

"Ebba, our Marshal, is beside him," George acknowledged.

"Soon...it'll be soon. Hold on," Ludwig said, sounding nervous. *"Elsie's at the front desk; she'll come get us when* he *arrives."*

A woman came into view, clutching her sword. *"I don't like this,"* she stated.

"Me neither, Ola, but it's our duty to be humanity's sword and shield, no matter how much we dislike what it demands of us."

Another finely dressed man approached Ola. Steven breathed a small sigh of relief. "Enzo," he said before George spoke.

Steven recognized the Grand Secretary from the many video calls and letters discussing Solis America's meeting minutes. He felt relieved to see Enzo alive and well after the Raptors made him reveal the Secretary's identity.

"We've done everything we could to prepare. It's all up to God now," Enzo said, resting his hand on Ola's shoulder.

Ola shrugged off Enzo's hand. She proceeded to a table and seated herself with a look of misery. Before anything else could be said, the conference doors flung open. In walked a group needing no introduction.

"Ah hell, what happened to Elsie?" the Historian grumbled.

"I hope she's okay," Enzo said.

"Focus!" Ludwig hissed.

Even with all the masks, Steven picked out Nythan, the boy behind all the madness. An army of Raptors flanked the Soulstealer, most of them armed with multiple guns and knives. Nythan chose a bone mask representing a vampire, a veiny piece of work with blood-red eyeholes and horns protruding everywhere. The woman on his left dressed in rags and a deer skull with antlers.

His eyes then fell on Raeleigh, trailing the middle of the pack, prodded by the Raptors behind her. Mia walked beside Raeleigh; they held each other's hand.

All but five Raptors broke from Nythan and made long strides across the ballroom to different spots. The camera angle didn't stretch enough to catch them all. The ones he did see stopped face-to-face in front of the other Ordo members placed throughout the room.

Nythan approached the tables, taking off his vampire mask and handing it to the woman in antlers.

"Greetings," Ludwig said without skipping a beat. *"My name is Ludwig, Worshipful Master of the Ordo Solis. This is Ola, our Senior Grand Warden. Here is Oliver, our Grand Historian; Ebba, our Grand Marshal; and Freddy, our Tiler. You've met Enzo, our Grand Secretary. I'll let our mutual friend here introduce himself."*

The camera panned to the left, showing a seated man in plainclothes that Steven hadn't noticed before.

"I'm Mr. Smith," the man said in monotone.

"This is P," Nythan said. The tuxedo-wearing figure called P made a terse bow. *"This is Raeleigh. She's from the Ordo Solis in America, and here is Mia. She's an associate of Mr. Smith."*

Steven's gut wrenched in agony. *You don't deserve to speak her name, you bastard!*

"Before we begin, can you please dispense with your guards?" asked Ola, the Senior Grand Warden. *"We'd prefer to discuss our agenda without your overbearing custodians."*

Nythan signaled to the Raptors to leave. All but one of them and the woman in deer antlers remained. The rest moved outside Nythan's immediate vicinity and planted themselves in front of other Ordo Solis guards scattered around the outskirts of the room.

"*I prefer my two friends stay here,*" Nythan said.

"*Shall we?*" Ludwig offered. The camera showed him gesture toward the table closest to Nythan.

Nythan took his seat, smiling that stupid smile he made around Steven whenever they walked in his pretentious garden. The lone masked Raptor pushed a chair in behind him.

"*I'm glad we could all meet here together,*" Nythan began.

Whatever, Steven bristled. He eyed Raeleigh, who stood, locked hand-in-hand with Mia off to the side. He found himself saying a silent prayer. *Please, God, keep her safe.*

"*I asked for this meeting so that we could settle our differences and come to an amicable solution,*" Nythan said.

"*I was very curious indeed, Bane. First at your return and now this meeting. Highly irregular,*" Ludwig replied.

Nythan's jaw clenched as he nodded.

"*Let's get on with it,*" Oliver griped.

"*Calm, Oliver. We'll have all the time we need to get to the heart of the matter,*" Ludwig said, looking to Nythan. "*What sort of arrangement did you have in mind?*"

Nythan nodded again. "*First, I want to begin with this. I'm not here to bring some apocalyptic end to the world. All these years we've been fighting have primarily been because you thought I was the devil, when all I wanted to do was survive.*"

Oliver lashed out, "*Ever since you destroyed the Zhōu in eighth century BC, you've survived off the lives of others. You still survive off others. How can you—?*"

"*Please excuse Oliver,*" Ludwig interrupted, "*He knows the details of our history better than most. As you say, the historical account of our conflict is open to interpretation. But as harsh as Oliver's words are, I have to ask: How can we come to an accord? We seem unequivocally at odds with one another.*"

"*The source of our conflict is with the suffering that it brings,*" Nythan said.

"That's putting it mildly," Steven said aloud.

George grunted in agreement. "You got that right, chap."

"I don't need or want the lives of everyone on this planet," Nythan continued, *"But I must eat to continue living, just as you do. Those who wish to voluntarily give themselves to me aren't those you defend. You just protect the innocent. So, you aren't opposed to what I am, so much as you're opposed to me destroying the lives of those who aren't willing. Can we at least agree on that?"*

"No, we can absolutely *not* agree on that," countered Steven.

Ludwig paused before answering, *"Agreed, mostly. However, we are chartered to stop you from consuming the lives of this world, good or bad. Your hunger knows no bounds. As our Historian, Oliver, can attest, you have before stated your wish to see this world burn."*

Nythan shook his head from side to side. *"My hunger has as much of a limit as yours does. If I can be satisfied by volunteers, then there need be no conflict between us. As for the whole* burning the world *thing, I get absolutely nothing from it. It'd be as if you cut down all the trees on Earth or drank all the water from the ocean. It's just not sustainable."*

So you'd have us believe, Steven thought.

Oliver grunted, still looking displeased.

Nythan narrowed his eyes. *"It's true."*

Ola spoke next. *"Part of our concern is that your…groups…lure unsuspecting victims into believing that you'll save them. I believe the phrase is, 'you will deliver us,' if I'm not mistaken. What're you delivering them from?"*

"Every organization needs its propaganda," Nythan said. *"The CIA, the Catholic Church…even the Ordo Solis, to support some narrative that furthers itself."*

"We had all the narrative we needed from your slaughter of countless civilizations through the centuries," Steven said, crossing his arms. "It isn't propaganda if it's true."

"Fair enough," Ludwig said. *"So, your proposal is what, exactly?"*

Don't fall for his trap, Ludwig, Steven thought.

Nythan inhaled. *"I can't change the past. None of us can. But I want to establish peace. Our people will no longer fight you. We just want to be left alone."*

"Hah!" Steven sneered.

"Cheeky little twat," George commented.

"You propose a peace treaty?" Ludwig asked.

"Yes," Nythan replied. *"Let's just step away from each other. You let me live in peace, no more innocents need be involved. As you can see, Raeleigh and Mia here are both unharmed. Steven, the other Solis dude, is safe with us as well. All of them can be returned to you, in good faith of our non-aggression pact."*

Nythan looked to Raeleigh.

Steven experienced a mixture of fear and intense hatred at the attention Nythan gave her.

"Raeleigh here will confirm my intentions and explain things from her perspective," Nythan said.

No one in the video said anything in response. Ludwig moved his arm over the camera, again shrouding the footage in darkness.

A few seconds later, a loud *clap* sound echoed through the speakers. Ludwig removed his arm in time to show Nythan snatched from the chair by the Raptor next to him. The woman wearing antlers clutched her neck, blood spewing out like a fountain. To Steven's infinite relief, Mia pulled Raeleigh to the ground. Yells rose from every direction.

Steven watched in shock as chaos erupted. The Ordo and Raptors guards were engaged in hand-to-hand combat and point-blank use of their weapons. The others next to Ludwig drew their swords. Ebba, the Grand Marshal, stood closest to where the Soulstealer had been yanked off his chair. She ran over and angled her sword to strike, but a luminescent silver stream dashed out of her mouth and snaked into Nythan's.

Steven couldn't spare the time to reflect on the first recorded taking of a soul by the Soulstealer. The antler woman stood back up, blood still everywhere, as Ola sliced upwards at her with her rapier. Ola missed, giving the woman a chance to slash Ola with a jagged dagger. A mist of blood flicked from Ola's throat and floated to the floor. As she fell to the side, Enzo took Ola's place, driving the point of his sword into the antler woman's chest. His victory proved short-lived as the Soulstealer bolted back upright, tearing Enzo's soul from his body.

Out of the corner of the screen, Steven saw Mia charge Nythan. Steven stopped breathing when Raeleigh stood and sprinted after Mia. The Soulstealer outstretched his hand toward the camera in what Steven assumed to be the final moments of Ludwig and Oliver. Mia, however, screaming at the top of her lungs, swung her leg into Nythan's side and threw an uppercut at his nose. The Soulstealer's smaller Raptor companion dashed to assist him before being tackled by Raeleigh from behind.

"Ahhh, go Raeleigh *gooooo!*" Steven bellowed at the screen, clawing his hair as he strained to see through the cluster of skinny tables.

Mia mauled Nythan as she straddled him, pounding anything she could make contact with. Raeleigh fared well too, landing a few hits on her masked adversary. Through the course of the brawl, Raeleigh and her opponent rolled on top of Nythan and Mia, all kicking and screaming.

"Ludwig, do something!" Steven screamed, jumping up. The camera remained still, panning the action.

Suddenly, a bright silver light flashed where the four battled. Steven froze, scrutinizing every detail of the footage. A second flash of silver followed the first, stilling all movement on the ground. Steven fixed his gaze on the pile of bodies, willing for Raeleigh to emerge the victor.

A sole contender of the struggle surfaced, bolting upright. Nythan glared straight at Ludwig, aflame with fury. Steven choked as his hyperactive lungs smothered his heart. He didn't dare blink.

Please, God. I'm begging you.

Nythan shut his eyes. A few seconds later, he started convulsing. Glistening pale silver streams shot from all angles, devoured by the Soulstealer. Ludwig's body camera panned left and right. Ordo Solis members fell all around him. The angle returned to the Soulstealer as he finished his foul feast. Nothing but silence remained.

The Soulstealer opened his eyes. Steven's eyes glazed, fixed on Raeleigh's immobile form on the ground.

Ludwig spoke. *"For this is the work of the Evil One. The apocalypse is the only fruit he bears!"* he shouted. Nythan watched without comment before outstretching his hand. Silver streams erupted from the point of view of the camera, barreling toward Nythan.

Ludwig and Oliver fell to the ground, lifeless. The lens settled on the floor, pointing into the face of Mr. Smith. The once-indifferent CIA operative's eyes reflected an empty shell.

"WE, THE RAPTOR'S CLAW!" came a cry.

"RISE FURTHER!"

Someone shouted for everyone to find cameras and witnesses. By that time, Steven wept nonstop.

"Re...rewin...rewind."

George, not having to be told where to go, rewound to when Mia charged Nythan. Steven watched in tragic silence, yearning for something different to happen. When it didn't, he demanded it be rewound again, again, and again. Neither George nor Mr. Hoche voiced any objection. They permitted Steven to relive the traumatic event until alas, he cried no more.

"So that's it then," Steven said. His chair creaked as his hands gripped it tighter. *She's gone.*

Mr. Hoche gave Steven a puzzled look.

In one fluid motion, Steven stood, raised the chair, and slammed it against the ground. It gave an earsplitting crack. Mr. Hoche jumped at the noise.

"AHHHHHHHHHHHHHHHHHHHHHHHHH!" Steven bellowed. His fingers gripped his head so hard they felt like needles in his skull. He turned toward the door, which already had a half-dozen people standing in it. In a fit of rage, Steven's burly form stormed forward. The group made a hole for him to escape, gentle hands attempting to offer sympathy. Steven felt none of them.

She's gone.

"AHHHHHHHHHHHHHHHHHHHHHHHHHHH." He tore down a framed picture of a member long since passed. The glass shattered, but it didn't break like he needed it to.

She's not coming back.

Another frame, another shattering. Still not enough.

"AHHHHHHHHHHHHHHHHHHHHHHHHHHH." He kicked at a closed door. It cracked, but didn't give.

More people came out of various rooms, peering at the disturbance. Steven made his way down the hall and toward the stairs. "It's okay!" George called out to them. "He's in a lot of pain."

More gentle hands touched him, far more than Steven thought lived in this picture-perfect house.

She's gone.

As Steven turned toward the stairway leading to the first floor, he found it no longer possible to move forward without running over a hallway full of strangers.

Steven released another fit of pain and rage as he crumpled to the floor, no longer registering the sea of hands cradling him. Steven wailed one last time, before finally succumbing to darkness.

CHAPTER 30

PONYHOF

Steven watched the crackling fire pop and churn. His senses tingled as he wiped away a tear.

Some Ordo members came to sit with him to express their sympathy; others made small talk. He ignored them all, deaf to any human interaction. George, one of the few people he liked, came and relayed how the new Worshipful Master eagerly awaited a visit. He said nothing to George either.

Steven established today as a day of mourning, as would be tomorrow, and the rest of the year.

His peripheral vision registered new movement in the mirror from the living room entrance. He refused to acknowledge the woman who seated herself in the armchair opposite him, and she made no effort to get his attention. Eventually, Steven looked at his latest guest. Adeline, the brash German fireball, glowered at the fireplace. Steven went back to watching it as well.

"My entire family vas murdered by ze Unas." When Steven remained silent, she continued. "Four years past, zey came into my home. A tiny village outside of Hanau. Ve never knew zem or ze Ordo Solis." She shook her head. "Zey did not care. Zey took our family, even my sweet *oma*, and threw us all together in ze living room."

Adeline trembled, clenching her fist as she fought back tears. Steven felt nothing, numb to her pain.

"Zey hit us vith sharp axes. Zey beat us vith hammers. I don't know vhy, I still don't know." She wiped her nose. "Vhen I vas taken to ze hospital by neighbors, I vas barely alive." She struggled to retell the memory but appeared committed to finishing. "Zey broke my body and hurt me everywhere."

Adeline stood and shrugged her shirt off, turning around. Steven couldn't help but look. Thick gashes skated across her back to her burnt upper arm. "I don't know if zey meant to kill me or left me alive by accident."

She slumped back into her chair, not caring to put her shirt back on over her bra. Steven's eyes wandered, and he noted other scars on her torso.

"My family did not survive. Not even our dog, Imre. I vowed to *get* zem. To *find* zem. To *hurt* zem," she choked. She opened her mouth a few times, but no words came. "To make zem hurt," she cried. They stared at each other.

"My girlfriends didn't understand my pain. Zey talked about babies, how ze men are, vhich dress zey will get. I wanted to talk about how many innocents ze Unas killed, and vhat could stop zem."

Adeline shook her head and put her shirt back on. "Zey didn't understand. I couldn't be myself, and ve grew apart. It makes me sad to zink about. Zen I found ze Ordo Solis, and zey helped me make ze Unas suffer ever since. Zis is my family now. *You* are my family too."

Steven returned his gaze to the fireplace.

"We have a saying in Germany. *Das Leben ist kein Ponyhof.* Life is not child's play. It is hard and not fair."

Steven grunted. Adeline offered a sad smile. They stared at the burning crevice until he noticed she had fallen asleep.

In the mirror, a figure moved in the doorway. Steven's gaze fixed on the silhouette, shocked to see Raeleigh smiling back at him. Her blonde hair flowed softly around her shoulders. He lunged from his chair and whipped his head toward the entrance, but she had vanished. Steven bolted forward, looking both directions down the hall.

Nothing.

You're seeing things, he concluded.

Steven trudged back to his seat, turned it facing the living room entrance, and sat, not daring to close his eyes.

CHAPTER 31

VAPOR

Today marked the 13th day since he saw the love of his life wrenched from this world. The Commandery grew more impatient with Steven each day. What began as willful disregard evolved into a vow of silence, much to the agitation of those who tried to console him. He moved around the house and obeyed requests to do chores, but didn't make conversation.

He spent his afternoons at the fireplace, eyes locked onto the mirror reflecting the doorway. Raeleigh couldn't come back, but his mind refused to accept it. He still expected her to walk through the front door, as he had hallucinated last week. Of all the people he chose to ignore, Adeline was the one he wanted to ignore least. Since telling him her family tragedy, she didn't speak to him again, nor try to get him to interact. Sometimes she'd just sit with him; other times she'd help him with his chores.

George would tell him the latest developments twice a day, growing giddier as the week progressed. Czech authorities launched an investigation into the local Unas there and its connection to the recent massacre. He mentioned a coalition task force formed from law enforcement of neighboring countries. The investigation itself became somewhat of a humorous distraction to the public at large. News agencies portrayed it as gang-on-gang violence, with only token mention of why they fought.

Steven intended for today to again be nothing special; just another good old-fashioned day of silence. He swept the long hallways connecting most of the house, doing his best to focus on the activity at hand. While the public acknowledgment of their fight piqued his interest, he expected nothing to come of it. The world's knowledge of the Soulstealer spanned centuries. The vast majority of people no longer considered the historical Soulstealer relevant. A revelation clicked in Steven's mind, overpowering his attempts to silence it.

It must've been deliberate. The Soulstealer *knew* it'd be forgotten if it became a scary tale of unverified doom. Sooner or later, human skepticism would relegate the source of the crusades into an amusing children's story.

We're visual beings; we believe what we can see. The revelation intrigued him, and he spent the next hour contemplating it while he swept. *It had to have been Alexios' death. He made it look like* that *was the final battle.*

Oral and written accounts of King Alexios IV Angelos' climactic end remained the most celebrated story among the Ordo Solis. In 1200 CE, the European powers first accused one of Saladin's brothers, Saphadin, of being the newest Soulstealer. The Fourth Crusade spawned yet another mission to destroy it. Along the way, word reached the Templars that the real Soulstealer possessed a member of the ruling family in the Byzantine Empire.

The Crusaders diverted to Constantinople, where an inquiry uncovered King Angelos as the new Soulstealer. A chaotic battle sparked in the Christian capital between the Soulstealer's cult embedded in city nobility, the Crusaders, and the confused city defenders who didn't know which side to help.

When the Templars slew the Soulstealer's vessel, a twisted assortment of ethereal colors ejected from its body. No one knew how to take this never-before-seen death. After years of fruitless search for its new vessel, the Catholic Church cited the bizarre end of Angelos as the final death of the Soulstealer. The depleted European powers, weary of more Crusades, gratefully accepted the proclamation.

Maybe it really did die. Maybe it took this long to come back. Maybe—

As Steven's focus reached the end of a hallway, he saw Raeleigh, her dark brown eyes filled with peace. He flung the broomstick and rushed forward. Ten feet away, she waved and dissipated into the adjacent room.

Steven barreled around the corner, charging into a tiny bedroom where three people lay on their beds. They sat up at the abrupt intrusion.

"Did you...?" Steven wheezed, putting his hands on his knees. His robust frame hadn't moved that fast since Texas.

"Did we what?" one asked.

"Did you see someone just now?"

"You mean, except you?"

Steven scrutinized the rest of the room. Disappointed he fell for yet another one of his hallucinations, he left and returned to retrieve his broom. *She looked so* real. He looked over his shoulder every few seconds. *She even waved!* When he picked up the handle, Steven found himself face-to-face with Adeline and her neutral expression.

"At first, I saw zem too," she said. "I thought it vas a trick. But it kept happening. Seeing zem walk out of zeir bedrooms, sitting at ze kitchen table, playing in ze yard. It goes away, but I haven't forgotten how real it felt." Adeline placed a hand over her heart, closing her eyes.

"It hurts too much," Steven said.

"I know."

"I don't want to talk about it."

"I know."

It dawned on him that he broke his vow of silence. Adeline walked past him. Steven found himself looking after her. Psychic shrapnel from his shattered heart still ricocheted throughout his body. On the days he couldn't bear it, he'd stop everything and crouch in the fetal position to cry.

He picked the broomstick back up and resumed assaulting the floor. He spun around and threw it at the wall. Tears seared down his cheeks.

"Show yourself!" he bellowed, balling his hands into fists and pounding the wall. He hoped no one came to investigate the disturbance. When no one did, he turned back around.

Raeleigh stood before him. Steven's eyes widened, first in terror, then amazement. She wore the same jeans and t-shirt she wore the day she died, but he saw through her like a ghost. A silver tint gave her the appearance of a sketch.

"Raeleigh," he choked. To his surprise, she smiled. "Can you...can you hear me?" She nodded.

Steven trembled. *I must be hallucinating again. Only crazy people see ghosts.* These sorts of things don't happen to regular folk.

Well, he countered, *we aren't supposed to see someone's soul ripped from their body either, yet here we are.*

Steven inched toward Raeleigh, not daring to blink. His hand moved for her cheek. She smiled even more, closing her eyes. As his hand reached the point where it would've met skin, her hand came to his, and her silvery, spectral form dissolved, whisked away as if by a gust of wind.

Steven didn't move. Instead of anger or sorrow, a warmth washed over him. Peace flooded his senses. "Thank you, Raeleigh," he whispered. He wasn't sure if he really saw Raeleigh, or a figment of his own imagination. But at this point, Steven wasn't sure it mattered.

CHAPTER 32

WHALESONG

Steven sat at the fireplace, contemplating his next move. He felt ready ever since his contact with Raeleigh, he just didn't know what to be prepared *for*.

In walked George with Adeline and the overly dressed Renaissance man, Mr. Hoche.

"Steven," George said.

"Yes?"

Mr. Hoche breathed a sigh of relief.

"We need your help. I know you're still mourning your loss, but it's time to do something."

"*Our* loss," Steven interjected.

"Pardon?" Mr. Hoche said.

"*Our* loss. Raeleigh wasn't just special to me; she was Ordo Solis. Those other people in that video, *they* were Ordo Solis. That was a loss for us all."

"I realize that 'ole chap, but we have to move on. You cannot remain paralyzed while we are beset upon," George said.

"Mmmm," Steven grunted.

"The Worshipful Master wants to have a word with you," Mr. Hoche offered. "There is much to discuss."

"I've met enough people for the time being."

Mr. Hoche crossed his arms. "Now Steven…"

"Stop feeling sorry for yourself," Adeline cut in. "Ve have something to show you. It's big, and ve need your help." She jerked her thumb at George.

Mr. Hoche looked bewildered. "Don't speak to him in that manner!"

Steven only smiled at the reaction, looking to George. "What could you possibly need from me?"

"Those discerning Yank eyes and that crafty Yank plan," George said, matching his smile.

Mr. Hoche and Adeline spoke in hushed conversation about her apparent misconduct. Adeline stood firm in her defiance of Mr. Hoche's disapproving frown.

Steven rose and put himself in-between Mr. Hoche and Adeline. "Let's see it."

Adeline gave no reaction. Mr. Hoche took a predictable step backward and smoothed out his jacket. "This way," he muttered without meeting Steven's gaze. "Mr. Weaver, if you would be so kind as to communicate to the Worshipful Master that we'll be there after a slight delay."

George nodded, going into the other room. Mr. Hoche led Steven and Adeline back to the surveillance room. There, Mr. Hoche attempted to access files on the computer. His clicks on the keyboard turned into aggravated thumping, confessing his technical illiteracy.

"Let me," Adeline offered.

Mr. Hoche waved her off, continuing to struggle.

"*Aufhalten!*" she exclaimed, nudging him away. She clicked her way into folders, pulling up a video. "Zere."

"The video we before showed you," Mr. Hoche said, "was not the entire video. It kept running, long after the battle was over, and it showed us this…"

Adeline pressed play as George reentered the room. The footage picked up in time to see the camera carted through the Unas catacombs. Amid the commotion blasting through the speakers, it seemed like the lens was inside something attached to a string, making the video bob up and down.

"*Search everywhere!*" shouted someone who sounded a lot like the Unas leader, Naked Man.

"*There's no more time,*" a second voice said. "*Forget the search. Call them all around me.*"

The seesaw motion finally ceased as the person held out the camera. It angled at the Soulstealer against a backdrop of the tunnels the Unas called home. The Soulstealer stood on a raised platform with the Unas horde behind him.

Steven raised his hands. "Wait wait wait. How is it that we're still seeing this?"

Mr. Hoche raised his eyebrows in triumph. George reached underneath the monitor.

"They watched," a scratchy voice said. The camera angle jerked and brought Nythan's face into view. His face contorted and his nostrils flared as he spit into the cracked red-tinted lens.

George pulled a leather bolo tie out of a black little grate box. He took the battered metal ends and held them apart, letting the ornamental clasp fall. The clasp held the shattered remains of a red ruby, revealing a tiny camera lens behind it. George smirked. "Not the brightest group of lads."

The footage fogged a bit, but a good deal of the spit fell away as Nythan apparently fashioned the bolo tie around his neck, just like Worshipful Master von Maur had done. It angled out toward the Unas horde.

The person who handed the tie to the Soulstealer immediately became the focus of Steven's attention. Standing erect, in full view of the camera, was the naked tattooed Unas leader with the fencing mask. When Steven first met him, he looked terrifying. Seeing him on film, however, made him look like a cartoon villain.

"All here," the Naked Man said, swinging his hand to indicate the crowd.

"Weird one, that," George commented from behind. Steven didn't hear him come into the room. "Never understood how that bloke stayed their leader."

Nythan held out a hand. *"Y'all have grown so much,"* he bellowed as a hush fell across the crowd. *"I've watched you grow from just a handful of loyal followers to an entire army of fearsome disciples. Wrath told me that you're the Widowed…"*

The throng sounded off with a mixture of shouts and grunts at the word.

"Do I have that right?" Nythan received no meaningful answer to his question.

"Okay then, has it felt good to see your Maker?"

The Unas responded with more hoops and hollers.

"The Maker—"

Whatever Nythan said next was drowned out by the commotion of the Unas' response.

"Well alright then, I guess it's time to make y'all Widowmaker."

The naked guy, whom Steven figured was Wrath, threw his fists in the air, shoving his hips forward. *"Widowmaker!"*

The Unas throng went into an ecstatic craze. They shouted, clamored, and jumped up and down like kids at a pop star concert, except the audience was a bunch of demented lunatics with clubs and dead animal masks.

Steven turned to George. "Widowmaker?"

George shrugged. "Some *thing* they have going on about them being widowed when he last left."

Thirty seconds later, swift change swept the Unas' demeanor. They began clawing and slashing at themselves, ripping their own clothes, and shook as if having violent seizures. Steven didn't know how to process it other than a mass exorcism.

Bright ethereal streams shot toward the camera. The lens panned the whole room as the Soulstealer turned all the way around. Wave after wave of vaporous silver erupted from the Unas crowd. Steven watched in incredulous revulsion as the Unas horde toppled over like the tipping of a domino chain.

When the footage came back around to where it all started, an ocean of bodies lay on the floor.

"Holy…*sheeeaaat,"* Steven breathed.

The camera swiveled to the Unas leader. His mask rested on the ground, revealing jagged facial features in frozen shock. "Amazing," he exclaimed. *"I saw Widowmaker!"*

"I feel them swirling about," Nythan said. *"You'll need to rebuild."*

"This not issue," Naked Man remarked.

The Soulstealer turned away and jumped down from the platform.

"*Maker,*" the Unas guy shouted. The camera again panned back to Naked Man.

"*One day, become Widowmaker.*"

The Soulstealer responded, "*If you rebuild the Unas to twice their strength, I'll come back, and you'll be Widowmaker.*"

Adeline stopped the playback as the Soulstealer stepped over the bodies and entered the long stone tunnel.

"And so, we acquire the best piece of evidence we could ever hope for," Mr. Hoche said.

Steven only nodded, his mind racing with possibilities. *Could it be? Could this be the key we need?* "What happened after that?"

"The Satan discards the bolo tie in those dumpsters outside the well entrance. Upon witnessing *that*, we immediately set about to recover the device. It'll be held until we have need of it," Mr. Hoche said.

Rage started boiling inside Steven. "You saw this all go down in real-time and you *didn't* get help? Like, the police?"

"We had *strict* orders from the Worshipful von Maur himself that if anything were to happen, it would be over before anyone could come help. He said not to do *anything* until we recovered the camera and found a way to use it to *destroy* the Satan."

"That's the stupidest thing I've ever heard."

"Don't you disgrace his name!" Mr. Hoche reprimanded.

"I'll disgrace whatever the f*** I want that contributed to Raeleigh's…" Steven's throat seized up, and he coughed to stop his grief from overwhelming him.

Mr. Hoche took on a sorrowful expression. "I understand. No one expected this to happen, and we have all done what we must to ensure their sacrifice was *not* in vain. But we've been discussing for far too long without a proper course of action. The Worshipful Master needs your assistance to leverage your past experience in informing the world of what has happened here. It's time to bring about the Satan's undoing."

Adeline shifted. Steven wiped away a tear before facing Mr. Hoche.

"*First*, his name is the Soulstealer, not *the* Satan. You won't ever get anywhere when you're calling this thing *the* Satan. *Second*, I—"

"It's his biblical title!" Mr. Hoche interrupted. "As for the word *the*, Satan is a *title*, not a *name*."

George sighed. "Don't get him started on that one, mate. You'll never hear the end of it."

Steven waved his hand. "Whatever. It doesn't matter. The modern world will still get mixed up. *Second*, I don't have to see s***." Steven pointed to the door. "Lead the way."

Steven saw the gears turning in Mr. Hoche's brain before snapping out of his trance, then moving to the door. George smirked as he passed, elbowing Steven. Adeline's expression didn't budge.

Seeing the confusion on Mr. Hoche's face caused Steven to swell. *Time to show these Euros some good 'ole fashioned Americanism.*

His mind wandered back to the words he wrote on the tunnel walls back in the Unas catacombs, and recalled a time when he and Raeleigh drew the short straws and had to attend Conspiracy Con on behalf of Ordo America. Raeleigh had convinced Steven to wear the traditional Ordo Solis while she wore a homemade version of the Raptor mask. They won fifth place for the Con's *Most Real Problem-Makers* contest.

The memory made Steven smile. *I'm coming for you. And I'll never stop.*

CHAPTER 33

WE UNHAPPY FEW

When Mr. Hoche had asked Steven to visit the Worshipful Master, Steven didn't realize it would translate into a six-hour road trip to a small German town. Steven sucked his teeth as he peered out the car window, face flush with anger.

"All I'm sayin' is, in our heyday, you couldn't hold a candle to our accomplishments," Steven said, refusing to look at Adeline. "Solis America was the best in every department. Full stop."

"Ve have been fighting longer and harder zan Ordo America," Adeline replied.

"Longer, yes, harder, no."

"You can't compare your hundred years of fighting to our zousands."

"No one here can claim that as part of their portfolio, Adeline. Anything done before we split into geographical regions belongs to us all, not just Ordo Europe."

"Ve certainly *can* claim zat. It is a part of Ordo Europe's legacy *in* Europe. *Ve* hold the leaders zat have built zis organization!"

Dang, she's good. "Sure, Ordo Europe kept the ritual alive. But it was Ordo America that brought the Order into the modern age, kicking and screaming."

"And embarrassed us in front of ze whole world!" Adeline exclaimed.

Steven pursed his lips. "That fake Soulstealer was as credible as anything could be. The Commandery itself gave us its blessing to sound the alarm. Don't fault us for *actually* doing something. Ordo Europe's been hiding under the bed this whole time."

"Ve have fought, just as you!"

"*Sure* ya have. I'm all that's left of the once goliath Ordo America. It wasn't long ago that we dwarfed Ordo Europe."

"Zat's debatable."

Steven puttered. "Hardly, our membership records clearly showed us twice as big as you guys. I've seen *your* membership count. No one truly ever knew Ordo Asia's membership; they were just as secretive as Sanhe."

"Vell, ve're slowly evening the score," Adeline muttered sarcastically. Mr. Hoche shot Adeline a look of disgust, but Steven smirked his approval.

She gets it. She knows how bad a shape we're in. "Yes, you are. But you better not keep this up, because Ordo Europe is all that's left. Once it's gone, the Order is gone."

"Zen get off your a** and help!" Adeline snapped. Her icy blue eyes filled with rage.

Steven shrugged. "We'll see. I devoted my life to Ordo America. I'm tired of fighting this fight. Been doing it most of my adult life."

"Just vhen it gets tough."

"It's *been* tough, Adeline. It was never *not* tough. Just because the world ignored the Raptors didn't mean that *they* ignored *us*. They murdered Jeff's entire family a month ago! Raped his wife for good measure. Then did it to a few more families. Made it into a bunch of robberies so the police wouldn't suspect what really happened."

Mr. Hoche interjected. "We were very sorry to hear about that."

"Yeah, I'm sure." Steven bit his lip.

"Zat's not fair for you to say," Adeline replied. "Just because *you* lost *your* friends. Everyone here in zis van can say zey lost someone to ze Unas. Zey're animals, in ze most savage of vays. A few years ago, zey kidnapped Ola's daughter and left her flayed body in a park in Paris. Zey only identified her through her dental records. George's cousin vas stabbed to death in London. Enzo's parents vere hung in zeir backyard, and you know what happened to my family."

"Jeez…"

"*Ja*. Similar zings happened to us all. You have no right to claim you've been only hurt. Ve all suffer."

Fine, I'll bite. "Then what do we do next?"

"We use zis opportunity to strike back. Get ze support of ze United Nations and make our resistance official."

Mr. Hoche interjected again. "Adeline, we've discussed this at length—"

Steven waved him off. "The United Nations is a hapless puppet with very little authority."

"Because it has no focus. All ze partisan interests of ze world collide in ze one place meant to bring ze world together."

"Yeah, and?"

"And all it takes is something to unify zem and ve can organize a resistance on a global scale. Ze UN is our solution; ve just have to show zem its potential."

Steven raised his eyebrows in surprise. *She's a far cry from the bimbo status George gave her.*

Mr. Hoche shook his head. "That is a waste of our resources. It's too far removed from our needs. We can't wait for the bureaucracy to act. *We* have to act *now*."

"Correct me if I'm wrong," Steven replied, "but didn't I just watch a video of the Order trying to act right now? It got us slaughtered." His thoughts lingered on an image of Raeleigh smiling at him.

"Their sacrifice will not be in vain," Mr. Hoche said.

"Oh, really? And how do you figure that?"

"Because we must win."

"That, my dear sir, is the language of losers. Victory doesn't come because you say so."

Mr. Hoche's eyes widened and his face contorted. "I beg your par—"

"No, no, no," Steven talked him down. "See what I mean? I don't even have to try. 'We gotta win' is what losers say, that's what. That's not how winners talk."

"And I suppose you know how winners talk? It surely didn't help Ordo America." Mr. Hoche's eyes went bug-eyed. George winced. Adeline stared at Mr. Hoche.

Steven resisted the urge to reach out and choke the squat man.

Mr. Hoche rested his hand over his chest. "I...I apologize for my words. They should never have left my mouth. Of course, I truly do not mean that in my heart. A loss to Ordo America is a loss for the entire Order. I apologize profusely." He turned back to face the front.

Silence hung in the small enclosure.

Adeline broke the hush. "You say zat, to say 've must win,' not vhat a winner says. Vhat does a winner say?"

Steven cocked his head back to Adeline. Her curious expression made him hope that what he needed to say didn't come out wrong.

He began tapping the window in sync with his response. "That I'll lose, and I will die, and I'll fail everyone I love unless I find *the way to win*."

"Those vords sound as though zey come from another."

"I heard it in a movie once and it resonated. It speaks to how victory doesn't come because you're owed it. It comes through action and providence."

"I see. Ve Germans have had our fair share of zis knowledge. Two times ve have been on ze losing side of major war. The first, ve thought it vas divine will zat ve vould win. Ze second time vas revenge. Each war, ve tried to find ze vay to win, as you say. It vas not good for us."

She should be in charge, not these other buffoons. "Sometimes, effort is still not enough."

"*Ja.* So, you say zat your language of winners puts ze responsibility for making ze win on you and no one else?"

"Sort of. It's the difference between believing the idea of victory has the power to win, versus knowing that it only greets you at the end."

George cut in. "What happens when defeat greets you instead of victory?"

"You lose. And if you're still alive, it's still up to *you* as to what comes after. It's not what *should* or *could* be, but what *is*."

CHAPTER 34

SOLIS EUROPE

They traveled all the way to the Solis Commandery in Dietzenbach and parked in front of a large white house with a coal-colored roof glinting under the rising sun. Behind the house, spacious farmland and a small forest lurked in the distance. Steven entered second, after Mr. Hoche; George and Adeline followed right behind. A faint smell of coffee greeted him, and across the living room he heard the back and forth of what he assumed to be other Ordo Europe members. Mr. Hoche led the group past the kitchen, down a hallway, and into a dustless dining room. Eight old men sat in their chairs. Some smoked a pipe, others murmured amongst each other.

All the men turned to face them. Mr. Hoche stopped several paces away from the group, only moving when the Worshipful Master, the only one with a hat on, ushered them closer.

Steven surveyed them. *This must be the new Grand Council.*

The group proceeded until they were a few feet away from the Worshipful Master. Steven kept a rigid posture, then brought the tips of his fingers to his adjacent palm, as was expected when meeting the Worshipful Master of the Ordo Solis. "Worshipful, I'm Steven Carpenter from Ordo America."

The Worshipful Master merely waved at Steven. His brown eyes lacked luster, blending in with the rest of his bland appearance. "There's no need for such formality here." The uninterested faces of the other Grand councilmembers also rebuffed Steven's gesture of respect.

Steven suppressed a scoff. *These old geezers aren't treating this seriously.* "Ooookay," he said. "I was told you wanted to hear about my experiences."

"Quite, yes," the Worshipful Master said. His tone made Steven think the guy had forgotten they were coming. Steven peeked at Mr. Hoche, who stared starry-eyed at the Worshipful Master.

The gentleman to the Worshipful Master's left spoke next. "Your experience with the Satan will be informative as we ponder our response. We have much work to do and not enough time to do it." His facial features sagged into a frown.

Ah. So that's why I get the feeling you'd rather be somewhere else. Steven shook his head. "Sorry, and you are?"

The guy straightened in his chair. "The Grand Historian."

"Ah. Apologies, Grand Historian. I'm ready when you are."

"Steven, if you please. Let's start with the Satan itself. We're ready to hear more about who the vessel is," the Worshipful Master said.

"Well, he's a kid. Sixteen, seventeen, eighteen—"

"A vessel with the memory of over one hundred lifetimes," the Grand Historian interrupted, the crow's feet around his eyes announcing itself as he squinted.

Steven grimaced. *That's your one.* "Sure, except that I got the feeling that the kid was disconnected from his thoughts. Raeleigh theorized that there was some sort of separation, but she didn't have the time to learn more."

"What kind of separation?" the Worshipful Master asked.

"I'm not sure. The kid is American, and he displays a certain amount of arrogance that borders on ignorance."

"How can that be?" one of the other councilmembers—Steven didn't care to know who—asked, leaning forward. The man squinted as he locked eyes with Steven.

"I don't know. I was only around him a handful of times, and each time was staged on some level—"

"Yes, tell us more about their safehouses," the Worshipful Master interrupted.

"Worshipful Master, I would appreciate it if the Grand Council would stop cutting me off."

Mr. Hoche, like a lap dog, came to the rescue. "The Worshipful Master may speak to you any way he wishes."

Steven shook his head. "No, he certainly may *not*. You people want to leverage my experience. That's fine. But stop interrupting me so I can tell you what I know."

The Worshipful Master glared at Steven with a stern expression that rivaled the look his dad gave Steven when he admitted to dropping out of college. Mr. Hoche's eyes bulged at Steven in silent fury. Steven caught George hiding his smirk and swore the side of Adeline's mouth twitched.

"Very well…please continue," the Worshipful Master muttered.

"I was only in four of their hideouts, I think. The first was an old house in Texas, probably. Big sprawling countryside out the window. Second one is a mansion headquarters of some kind, next to a forest. Has a huge garden with hedges and a historical museum of grass statues. Another was a really dusty airfield, and I'm not even sure it's in the United States. Probably not, as my next stop was the Unas headquarters. It's clear that the Unas have a different definition of 'hideout.' Pretty much a different definition of everything."

"What would that be?" the Grand Historian asked.

"Take the Raptors. They're killers, but they're smart. They grew their cult into a disciplined and professional machine. Their leaders aren't naked lunatics with kitty-cat fingernails. They're business owners, politicians, community organizers, philosophers…they even have cops. The Unas seem like amateurs. Just kinda doing things in underground caves running around in gangs like they're a bunch of Vikings."

When Steven stopped speaking, the Worshipful Master rubbed his bearded chin. "We recall there being a master plan you designed to convince the world that the Satan had returned. Care to expound upon this?"

Steven considered the request. *It can't hurt.* "Well, credit goes to the Freemasons in the USA. The Knights Templar called it the Sparrow's Roar. It works like this. We compile a package of evidence that so overwhelmingly exposes the Soulstealer—that's what we call it in Ordo America—that its existence can't be disputed. Next, we identify an influential figure that has a huge following.

Then, we pen a call to action, sign it in that individual's name, and release it to every news outlet we have. When it catches national or global attention, we quickly leverage the situation to enlist the aid of the United Nations."

At the mention of the UN, Mr. Hoche's head whipped over to Adeline, then back to Steven. Adeline stared straight at the Worshipful Master, her face betraying no emotion.

The Grand Councilmembers all began blurting questions at the same time. The Worshipful Master hushed them, pointing to a councilmember who had earlier displayed the most interest. "Grand Warden."

"Steven, that sounds dubious, at best," the man said, whose interest-turned-holier-than-thou attitude made Steven clench his fists.

Steven regarded him in an equally unwelcome tone. "I didn't hear a question there, Grand Warden."

The Grand Warden grunted, looking at the other councilmembers. "Where to begin?"

"Start with the first question."

The Grand Warden gritted his teeth. "How do you intend to perform this incredible feat?"

"With the Order's help, we'll find the most appropriate person."

"And what about this lofty plan makes you think it will work?"

Steven kept his tone even and calm. "A number of factors. It's unexpected, and it's uncontrollable once spread. Groupthink will do the work for us, fear will be the driving factor, and it'll leverage the whole population rather than continue to work us to death in isolation."

"How could you think the UN is the solution to our problem?"

"Because the UN is what the Pope was during the Crusades: a unifying force, a reasonably objective party. Every major nation is linked to it. When the call of support comes from the UN, it comes from a neutral position, not partisan to anything except humanity. It's the perfect venue to call for another crusade. A lasting crusade."

"Or it could be another League of Nations. Much ado about nothing," the Grand Historian said. "Was this your idea?"

"Like I said, the Templars came up with it."

"No, I mean, who suggested the United Nations be the organization to contact?"

"This idea was one of the stronger candidates that we threw around when devising the plan. Adeline here was the one who helped me see its true potential." He glanced at Adeline, who was still stone-faced. "Speaking of which, you all should give her a promotion. It's clear she has a firm grasp on Ordo Europe's predicament, in addition to her uncanny insight and innovative solutions. You should pay her more attention."

Mr. Hoche's face grew redder by the second as he seethed with fury.

"We have doubts about her…potential, to serve in the higher grade," the Worshipful Master said. It didn't seem to matter that she was standing ten feet away.

"I don't," Steven shot back. "If anything, she'd have figured out a plan the day the attack happened."

"That was a *very* tough decision, Steven. One you were not here to make. Late Worshipful von Maur's insistence that we recover the device and formulate a plan if anything went wrong was the most reasonable course of action in our consideration."

"Yeah, and you've spent *considerable* time *considering*. Adeline should have been involved from the beginning."

The Worshipful Master made brief eye contact with Adeline before raising his head and returning his attention to Steven. "She was."

Steven looked at Adeline, still stony-faced and not meeting his gaze. "Uh huh. And I'm supposed to believe she advised you to follow those *strict* orders from Worshipful von Maur to not do *a single thing* until you recovered the footage? A whole room full of Ordo Europe gets slaughtered on video, and you all are just sitting here talking like we're having a reunion meeting." Steven crossed his arms.

The Worshipful Master dismissively waved his hand. "Of course we have a plan, Steven. The Order *had a plan* for over a century. But that plan needs a new face, because our *previous* plan was spent on a Raptor trick foolishly championed by Ordo America, which so convinced itself of the ruse that we spent all available political capital to tell the world of a threat that didn't exist. Not only did it eviscerate the credibility we so carefully earned since the birth of our Order, but also of our friends, who endorsed our message to their secular peers."

Steven gritted his teeth. "That was seven years ago."

"And still follows us *to this day*." The Worshipful Master sunk his index finger into his armrest. "So, you'll excuse us if we need more time than the couple of weeks you've impatiently given us."

Silence lingered as the two stared each other down.

"Grand Secretary," the Worshipful Master said. "I believe you've yet to have a turn."

The Grand Secretary sighed. "Well I…I can't dispute what we've seen happen in Czechia, but I don't know if anyone will believe it."

Steven's mouth dropped. "*What?*"

Multiple pairs of eyes shot daggers at him.

The Worshipful Master held up a hand toward Steven. "Grand Secretary, if you please."

"We've done this before," the Secretary continued. "It did not end well. Even with the bodies the Satan left behind, it looks like it could be a science fiction TV show. It's easier to explain it away as a new biological weapon, "

A few other councilmembers voiced their agreement.

"Not to mention," the Secretary continued, "save for the Unas, we have yet to produce any clear linkage to these cults. All we have is an interview with video only, some newspaper clippings, a phone conversation, a fantastical looking fight, and a massacre that looks like it could be a scene from *Lord of the Rings*."

"You sound like you don't believe it yourself," Steven accused.

"Surely there's something in all this that could substantiate our claims," the Grand Historian said. "With the combined material we've collected and the bodies found in the Czechia catacombs, it must be enough."

"I'm just saying," the Secretary continued. "Everything we have can be explained away. The Unas is a reclusive goth underworld who have been known to practice sacrifice, the Raptors have taken over the American government and can suppress the truth, and the Sanhe looks to have disbanded from inactivity."

Steven blinked. *Everything he just said is wrong. This whole Grand Council is wrong. The Order's in big trouble with these old goats in charge.* He opened his mouth to speak and was met with yet another raised hand from the Worshipful Master.

"No one is taking the position that we act rash," the Worshipful Master said, eyeing Steven.

Steven frowned at George. Mr. Hoche ogled the old man and his rabble of "yes" men with nothing short of infatuation. Adeline remained silent, but kept eye contact with Steven.

"Well, like I said earlier...you need help. *We* need help." Steven cleared his throat. "And if you do this without Adeline, you'll be spinning your wheels."

The Grand Warden cleared his throat. "We'll determine her suitability at a later time." He rubbed his two index fingers together. Steven imagined the Grand Warden twirling his mustache with them.

Steven grimaced. "That would be smart. There are *a lot* of things around here in need of a suitability determination."

CHAPTER 35

THE PIN DROP

Following Steven's testy meeting with the Grand Council, they took the rest of the day to deliberate. They called him back the next day, to the same white house. The resulting conversation did little to clear the starkness of their disagreement. Steven became convinced the Grand Council held an unrealistic perspective and zero decision-making ability.

Two days later, they again debated what the Order needed to prove the return of the Soulstealer. Adeline received two reprimands throughout the conversation for speaking up without being invited to participate. They only allowed her to stay at Steven's insistence.

"Gentlemen, there is no need to be hasty," the Grand Warden mused. "Ordo Europe has kept the Satan in check for centuries. Now that it has returned, we simply need to gather our strength and wait for the world to see they need us once again."

We'll be dead by the time they figure this out, Steven concluded. *They need to step aside.*

"Quite so, yes. Just this morning, I reviewed the effect of our courageous assault on the Unas headquarters," the Worshipful Master crowed. "The one that released you from your bondage, if I'm not mistaken. Reminded me of another legendary tale, when, in 12th century AD, our ancestors brazenly uprooted the Satan's hideout among the heretical Cathars—"

"Are you guys Nazis?" Steven cut in.

The room gasped. Steven didn't wait for a response.

"I'm American; we deal in what's real. It's why we're back-to-back World War champs. And I really, seriously, want to know. Are you all Nazis? Cuz I haven't heard delusion of this magnitude since World War II. 'We're the best,' the Nazis said. 'No one can match us,' they said. Let's voice some inconvenient truths."

The Grand Secretary tried to cut back in, but Steven bellowed over him.

"First, Ordo Asia didn't dissolve like a broken-up rock band, it was *eviscerated*. We have, absolutely, positively, zero contact with *anyone* there. I can tell you without a doubt that Kaiyue's little ninja clan didn't just abandon our cause. Someone *made* them disappear. Second, we beat the hell out of you pipsqueaks up until the 21st century in membership and financial contribution to the cause. The numbers aren't even close. The only incompetence here is you all insisting that you can just waltz around like the blind 'ole geezers you are and make everything go your way. You think you've seen it rough in your cozy town? Wait until the Raptors collect themselves and turn their attention to you. You've never felt fear like a dark room full of black reflective masks staring at you as they cut the throat of a mother of three." Steven exhaled. "The Unas, they're predictable beasts. The Raptors—those cunning bastards are Satan's heavyweights."

He threw his hands up and walked toward the door, then turned back around. "Get your s***t together and come down from your ivory tower. Or else we'll all die, and you'll be the last disappointing chapter in the Order's very sad story."

The faces of each councilmember showed nothing short of shock and disgust. Steven turned to leave.

"You have some nerve!" someone called out after him.

Steven threw up the bird as he thundered out of the room and didn't stop until barging out the front door. He looked left and right, settling on a nearby crop clearing. On the far side stood a lone observation tower that looked like a black spiral staircase leading to the sky. Steven thought it as good a place as any for a stroll, so he began walking. Someone yelled behind him as he made it across the field to a small forest. He turned and saw Adeline sprinting, but Steven kept walking through the woods until he reached the tower entrance.

Adeline caught up with him and grabbed his arm.

"Halt," she wheezed.

Steven ignored her, entering the building and climbing the darkened winding stairs. Adeline could only follow if she wanted to keep hold of him.

When Steven reached the top, he leaned over the bar and looked down at the town. Adeline plopped down beside him. She blew her disheveled hair away from her eyes.

"*Die Arschmade!*"

Steven made no comment. A sea of maroon rooftops cozied up against a backdrop of forest and farmland. The silver-lined clouds blushed gray, casting a gloomy shadow across the area. The sleepy town proved a fitting gesture for the Order's predicament.

A few minutes later, Adeline stood, and punched Steven in his meaty arm. "*Arschloch*," she said.

Steven chuckled. Whatever she said, she looked the tiniest bit cute when speaking German.

"You didn't have to say zat," she added.

"I know."

A faint smile crept along the edge of Adeline's mouth.

Steven narrowed his eyes. "You liked it!"

"Did not! It vas rude, and as a German, I should be so offended."

"Should be, but you're not."

Adeline now made no attempt to hide her joy. "The Nazi reference vas excessive."

"What I really wanted to say was that some of them could be an agent of the Soulstealer. That's how the Raptors crippled Ordo America."

"I have considered ze same ever since I have heard zeir views. But without evidence, my claim is not credible."

"Speaking of credible." Steven leered at Adeline. "I've been wondering as of late…why do you fake so much?"

Adeline's head snapped toward Steven. "Vhat did you say, you bastard?"

Undeterred, Steven continued. "You're abrasive, you look like you've seen better days, you talk as if everyone on Earth has offended you, and you pretend that most of this stuff is way above your capability to understand. I'd be fooled too, except that your keen questions all show something you refuse to let others peek into. You're super intelligent. And when I care to pay enough attention, you even *look* like you have a plan. For some reason, you hide it. You instead embody this haphazard bimbo stereotype we both know is bulls***."

His fingers drummed the metal railing. "So, why *is* that? Why does Adeline feel it necessary to put up a front? Is it because you scare all the little boys?"

Their eyes locked in a stalemate. Steven smiled, unable to contain how humorous he found all this. Adeline stared back with the blankest of expressions.

"No," she snapped. "I can't question everything given to me."

"So you're a 'yes' woman." Steven raised an eyebrow. "A company woman."

"No." Adeline flipped her long blonde hair out of her face. "It's just zat our leaders need to feel confident in zeir decisions."

"That sounds like an excuse. Why do you need them to feel confident? Why can't you question everything?"

Adeline's shoulders tensed. "Zey get distracted and make poor decisions vhen zey feel threatened."

"That's because you're better than them."

"*Nein*, it's because zey have access to all ze information."

"See now, I don't buy that for one second. No offense to Mr. Hoche, but he isn't the genius he assumes he is, and the Worshipful Master is anything *but* omnipotent. The first ten minutes with those guys told me that. They need help from people who can discern good information from bad. The Ordo Solis has been suffering from people like you just standing idly by when you could be making a real difference."

"Hey, zat's not fai—"

"It's not about what's fair. It's about accomplishing our mission, ensuring the human race survives. It's worth bruising a few egos, especially if those egos are getting people killed."

"Zey've gotten us this far."

"And where's that, exactly? The Ordo Solis has been obliterated on every front except this one, and this one's on the verge of collapse. Hell, the things they were telling me earlier will only *ensure* that it collapses."

Adeline drew her eyebrows together. "Ze new Grand Council is doing zeir best. Zey didn't ask for Ludwig von Maur and his Grand Council to sacrifice themselves." Her expression froze, eyes locked onto his.

"Well, unfortunately, their best isn't good enough," Steven retorted. "You, however, can up their game. *You* can lead these people out of the abysmal black hole in which they currently find themselves."

After she stopped fidgeting, Adeline turned quizzical. "Vhy do you keep saying 'zey'?"

"Because after today, I'm retiring." Steven slapped the railing. "I've had enough. I'm done. I've sacrificed enough; you all can continue on without me."

"You're going to abandon us and leave us to our fate?"

"Yup, I'm not even going to sugarcoat it anymore. I'm leaving you all to your fate. Done my part. Finished." He crossed his arms.

"Please don't," Adeline pleaded.

Steven paused. This marked the second time she let some of her vulnerability show. "You all don't need me any—"

"If I'm to 'make a difference' as you say, zen you'd better be here next to me. You're a difference-maker too. And if you believe ze things you just said, zen you'll take your own advice, set your ego aside, and accomplish our mission."

Steven felt paralyzed in an endless loop of disbelief and embarrassment. "S***," he muttered.

Adeline beamed. "*Wunderbar!*"

She returned her gaze to the landscape and let out a light sigh. "I've stood here a dozen times. Mainly zat one, though." She pointed to an observation deck on the other side of the city. Steven paid little attention what she said next, his thoughts elsewhere.

Damn her. He wrestled with her surprise assessment of his hypocrisy. At the end of the day, what excuse did he give for leaving the Order? It was about him, Steven.

Maybe I should just accept that I'm a hypocrite and be on my way.

And do what, Steven argued with himself, *hide away in small corner of the world and wait until the Soulstealer takes over?*

Yes! I don't want to do this anymore.

The fight or flight instinct raged inside him; his thoughts felt like a game of tug-o-war.

Yeah, you do. It's just much harder to stay and easier to leave.

A whole life devoted to the Order gave him lots of experience and ideas. The thought stung as they shifted to Raeleigh.

He glanced to his right and found himself face-to-face with Raeleigh's spirit. Steven didn't jump this time. She too leaned on the railing, looking out across the city with the most beautiful of smiles. The evening breeze whisked her away into the night a few seconds later. Steven held his gaze as his hate and bitterness left with her, filled in its stead by steady resolve. Resolve to finish what he started all those years ago.

Steven recalled the words he wrote back in the Unas' tunnel. *I'm coming for her.* He pictured Nythan, not as a naïve kid, but as the Soul-stealer. As the thing that took life. *And I'm going to go through you to get her.*

"Do you still see her?" Adeline asked.

Steven continued looking at where Raeleigh left him, a gentle smile on his face. He nodded. "Do you still see yours?"

"Not in a long vhile."

Steven glanced over at Adeline. "I never stopped seeing her. At first, it was too much to bear, but now she gives me strength."

"Ze strength to stay and fight."

Steven grunted. "I'll sleep on it and get back to ya."

Adeline nodded and went back down the stairs.

Steven stayed atop the observation deck until dusk, peering across a landscape of chilled rolling hills. He thought about nothing in particular and immersed himself in the joy of the moment.

It occurred to him that Ordo members, back during the crusades, probably felt this way too. The real Knights Templar fought an enemy with abilities they didn't understand that shook even the most devout believer. They also lost loved ones. He wondered how they gathered the strength to go on.

Every inch of him screamed to call it quits and go home. He recalled the words of Winston Churchill. *If you're going through hell, keep going.*

But that's the wrong answer, Steven thought. *The* right *answer is to keep going and kill that son of a b****.*

CHAPTER 36

THE WHEN

"So how do you vant to do zis?" Adeline asked Steven at breakfast. Sweat glistened down her neck and forearms from her morning jog.

"Gotta rip it off," Steven said mid-chew at the kitchen table. "Like a band-aid."

"Zey're not going to like zat." She didn't mask her approval very well.

"Doesn't matter," Steven said, still chewing. "Out of time. Soulstealer knows. We have the stuff to expose him. All those years wasted. He'll do something drastic. About to lose the element of surprise."

"How do you know?"

"Cuz. The little brat. Been planning this for hundreds of years. Doesn't want to see his hard work go to waste. Lots of death, now we have proof." Steven finished the last scoop of cereal and lifted the bowl to his mouth.

Adeline leaned against the table's wooden surface. "Ve're in danger then."

Steven wiped his mouth and shook his head. "Sure, but not really. You saw. Took out the whole Unas. Up and killed 'em. He's not coming after us. He's running. My guess, back to Raptors, or Sanhe."

"You don't believe ze Sanhe are extinct?"

"Zero chance of that." Steven leaned back and patted his robust belly.

"So vhich one, ze Sanhe or ze Raptors?" Adeline's forehead wrinkled.

"That's the thing we'll need to figure out. I put it at sixty percent Sanhe, forty Raptors."

"Vhy so close together?"

"Well, his host is American, so he has home field advantage there. But we don't even know where to begin with Sanhe. We don't know the first thing about them, to be honest. He has *complete* advantage there. I guess if I had to choose, it'd be Sanhe."

Adeline frowned. "Ve haven't had a presence zere in over a decade."

"Yup, he has it all. Except the Chinese government. They have the resources to find him…if it was in their interest to do so."

"So vhat could ve do to make it in zeir interest?"

Steven scrunched his face. "Good question. Your idea with the UN is probably our best option, but we'd need to take it a step further. Convince the Asian powers, particularly China, that the Soulstealer poses an immediate danger to them. At the very least, they'll likely search for him on their own. Failing all that, we force an intervention on their behalf. Either way gets us what we want."

"Do you zink ve have enough proof to convince zem?"

"Sort of, but by itself, those videos only create curious interest. We need another bang to go along with it, something that creates interest and is associated with fear on a level they can understand. Fortunately for you all, I have that bang."

"Vhy didn't you say so sooner?"

"Because, in all honesty, I wasn't sure how much I could trust Ordo Europe. You though—you're someone I can work with. With the film and other stuff, it'll be enough to cause a serious investigation into the Soulstealer's operation. With any luck, authorities will substantiate our claim and take decisive action to kill him."

"*Wunderbar*! Vere is zis information?"

"Uh, that's the problem. It's not exactly *where* it is, but *when*."

"Vhen?" Adeline tilted her head, causing her light blonde ponytail to sway behind her softly.

"*Ja.*" Steven chuckled. "When. I needed to make sure that the evidence would be near impossible for the Raptors to get a hold of. So I cashed in a favor with an old friend to make the package get lost until the time was right."

"Vell ze time is right now."

"Yeah. Unfortunately, all we can do is go to where the package will end up. I've no idea when, or even if, it'll ever get there."

"You didn't try burying it?"

"No," Steven lied.

"Vhat exactly vere you zinking vhen you did zis?"

"I was on the run, Adeline, being hunted by an enemy I couldn't see. I had to do something they wouldn't be able to trace."

Adeline sighed. "Vhere do ve have to travel now?"

"To a place very, very far away."

"Vhen do we leave?"

"Depends on how soon we can book a flight out of here. Problem is, I don't have anything with me. No identification, no passport, no money, no nothing. Trying to get a replacement passport and flying will generate lots of questions about how I got here in the first place."

Adeline perked up. "I know how ve can get into ze United States, but it vill take a couple of veeks. Ve can get zere faster if ve ask for aid from ze Order; zey have ze resources."

"I doubt they'll help us much."

"Perhaps you should ask zem nicely."

"I called them Nazis." Steven failed to stop himself from laughing.

"*Ja, ja.* However, I believe zey vill look past vhen zey understand vhat you intend to do."

Steven shook his head. "I have *zero* intention of telling them what I'm doing. For all I know, some *are* traitors. If the Raptors know where I'm going and what I plan to do, they'll drop all pretense and take me out."

"You mean zey'll ambush *us.*" Adeline pointed at him. "Don't you even zink of going without me."

"Fine, they'll ambush *us.* But we need to get there without the others noticing."

"Zat will be of some difficult. Not only are ze Unas and Raptors after us, but ze Order vill vant to impose themselves in zis process. Zey could complicate us."

"That's true. Which's why we should leave right *now.*"

Adeline recoiled. "Now?"

"Yes. Five minutes from now. You said you knew how to get into the United States. How can we do it?"

"I, I don't have anything prepared—"

"We have to ditch anything that can trace us. Cell phones, credit cards, geographical or GPS enabled devices."

"But, but...hold on—"

"There's no more holding on. The Soulstealer's minions have been one step ahead of us this *entire* time. No more. They react to *us* from now on. Are you coming with me or not?"

Adeline took only a moment to answer, nodding her head solemnly. "I need to vithdraw my savings and grab my passport. Zis we cannot do vithout."

"Let's do it and get the next train out."

Adeline strode out of the room and bumped into George. He passed her and proceeded into the kitchen, pacing back and forth a few seconds before looking at Steven.

"I heard you both talking," George said, fumbling with his hands.

Steven eyed him, his body tensing. "What'd ya hear?"

"Enough."

"Am I going to have to fight my way out of here, George?"

George looked at the doorway. "I disagree with the *how*, but I share your concern. If you *are* intent on doing this, Adeline is the right person to help."

"I thought you said she was a bimbo?" Steven reminded him with a grin.

"*Your* words. But I also said she makes our problems go away post-haste. This looks like a problem."

Steve nodded. "Anything I should know before we leave?"

"This area has a large presence of Unas and the Order. The further North you go, the less of both."

"I need copies of those two videos with the Soulstealer."

George left the room without answering, leaving Steven wondering what he intended to do next.

Adeline walked in a few minutes later with a backpack. "Ready."

Steven signaled for her to wait. George returned and handed him a thumb drive. He eyed the two of them, opening and then closing his mouth without speaking, then left the room.

Steven nodded at Adeline and jumped off the stool. They left the house without attracting much attention. At George's suggestion, Steven and Adeline boarded the next train heading north.

CHAPTER 37

BREEZING THE SEA

Steven stood on the deck of a white luxury Trimaran yacht humming across the ocean. Equipped with everything a crew needed for a two-week-long expedition, the wind generators, solar panels, and water turbines kept the *Seabreezer* cruising at a steady 41 knots.

Adeline's getaway belonged to a wealthy Belgian yachtsman and his crew of sailors. The sailors enjoyed voyaging out into the ocean for long periods, and the yachtsman turned out to be an Ordo Solis donor with money to spend. She described Nikolaj as "an acquaintance," but the acquaintance introduced himself as Adeline's "close friend."

Adeline offered Nikolaj a vague explanation for their journey; something about being on the hunt while running from danger. She sweetened the pot by promising to tell Nikolaj the latest Ordo Solis gossip on the Soulstealer. Nikolaj moved mountains to get them to the nearest American port, eager to get the scoop. He showed them the permit papers for their Transatlantic voyage as if presenting an award. Nikolaj explained how another aquatic journey would be a welcome respite for his crew.

Nikolaj and Adeline chatted in French over a few glasses of wine. Steven found himself helping another crewman adjust the boom as the winds shifted.

"Me very glad you did this travel," the crewman said in a heavy Belgian accent.

"You're glad I'm here?"

"Of course, glad we to do this, needed to do this for high time now."

Steven offered a polite smile, not quite sure what the sailor meant. He tried to unfasten a latch the crewman pointed to earlier, but it didn't budge.

"This opposes you greatly, yes?" The crewman nudged Steven aside.

"Yes, it opposes me," Steven laughed. "How long have you been doing this?"

"How long?"

"Yes, when did you start?"

"Oh, seven of years. We make travel all over this house."

Steven pointed to Adeline's glass. "Do you all have anything stronger than that red spit water?"

"Ah, yes, we have that, would you like?"

"No, no, no, I mean, do you've…anything else? Cognac? Wild Turkey?"

"Moët, we have."

Steven shrugged. "I don't know what that is, but sure."

"I'll get you. Please, be here while I get."

Adeline laughed loudly.

The sailor returned with an engraved flask of sterling silver. Steven drank it down, then handed the flask back. "Bring two." The crewman grinned and left.

Steven made his way back to Adeline and Nikolaj, who were still engaged in a rapid-fire conversation in French. The crewman came back, handing him two flasks.

"Thanks." Steven chugged the first, then started sipping from the second. "Hey, Nick. You two know each other, right?" He twiddled his fingers between them, taking another sip.

Adeline shot Steven an annoyed look. Nikolaj switched to English. "Yes, my friend, yes! We've known one another for many years."

Nikolaj's rich brown hair was slicked back out of his face and curled softly under his ears. He had a rather large nose and a strong jawline.

Adeline turned her head back and forth, letting out a 'pffffft!' "Viry long?" The wine made her German accent impossibly thick. "Ve've *known* eich ozer, Niko."

"I'll bet. How many of those have you had?" Steven asked Adeline, pointing to her glass. He absorbed this new insight into Adeline with curious amusement.

"Pffffft!" she puttered.

Steven took a couple of large swigs from the flask before turning his attention to Nikolaj. "So...Niko, you two seem cozy."

Adeline's head fell back; a few seconds later she let out a loud-speaker laugh.

Nikolaj stole a glance at Adeline before placing his hand alongside his mouth as a shield. "We used to be engaged," he tried to whisper.

Adeline pulled her head upright. "Vhat!" She then fell still, eyes drooping.

"That explains it," Steven yelped, slapping his upper thigh. "Here's what I don't get." He gestured to Adeline. "She puts on this front...like she doesn't know what she's doing. But clearly, she does. What gives? Why does she hide?"

Nikolaj looked to Adeline before returning his gaze to Steven. "I think you are asking me why you don't see...the *real* Adeline."

Steven slumped, letting the chilled Moët tingle his senses. "Yeah. She keeps talking about how she's giving our fearless leaders an ego boost."

"She's sensitive..." Nikolaj grinned, revealing a small space by his upper right canine. "Doesn't want folks to know it makes her angry." Nikolaj shook his head. "Bothers her that people see her face." Nikolaj reached out, imitating himself squeezing Adeline's cheeks. "And they don't acknowledge her brilliance!"

Adeline bared her impeccably straight teeth at them. "You two..." was all she managed.

"Hmm. And here I thought—she had a master plan..."

"She does!" Nikolaj bellowed. "Oh, she does! Has a plan...for *everything*," he tapped his temple. "Right up here. Always planning. Wants it all done herrrrr way!" Nikolaj grew still. "That's why we stopped. Her plan didn't include me."

"Ssssstaip...you two," Adeline murmured.

"It wouldn't have worked out," Nikolaj continued. "She manages everything, all details. Didn't trust me. She does that. Thinks everyone wants to hurt her, and the rest want to use her." Nikolaj threw his hands up, gesturing to the wind.

Steven bobbed his head in agreement. "Makes sense. Beautiful girl. Big brain."

"Dead family."

"Mmmph," Steven grunted.

"Unas made her think that, of course. Bad people, good people. All look the same to her."

"Bummer."

"That's what I said!" Nikolaj shouted, then whispered. "That's what I said. She got what she wanted. Stayed safe. Didn't get hurt. All part of the plan."

"She got hurt tons, though."

"Sure did," Nikolaj said. "What about you? Unas hurt you too?"

Steven gripped the mast to stop himself from swaying. He stayed silent a few moments, then upended the flask and drank the rest.

"Something like that," Steven said, stretching. "It's a sad story, though. Much sadder than I want to get into."

"Pffffft!" he let out. "Life is—"

"Don't pffffft me," Adeline blurted back.

"Mmmph," Steven grunted again. "And on that note, time to catch some Z's."

Nikolaj offered a smile. "Tomorrow, then."

Adeline poked Nikolaj. "Tomovrow, zen!"

Steven's gaze bounced between them before turning around. He wandered to the bottom deck and his enormous, fluffy bed, belly-flopping on the top cover. He didn't bother to crawl under the covers as his vision faded to black.

CHAPTER 38

TACKING

As soon as they docked in Baltimore, Steven approached immigration and recited the story he, Adeline, and Nikolaj rehearsed earlier that morning. Since everyone but him had proper identification, authorities didn't ask an unreasonable number of questions. He gave a statement while a search of the police database confirmed his citizenship. Adeline's German passport didn't expire for another year, so she faced the standard inquiries about her reason for coming.

Hours felt like days until immigration finally granted Steven and Adeline entry into Baltimore. Steven found the nearest library and used a computer to reorder his passport. They bid farewell to Nikolaj and the crew, zooming away in a rental paid with cash loaded on a Visa gift card. Steven told her they traveled next to Northern California, but refused to say anything else. She expressed her frustration at being kept in the dark.

After a couple of hours on the road trip and a few rental car exchanges later, Adeline demanded, "Spill it!"

Steven shook his head and put a finger to his lips. *Not yet,* he mouthed. Adeline huffed.

Steven had already explained how different the Raptors were from the Unas. They no longer faced raging, naked lunatics with axes. They squared off against a deeply rooted, professional group of killers with a lot to lose if Steven and Adeline got what they wanted.

Steven drummed his fingers on the steering wheel. *I hope we got through unnoticed.*

"Can you at least tell me vhat city?" she asked.

Steven again shook his head, putting a finger to his lips.

"Zere's no one listening!" Adeline raged. "Ve switched cars three times!"

Steven grimaced. *Dang, maybe she really* doesn't *have respect for the Raptors.* "Let's talk about something else."

Adeline turned her head out the passenger window. "Stupid."

Steven chuckled. He saw a twitch at the corner of her mouth. "You're laughing!" Steven pointed at her face.

"Am not!" Adeline refuted, turning back to him. A broad smile crept across her face.

Steven shook his head, returning his gaze to the road. "You get it. I knew you would."

"Yes I understand, but it's still silly."

"Well, I'm willing to bet that sometime in the near future you'll understand even more why I can't deal with the Raptors the same way you dealt with the Unas. These Raptors…I'm not kidding when I say they're trained professionals."

"*Ja*, you keep saying."

"I'm saying because I don't want you to make the same amateur mistakes we did, thinking they won't notice."

"*Ja*, I get it. Zey good. Very good. *Wunderbar*, even! Vhen are you telling me vhere ve're going?"

"Just be patient; we'll get there."

Steven told Adeline to drive to Salt Lake City while he slept. They drove most of the way without stopping, only pulling over to get food and gassing up. She eventually shook him awake.

"*Wir sind hier!*" she exclaimed. Steven stretched his neck, working out the kinks. He looked out the window into the dead of night at the familiar silhouette of the Rockies.

They spent only as much time as it took to find a new rental, at which time Adeline demanded their final destination. As they reached the outer suburbs of Salt Lake City, Steven turned the car north and made his confession.

"We're going to Washington, the state," Steven said.

Adeline clapped as she squealed with delight. "I *knew* it!"

"Well, we're still about 15 hours away. I'll wake you when we get close."

Adeline wouldn't sleep for the next couple of hours, but at last, she dozed as they sailed into the night.

Steven rolled down a window to let the fresh spring breeze rustle his hair. His thoughts drifted to Jeff, Sara, and Trista. He fought back tears as he reminisced through the good times: BBQs, movie nights, horseshoes, karaoke, and baseball games. All with the best friends a guy could have. A knot formed in his throat.

His thoughts again lingered on Raeleigh, his eternal soulmate. He glanced in his rearview mirror, not the least bit surprised to see her silvery spirit in the backseat. She grinned and waved.

"I always loved you, you know that, right?" Steven breathed, doing his best to not run off the road while trying to look at her.

Raeleigh nodded, turning her head to peer out the window. She extended both arms and arched her back. Steven chuckled before growing stern.

"I did fail you though," he choked. Raeleigh's shoulders dropped with a gentle sigh. "I left you to the Raptors, thinking how I was choosing the more righteous path by trying to expose the Soulstealer. But I was too cowardly to try and save you. I see that now."

Her expression took on a sympathetic look as she gently shook her head.

"It's okay. I'll make it up to you by ensuring the Soulstealer wasted all those years he silently schemed away."

Raeleigh's dark eyes widened, and she shook her head more fervently.

The car began to rumble. Steven's attention jerked back to the road, finding the vehicle crossing over the outside line. He eased the car back over.

"Thanks." Steven peeped into the rearview mirror but didn't see her anywhere.

His gaze slid back to the highway. "What a woman," he whispered. "Even in the afterlife, she's *still* looking after me. What a woman."

CHAPTER 39

FEATHERFEET

Steven walked up the driveway to the picture-perfect cottage in the middle of a forest outside of Ashford, Washington. The porch light shone through the night like a lighthouse. Adeline hid in the bushes within sight of the door, keeping a watch out. The two-story cottage and its surroundings looked as peaceful as he remembered, but Steven's new experiences caused him to question everything he thought to be true.

He ascended the porch steps, hunting for anything amiss. He tried not to make it obvious when he lowered his eyes to search for delivered packages. Satisfied there was nothing outside, he reached into a flowerpot on the far side of the door and dug out a key. He unlocked the door and entered the cozy home, flicking on the lights.

Grief overwhelmed him, and he couldn't stem the tears that followed. Steven wiped them away with embarrassment, glad Adeline couldn't see his moment of weakness. A calm enveloped him, as did every time he stepped foot into this house.

It shouldn't have taken me this long to come back.

Steven walked through the cottage, stopping in the living room. A dull gray package rested on top of the glass table. A note leaned against it.

Hiking trip in Asia.
Stay as long as you like.

Larissa

Steven admired the letter, then snapped back to reality. He returned to the front door and flicked the porch light four times. Minutes later, Adeline ran inside.

"Is all zis necessary?" she asked.

"Absolutely."

"Can you tell me vhy ve're here now?

"Come in here."

They sat on the soft couch, and Adeline read the note as Steven tore apart the gray wrapping.

"Who is Larissa? Vhat is zis place?"

"In a minute," Steven muttered as he struggled with the tape.

"*Nein!*" Adeline snapped. Steven arched his eyebrow. "Tell me now, from ze beginning."

Steven set the parcel down. "Fine." He turned to face her. "I already told you and the Commandery about the Templars. What I left out was that while I was on my way to Texas, I made copies of everything I had and USPS'd it here through a convoluted daisy chain. I had never told anybody about this place, not even Jeff, so I was confident the Raptors didn't know about it either."

"If so confident, vhy is all the precaution getting here now?"

Steven wagged his finger. "Can't be too careful. I've been in a bunch of recent situations where surer things failed."

"So if ze Raptors had known about zis place, vouldn't zey have come here looking for you and found ze items?"

Damn, she's good. He smirked. *I guess there's no harm in telling her.*

"Well, I thought of that too, so I packaged boxes within boxes, sent it to an address I knew would be forwarded to an undeliverable place, causing the package to be returned unsent to a friend, and wrote him instructions to send it here. Because the USPS takes the longest, I figured the whole process would take at least a month or two. It bought me a lot of time to wait out any Raptors hunting for extra copies."

Steven expected a barrage of questions, so he prepped himself to withstand the onslaught. Instead, she only said, "Impressive, vhere is here?"

"Ahhh," Steven sighed, leaning back on the sofa. "The note you just read, it's from the most bada** old lady I've ever known. Met her six years ago while biking across the U.S. We were inseparable after that. She's this rich lady with a knack for dangerous things, like hiking in the wilderness, skydiving, hunting, biker bars, sailing, even boxing. You name it, she's done it. So *rad*."

Adeline beamed. "My kind of woman!" She pointed at the unlit fireplace. "I suppose zat's her zere?"

Steven admired a picture of a lean black woman with braided white hair. She held up an oversized trophy belt and touched gloves with an even more oversized boxer.

"You bet it is."

"She wins against big boxers?"

Steven let out a laugh. "Nah. Probably paid him to let her beat up on him."

Adeline looked back at Steven, then the package. "Okay, so vhat did ve travel here to get?"

"Instead of telling you, how 'bout I show you."

CHAPTER 40

SPITEFULLY LACED

Steven laid the box contents on the table, starting with a picture of Ordo American members. "That was us a little over ten years ago."

Adeline tucked a section of loose blonde hair behind her ear, her almond eyes narrowing. "You vere much thinner."

"Many, many pounds ago, yeah," Steven remarked. "That person on the far left is Raymond. He disappeared not long after this was taken. We never figured out what happened. The dude to his left is Garrett, the little rat bastard who'd been betraying us the whole time. There's me, then Raeleigh."

Steven glanced up, hoping that by somehow speaking her name, she'd appear once again. Not seeing her, he continued, pointing. "That's Jeff—he was kind of like our leader. Sara, his wife, they were newlyweds then. She wasn't part of the Order but happened to be there that day. Jessica, Maggie, Jayce, Myrka, Ra'ef, the Mayhle brothers, then Monti, and finally Vincent. Except for Raeleigh and Jeff, the rest ended up distancing themselves from us over time."

Adeline nodded. "I understand."

Steven took hold of the USB clip. He walked to an LCD TV and inserted the device, accessing the videos.

Adeline watched the exchange between the Soulstealer and the Gatekeeper in New York. She read the dialogue, the news article depicting Jeff's murder, and the article about the deaths of the Masonic Templars in Texas. At the end of it all, she peered at Steven.

"Vith vhat ve brought from Europe, it vill be enough. How can ve get zis into ze hands of someone who vill do something about it?"

Steven bared his teeth. "Now *that* is the right question. The answer is us doing a whole lot of thinking to figure out which person has the right amount of influence and too much time on their hands. That, or someone who's a pushover."

"Zat is manipulative."

"Yup, and I'm not going to apologize for it. This threat is real. There's too much at stake. I've made some terrible choices to get this far; I have to keep doing whatever it takes."

"Even if it brings more death?"

"Better a few deaths than the whole world."

"You believe zat?"

Steven narrowed his eyes. "Don't you?"

"More zan you, *ja*, but I do not zink you know vhat you mean."

"What?"

"Have you ever taken life?"

Steven scratched his chin. "Uh, no."

"Have you slept out in ze cold?"

"Yeah."

"Vas it recently?"

Steven drew back and crossed his arms. "Ish."

Adeline frowned. "You do not yet realize."

"I realize it enough to take action."

"Young boys hoping to fight war do zis as vell."

"Which person should we target?" Steven said, changing the subject.

Adeline paused for a while. "Do not phrase it like zat. Ve want cooperation."

"Sure. As long as we get what we want."

Adeline shook her head. "Ve must be careful, Steven."

"Sure, careful is my middle name." Steven clasped his hands together. "Let's get to it. Who should we make cooperate?"

"I zink you are proceeding in ze wrong way. Your plan to vrite an article by someone else is unnecessary."

Steven pursed his lips. "How so?"

"Ve are in ze age of Twitter. Zings can go viral in a matter of days if ze right person endorses your message. How about ve upload all of zis to a vebsite and tweet to someone with many followers. Vith luck, it vill be retweeted to followers, and ve vill have achieved ze popularity ve vanted."

Steven scratched the scruff of his stubble. "I never messed much with Twitter."

"It's okay. I do. All ve need is ze right retweet."

"What's a retweet?"

"It's a rebroadcast of ze original. Like a story republished in a more read section."

"That's good, but I need this to *actually* spur some backing by the U.S. or the UN."

"Perhaps one of ze United Nations people vill see ze articles and take action?"

A smirk crept across Steven's face. "Orrrrrrr, we get that retweet thing you mentioned, and *then* I pen that article in someone else's name."

Adeline shook her head. "I'm saying you do not need to coerce. You can do it better another vay."

"And I'm saying, *por qué no los dos*?" Steven laughed.

"Vhat is zat?" Adeline asked without expression.

"It means, 'why not have both?'"

CHAPTER 41

ILLUMINATE

Steven and Adeline spent the better part of the week discussing who'd be a suitable candidate for making the plan work. As for the Twitter thing, Adeline convinced Steven of the value in getting that viral Retweet. After looking on Twitter's top #100 personalities, they found plenty with millions of followers. Steven quickly discovered the most challenging part was figuring out who'd take the bait.

They came upon a few potential candidates, but Steven still struggled to find the right person to champion his letter. Without that final piece, he argued, everything would crumble. Steven sat on the armchair couch watching the news.

"Steven."

"Mmmm?" he said without looking over.

"Steven."

"Yup?"

"Ve must eat. Ve have worked on zis all day. It is almost dinner and ve have not had lunch."

"One more hour," he said, concentrating on the news reporter.

"*Nein*! Ve go now." Adeline poked him several times.

"Ugh, fine, woman!"

Adeline's poke turned into a hard punch. "Don't you say zat to me, you American pig!"

"Whatsa matter, not used to a man talking to you like that?"

"Not one I want to be vith." She blushed.

Steven cocked an eyebrow. "I've never seen you blush before."

Adeline stood, unable to contain her frustration. "Ve leave to eat now!"

Steven laughed, grabbing the car keys.

Adeline gave him the silent treatment the whole way to their favorite diner. Steven ordered his usual while Adeline turned to a televised hearing of Ashford's local news.

The waitress came over, her long black braid swaying behind her. Silver streaked through her dark hair. She smiled and poured Adeline a cup of coffee. "That screen says, 'Gender Law.' What is zat?" Adeline asked.

"Oh, it's what Congress has been trying to pass," the waitress replied. "Something about referring to people as something different than 'he' or 'she.' That's Dr. Jodyn Tyson there talking. He's been quite the opponent, calling it a 'mask of evil.'"

Steven's head jerked toward the TV.

"*Danke schön*," Adeline replied, tucking her hair behind her ear.

"Let me know if you need anything else," the waitress said, walking back behind the counter.

Steven focused on the guy speaking on TV. "Excuse me, miss. Could you turn the volume up?"

She did so, and for the next ten minutes Steven listened to Dr. Tyson. He explained how he believed this law to be the latest in an ideological war, pushed by a gang of bad actors to cement subversive legislation.

The moment Dr. Tyson said those words, Steven knew he had found their guy.

"Excuse me, Miss. How far away is Sacramento?" Steven called out to the waitress.

"Hmm, about a 12-hour drive."

"Thanks."

Adeline nudged Steven. "Vhy is zis?"

He pointed to the TV screen. "Found him."

"How do you know?"

Steven peered back at the screen. "I know."

Adeline shrugged. "You could be vrong."

"Yeah. But it's worth a shot. I like what he says." It struck Steven that his plan changed without him realizing; he was going to Sacramento to meet this guy.

His attention settled on Adeline as she ate.

Adeline glanced up, catching him mid-stare. "Vhat?"

Steven arched an eyebrow, shaking his head. "Just looking at you."

"I don't like ze vay you do zat," she said, holding his gaze.

Steven shrugged, breaking the staring contest to scout the empty diner. He found Raeleigh seated at the table on his left. She smiled, a mischievous glint in her eye.

Steven let out a stifled laugh. *I know what you're trying to do.*

Raeleigh's gaze flicked between Adeline and Steven.

She's not my type, Steven mouthed at her.

Raeleigh only cocked her head to the side and stuck out her tongue. A pang of guilt struck Steven.

Her sly grin transitioned into a somber smile, and she nodded empathetically.

He bit his lip to distract the tightening of his throat. In the blink of an eye, Raeleigh vanished again. Steven's eyes lingered on the spot before he returned to look at Adeline. She was staring at him.

"She vas here," Adeline commented, glancing around.

Steven forced a smile. "She never left."

CHAPTER 42

TYSON

Steven set foot into the vast and overcrowded auditorium. On the stage stood Dr. Tyson giving his latest lecture on the psychology of the Bible. Steven waited for almost two hours as Dr. Tyson explained the relationship between Noah, the Flood, and societal evolution.

After the waitress in Ashford pointed them to Dr. Tyson, Steven's plan morphed from a surprise attack on a random celebrity to a rational appeal to an intellectual. Steven felt pretty confident he and Adeline would continue to be a needle in a haystack as far as the Raptors were concerned. On the long trip to Sacramento, Steven familiarized himself with Dr. Tyson and his online lectures. He found himself almost entranced by the way the professor articulated his perspective. Almost.

Steven didn't know what to expect, but hoped it brought them one step closer to exposing the Soulstealer.

After the lecture, Steven inched his way through the crowd toward Dr. Tyson. The man engrossed himself in conversations with fans.

Just like you practiced, Steven thought, stepping forward.

When Dr. Tyson turned to him, Steven took a huge breath and dived in.

"You've been exploring the phenomenal story of the Bible. Here's the next story you should consider." Steven handed Dr. Tyson a small envelope labeled 'The Soulstealer.' "It's interesting, risky, and things are still occurring as recently as last week. I look forward to your thoughts. Thank you."

Dr. Tyson considered the envelope for a moment. "I'll see what I can make of it."

Steven nodded, turning and wading back out of the crowd toward Adeline.

"*Ja?*"

Steven bobbed his head.

"Vhen vill we know?"

"Soon," Steven said.

"Vhat now?"

"Now we go sightsee."

CHAPTER 43

LIGHTS

A few days later, the call came through.

Steven fumbled the burner phone out of his pocket and mashed the accept button. "Dr. Tyson."

"Yes, hello. How did you know it was me?"

"You're the only one who has this phone number."

"Strange. I reviewed your material and did research of my own, and it's by no means obvious to me what you're up to."

"Do you have 20 minutes where me and my friend can help clear that up?"

"I have to leave town in the near future. I only have availability for lunch."

"Name the place."

"There's a diner called Sazzafraz. I can be there at noon."

Steven and Adeline hurried to the diner. They scouted the area, noting every escape route possible. At noon, Steven got them a table near the back-emergency exit.

Adeline faced the door, so she saw Dr. Tyson first. He approached when Adeline got his attention.

"Greetings," Dr. Tyson said. "May I sit?"

"Please do," Steven replied.

Dr. Tyson sat, but didn't touch the menu. "I read through your material. I'm not sure what to make of it. I can determine that bad things have happened, but their connection is unclear."

"*How* is it unclear?" Steven asked, keeping his emotions in check.

"Well, for one, I don't have the expertise to verify its authenticity. As for the second, it seems to revolve around the mythology of Satan. I must say, it's seen innumerable iterations over the course of time."

"Iterations of the same thing, yes," Steven explained. "All of them point to the same phenomenon. Satan came to earth in physical form, just as Jesus did. Except that Satan, the Soulstealer, didn't just come once. He kept coming and is still here."

"An interesting hypothesis, one with little empirical evidence."

"I'd say I have all the empirical evidence I need in the videos I gave you. It has historical precedence from the dozens of independent testimonies ranging from the Mongols to the Aztecs. There's a common theme among them all. They reinforce the same struggle that birthed the Holy Crusades."

"If what you say is true, and that's a mighty if, what makes you so certain this young man is Satan?"

"The Soulstealer," Steven corrected. "Because the conditions that'd bring him back are perfect. No one alive today has seen the carnage he wrought centuries ago. Popular culture no longer believes he ever existed. If you were the Soulstealer, what could be better than convincing the whole world you were a fairy tale?"

"There's a lot to be gained, sure, but that doesn't make this young man the apocalyptic demon you assert him to be. And I'd like to hear from your colleague."

Steven suspected Dr. Tyson evaluated them for any indicators of hyperbole or deceit.

"*Ja?*" she replied. Her hair was neatly twisted behind her head into a firm bun.

"What part do you play here?"

"I am from Germany. Ve fight Satan…" Adeline peered at Steven. "Ze Soulstealer's minions zere. Zey are Unas. Cult fanatics. Zey are vell written in today's news."

"Have you seen these people?"

Adeline's face flushed, causing Steven's eyes to widen. *Please don't blow up on him.*

"*Ja.* Zey have destroyed many friends and families."

"I'm sorry to hear that," Dr. Tyson noted. "Your organization…you are a member of the Ordo Solis?"

"*Ja,*" Adeline responded. "He is from United States; I am European group."

"Where are the rest of you?"

"Most have disappeared or died."

Dr. Tyson straightened. "This is far darker than anything I want to be involved in. Why did you contact me?"

Steven cut in. "Because very soon, this will be made public. Things will unfold, and the truth will set us free. I'm not asking you to do anything except what you always do. Critique, analyze, and comment. That's all. It's too dangerous for you to be our advocate. But what isn't dangerous is you commenting on this once it has the world's attention."

"You're asking me to address it once it becomes public knowledge."

"Yes. I want you to intentionally address it as an issue worthy of your attention. It's the epitome of the very thing you speak about. A thing of malevolent intent. A destructive force that revels in suffering and contributes to a harmful mode of being," Steven recited.

Dr. Tyson looked down at the table for several seconds before he spoke. "I'm not making any promises. All I'll say is that I will give it some thought and make appropriate comment as I see fit." He stood from his chair.

"That's all we can ask," Steven said as he rose to his feet. "Thank you for your time." He extended his hand.

Dr. Tyson's spidery fingers wrapped around his. He regarded Adeline for a few seconds, then left.

Steven breathed a deep sigh of relief.

"Zat vas no good," Adeline commented.

Steven shook his head. "No, it was *very* good," he affirmed. "We have Dr. Tyson's attention. Now we need to drop the bomb and pen the letter."

Adeline crossed her arms. "You're still going to do zis, pretend to be him to drag him into zis?"

Steven shrugged. "We need someone like him. Whether he wants to help or not. This goes beyond any of us."

"Zen *you* should be out zere in the open. Not hiding and running, hoping on your plan of deceit."

"It's going to work." Steven winked at her. "Just trust me."

"You say it vill vork, to trust you, but still not listening to others." Adeline gave him a dark grin. "I zink you could be mistaken for ze Worshipful Master just now."

Steven's happy demeanor went stale. "Not funny."

Adeline smirked. "But oh, so true."

CHAPTER 44

CAMERA

Steven placed one of Larissa's fountain pens down on the paper, looking to
Adeline. They were sitting on Larissa's living room couch back in Ashford.
The fire crackled every few seconds.

"Told you," she said.

Steven grunted as he crumpled the letter. "It just needs some revising."

"Ve should not be fake, Steven."

Steven threw up his hands. "Then what?"

"Be you."

"What does that even mean?"

"Let it come from you. You're ze best to tell zis story."

"The Raptors will be all over us if we did that."

"Zey are *already*. Put zis video out zere for ze world to see, and you
be ze author."

Steven saw a figure move out of the corner of his eye. He turned to see
Raeleigh nodding at him empathetically. "You too?" Steven asked.

"*Ja*! Even she agrees vith me!" Adeline declared, pointing in a
random direction.

Steven raised an eyebrow. "I'll need to draft up what I'm going to say."

Adeline bolted upright. "*Nein*, go now, ve do zis now!" She tugged
at Steven's arm.

Steven let Adeline do whatever she had in mind, remembering Nikolaj's comment about her never-ending planning. After ten minutes of rearranging and setting up, Steven surveyed the homemade movie set. Adeline swiveled Larissa's high-end laptop around, aiming the webcam at the scene.

Adeline pointed to the chair. "*Dort.*" Steven walked over and sat. Adeline clicked a few buttons, looking at Steven. "Okay, now it's time. Tell ze vorld vhat you vant zem to know. Let it come from *you.*"

We believe what we can see. Steven stared at the floor in silence as a tsunami of memories crashed into him. He let the images flow through him, experiencing every emotion daring to reveal itself. When his memory caught up to the present, a sense of calm washed over him. His eyes slid up to the webcam, where he saw Raeleigh standing beside Adeline. They both shone with delight.

He fixed his gaze on the tiny black orb affixed to the laptop casing. "My name is Steven Carpenter. Lots of people gave their lives that I might sit here now and tell you something terrifying. And I wanna make sure their sacrifice wasn't in vain." Steven sighed, clenching his hand to keep the trembling under control. "Let's start from the beginning."

CHAPTER 45

THE EMERGING SHADOW

Pandemonium.

That was the word Steven would use to describe what he and Adeline set off. They posted the videos for public consumption and sent media packages to every major news organization they could think of.

The phrase #SoulstealerSurvived trended Top Ten on Twitter, garnered 78,000 upvotes on reddit, and racked up 6.7 million views on YouTube. Dr. Tyson retweeted the unfolding drama, adding a bit of welcome fuel to the fire.

The whole ordeal surpassed Steven's wildest dreams, but he still needed to be honest with himself about the reaction. Despite all the publicity, the U.S. Government issued no statements, except for an all-points bulletin put out for Steven as a "Person of Interest." The few American politicians commenting on the matter "awaited an investigation." Meanwhile, the CIA, FBI, and Homeland Security "refused to speculate."

Across the Atlantic, however, his post had set Europe ablaze. Its deep-rooted history with the Soulstealer and the violent Unas proved kindling to a fire Steven thought burned out over a century ago. The government of the Czechia threw themselves into a frenzy after construction workers happened upon the gruesome aftermath of the Soulstealer's meeting at an unfinished hotel, and that was *before* police discovered hundreds of

Unas bodies in the catacombs of its capital. Germany pushed a resolution through the European Union, calling for the EU Special Investigative Task Force to examine the matter without delay. While EU SITF hunted for the Unas, journalists were already publishing pieces on the Raptors and Sanhe, despite the scant details on both.

The initial mocking undertone of cult-on-cult delusion transformed into a full account of the shadow war affecting countless lives. People came out all over the world to tell their story of how the Soulstealer cults had hurt them. Victims of Unas violence in Romania talked of the barbarian practices that had become commonplace in several parts of their country. People in Nicaragua reported family members disappearing after joining the Raptors. And while most public sentiments judged the videos to be deepfake or CGI, no one doubted the bodies left behind and the criminal nature of its cults. It made no difference to Steven; finding *them* meant finding *him*.

Everyone wanted to find the guy who introduced the conflict to the world. Half of the news headlines commented on Steven's whereabouts and association with the Ordo Solis. The Commandery hilariously failed at public affairs, giving one confused response after another.

Steven hit refresh every few seconds, much to Adeline's irritation. "Can you please stop zat?" she scolded, ringing her wet hair, fresh from a shower.

Steven closed his eyes for a few heartbeats, cursing silently. He reopened them and stared at the bathrobe wrapped around her glistening skin.

"Keep your attention zere," she said, jerking her head at the screen.

Steven's gaze didn't budge. Adeline narrowed her eyes, returning to the bathroom. Steven looked back to the laptop with a triumphant smirk.

He clicked on one of *Vice News'* recent video uploads about the Unas, which featured a thumbnail of a dark and dreary pebbled tunnel with a light at the end. The video opened up with the camera crew and correspondent panting as they half-jogged down a dark passageway. Steven pegged the location; the long hall the Unas had dragged him through to the main cavern. One of the *Vice* correspondents outpaced the camera as he braced himself against the wall.

"Took some time for the police to leave. They wouldn't let us in earlier, but we found a way inside," the correspondent said as he looked behind him at the camera every few seconds. "We barely know anything about this group. The Unuh, I think—"

"Unas," the cameraperson corrected.

"The Unas. We know they have a violent history and are on the watch list for several European governments as known cults. Tons of accounts of their involvement in criminal activity. Very dangerous people. We're still piecing together how they're connected to this Soulstealer and the Ordo Solis. Here we are at what looks like some kind of cavern…"

The camera approached the end of the tunnel; yellow crime tape stretched across the doorway. A dozen or so construction lamps lit the area. Beneath the lights, neat rectangular clusters of stacked body bags made a makeshift path to a mountainous heap of things on a platform in the middle of the area. The camera zoomed in and out, focusing on the pile.

"What *is* that?" the correspondent asked aloud.

The camera zoomed in on the pile, revealing discarded disguises, clothing, and other indistinguishable items.

"They look like disguises and clothes," the cameraman replied.

The correspondent raised the crime tape and jumped down, proceeding through the narrow pathway toward the center platform. The cameraman followed, panning left and right across the ocean of black body bags.

"There are *so* many bodies here, must be hundreds. And the stench…" The guy coughed. "According to those videos, all those people were standing here when they died." The correspondent motioned around the cavern. "And the camera's point of view was from over here." He gestured to the heap in the middle.

The correspondent reached out and picked up the closest object. "It's a…mask made from the skull of an animal." He grabbed something else. "This is some curved dagger. Has dried blood on it. Maybe a ritual item?"

"Look at the thing next to your feet," the cameraman said, panning the lens down. The correspondent bent and picked it up, twisting it in his hands.

"It's a bone club with nails coming out of it," the correspondent said before dropping it to the ground. He slapped his hands together, wiping off the dusty bone debris. "This is so creepy. It's all very cultish."

A scream echoed in the distance. The camera jerked to the far side of the cavern.

"Holy s***," the correspondent said, grabbing the cameraman. "Man, run!"

The camera turned back to where they came from and shook as the crew ran back toward the exit. The video went black and cut to the outside with the correspondent in front of the well.

"That was terrifying," he said. "The bodies, all those weapons, the catacombs, the masks of bone. It looks like some ritualistic mass suicide took place. That scream at the end—we're going to need to alert the authorities that someone else is down there. We definitely need to find out more about this."

Steven closed the lid of the laptop with a smile. He walked into the kitchen where Adeline chopped chives into a beef stew.

"I'm not good at zis." The sawing sound of her serrated knife made her skill level obvious. She wore grey sweatpants and white slippers, her damp hair clipped loosely out of her face.

Steven stopped beside her, grabbing a sleek knife to slice the carrots. The sweet smell of mint surrounded him. He glanced at the counter, confused, not seeing the herbs. It dawned on him that he was smelling Adeline's shampoo.

A few seconds of silence, then, "Vhat did you see?" Adeline asked.

Steven grinned from ear to ear as he continued chopping. "It won't be long now."

CHAPTER 46

TOUCHPOINT

Steven awoke with a start upon hearing a series of thumps on the door and shouting. He bolted out of his room and barged into Adeline's. She jolted upright, tearing off her sleep mask.

"We need to go!" Steven hissed. There was a crash, followed by an army of footsteps storming the house.

Adeline undid the latch and flung open the window.

"Go, go, go!" Steven urged, and helped her down and let her drop to the ground below. He pulled the window back into place as the door swung open behind him.

"Police! Put your hands up!"

Steven went wide-eyed.

"I said: Put your hands up!"

Steven threw his hands up, keeping his robust frame in front of the window.

Please, God, help her get away.

The cops frisked Steven before bringing him downstairs. It seemed like the whole Ashford police department swarmed the home, bagging computers, notepads, and newspaper clippings. They brought him outside and into the back of a police van. He found himself staring at Adeline.

She raised an eyebrow at him, lips forming a thin line. The van started and sped away.

"What?" he said, shrugging.

"Nothing."

"Look, how was I supposed to know that was gonna happen?"

"It's fine," she said without emotion.

Steven pursed his lips. "I know that trick. Spill it."

Adeline let out a sly grin. "You never could have fit zrough zat vindow."

Steven rested the back of his head against the steel interior of the van and chuckled. "Well, that's rude," he said, unable to hide his smile.

At the police station, Ashford police uncuffed and separated them. They were each interrogated for a few hours. The examiners got *way* more than they bargained for. Steven told them everything he learned from Nythan's blabbering, leaving out specific names that put other friends in danger. Like the detectives back in Texas, these detectives asked him the same questions over and over. His response stayed the same, every time. Steven didn't waver. He did snicker whenever Adeline screamed something in German through the plain white walls.

One of the examiners placed his hands on the aluminum table and bent toward Steven. The bright fluorescent lights put a spotlight on his thinning blonde hair. "We *will* figure out what's going on here."

"I wish you would." Steven crossed his arms as his examiner turned to the door. "Hey!"

The examiner turned around.

"Make sure you bring in extra security. It won't be long before those killers on the news find out we're here. They'll come after us, and they don't care about anyone who gets in their way."

"That won't matter soon," the detective said. "You'll be out of here in no time."

Steven cocked his head. "Got something special planned?"

The detective shook his head. "Nope, but someone else does."

Steven raised his eyebrows. "What do you mean by that?"

The detective ignored him and left.

"Hey! What do you mean by that?" Steven shouted as the door slammed shut.

Steven paced the room. *Better not be another damn Raptor trap.*

He sat, scrutinizing the eggshell-colored walls and matching door that kept him locked inside, until the silver handle twisted open. In stepped a man wearing aviator sunglasses and a cheap suit.

"Mr. Carpenter, please come with us."

"Where's Raeleigh—" Steven cut himself off. "I mean, Adeline. Where's Adeline?"

"She's being questioned."

Steven crossed his arms. "She and I stay together, or I make this difficult for the both of us."

The man regarded Steven and whispered into a lapel microphone. Soon a guard brought in Adeline. They were led to a garage without being cuffed again. Before Steven got into one of the unmarked SUVs, he turned back to the officers.

"Please, listen to me when I say this. The Raptors may not know we're leaving. You've *got* to be careful. They're professionals who don't care who they hurt. Just watch your backs."

"We will," one of them replied.

Steven got into the SUV and sat next to Adeline. Their convoy pulled out of the garage and under the night sky. Steven expected yet another long road trip, but twenty minutes later, they arrived at the airport.

"Where're we going?" Steven asked as his feet touched the tarmac.

"This way, please." His escort ushered him toward a medium-sized plane. He sighed, went up the aluminum stairs with Adeline, then took a seat. The plane wasted no time taking off. When it became clear their destination wouldn't be as short, Steven fell asleep.

He jerked awake as they landed at Dulles International Airport in Washington, D.C., were ferried into another convoy of SUVs, and traveled east until hitting the Potomac. At first, Steven didn't know where they were. Then he saw the unmistakable sign of the bald eagle resting atop a white block and red star.

The Central Intelligence Agency.

Steven's lips curled into a grin. "Well damn, it's about time."

Chapter 47

Only A Messenger

Steven and Adeline sat in a conference room deep within the CIA's headquarters. Across the oblong cherry oak table were representatives from the Federal Bureau of Investigations, the Defense Intelligence Agency, Homeland Security, National Reconnaissance Office, and the Secret Service.

They first questioned Steven and Adeline on their backgrounds, as if these particular agencies didn't already have access to a person's entire life history. Next, they went through everything leading up to the present day in excruciating detail. Steven revealed everything this time, even the identities of those he concealed from Ashford authorities.

The next couple of hours were a series of rapid-fire questions attempting to clarify everything from where Steven had been to what the Soulstealer was. Steven hoped the agencies did more investigative work than what the interrogation led him to believe. The CIA wanted *every* detail surrounding the deaths of their three agents: Mia, her accomplice, and Mr. Smith.

One by one, each agency representative left, leaving only the agents from the CIA and FBI.

"So, tell me," Steven said. "What do you make of all this?"

"It's surreal, that's for sure," the CIA agent commented.

"Uh huh. But beyond that, is the Agency going to do anything more than question us?"

"We'll see."

"What an ominous reply. At least tell me that you confirmed the death of your two agents in the videos we release."

"I don't have an answer for you."

Steven sat back, folding his arms across his chest. "This relationship is going to be short-lived if you don't start working with us," he said, turning to the FBI agent. "Is the Bureau going to take a deeper look into the murder of Jeff and his family?"

"That's not a decision I can make," the agent answered.

"Well then, why am I talking to *you*?"

The agent shrugged.

Steven sighed. "Fine. Are we free to go?"

"Yes, but we'd like you to stay close by. You mentioned the Raptors are coming after you. We can offer a safe location."

"I mean, thanks, but no thanks. If you guys aren't gonna tell me how you plan on helping us, we'll figure that out on our own."

"We'd like you to stay close," the FBI agent repeated.

"I don't care *what* you'd like us to do. I know the threat. I've *seen* the threat. Now you see the threat. So either help us find this kid or do whatever it is that you do instead. We keep going, with or without your help," Steven asserted.

"We don't think it's a good idea for you to go out there on your own. We have a validated threat on your life."

"Oh really? That's great. At least now you've caught up to where we are," Steven fumed. "Also, you were going to tell us this…when, exactly?"

"I just did."

Steven shook his head. Adeline broke her silence and reached over to squeeze his hand.

"*Ja*," she began. "Do you take zis seriously?" she asked the agents.

"We're looking into it," the CIA agent evaded.

Adeline raised an eyebrow at Steven. "It isn't a no," she said.

"It isn't a yes, either," Steven replied. "They've had time to get into this and be less wishy-washy than they are."

"Zey are probably slow, Steven. It's been one veek since ve posted ze videos."

"All I'm sayin' is, that's fine, but we're not slowing down. We need to keep going while we still have time on our side. They know everything we know."

Adeline shrugged.

Steven stared the two agents in the eyes. "If we leave, are you going to stop us?"

The CIA agent opened a brown folder in front of him, skimming some text. "No, not that I can see."

"But we advise you to take advantage of our offer," the FBI agent added.

"I appreciate the offer, boys, but unless that protection means you put trained bodyguards on us as we go back out there, I can't accept."

The CIA agent nodded to the FBI agent, who again shrugged. Steven took that as his answer.

"Just to let you know, we're probably going to travel back to Europe. We'll try not to hide our movements. That way, if we get into trouble, you'll have some way to see it. I just hope you guys are paying close enough attention to the Raptors and the Unas to take notice. Also, have you guys looked into Sanhe? Soulstealer is called Yaoguai in that part of the world."

The FBI agent gave Steven a blank stare. The CIA agent offered a terse response, "We don't have an answer for you."

"Of course not, neither does anyone else, it seems." Steven stood. "Well boys, it's been fun. I hope we were helpful, and I hope this gives you dudes the stuff you need to get your rear in gear."

"This isn't an easy decision to make. You've given us a confusing and unusual message," the CIA agent stood, offering his hand.

"The message existed long, long before us," Steven told him. "I'm just the messenger."

CHAPTER 48

CATCH UP

Steven and Adeline made their way to a nearby motel and paid for a bottom-floor room with cash and a fake name. On the way, Steven stopped by his bank, verified his identity, and withdrew another stack of bills. They spent a few hundred dollars on a new laptop and accessed the internet. A quick search of the latest news left him encouraged. The EU Special Investigative Task Force reported violent clashes with local Unas gangs across several countries.

Vice News published a litany of pieces on the Unas. The BBC, *The Guardian, Der Spiegel, Le Monde,* and *la República* all devoted investigative articles digging up the Soulstealer's long and bloody history. American media relegated the Raptors to minor segments, but Asian outlets didn't report much on Sanhe.

Burn it down. Steven smirked when he noticed Wrath's face plastered all over the news. Underneath Nythan's portrait read "Nythan Dwienz" and "Ştefan Černý" under Wrath's.

No wonder you went by Wrath. Not much cult credibility in a name like Steh-fawn.

He clicked through the trending section on Twitter, happy to see #SoulstealerSurvived still in the Top 10. Steven made a little hop, pumping his fist. "Yesssss!"

Adeline beamed. "Zey still see us."

Steven pointed to a BBC article headlined, *Ordo Solis Leaders Urge Caution Amidst Chaos*. "Let's see what the buffoons have to say."

He took a moment to read. "They're saying that we all need to remain calm," Steven sneered, reading further into the Solis Commandery's statement. "They call upon the EU to continue investigating and for the United Nations to have an emergency session to discuss what must be done about the followers of the Soulstealer."

"Not a bad response," Adeline said.

"Sure, but I want *us* to be there to broker that deal. They'll just screw it up."

A gentle knock on the hotel door made them both turn their heads.

A few seconds of silence ticked by. Steven motioned for Adeline to hide in the bathroom, but she instead rolled her eyes and followed him as he tiptoed toward the door.

He positioned himself up against the wall next to the handle as Adeline went to the left corner window, peeking through the curtains. Steven leaned over and peered through the peephole, seeing two figures in dark clothing. A chill shot down Steven's spine.

He pursed his lips. *This doesn't feel right.*

Steven quietly cleared his throat, and in the womanliest voice he could muster, snapped, "Who *is* it?"

Before either of the newcomers could react, Steven heard a loud "Scuse me!" echo somewhere from the right hallway. The two figures looked down that way, then turned in the opposite direction and hurried to the left.

A few seconds later, a motel night guard passed by, presumably following the newcomers. Steven looked over at Adeline, whose gaze slowly tracked the night guard. Steven peered back through the peephole, when a weathered face he hadn't seen in more than a decade rushed into view.

A series of frantic knocks beat against the door.

"Steven!" the man hissed in-between knocks. "Steven, open up!"

I'll be damned. Steven narrowed his eyes, suddenly recalling how Garrett had used Raeleigh as bait.

"Steven!" the voice said louder. "You're in danger. I bought you a minute, maybe two."

Steven's head jerked as Adeline backed away from the window and ran to the first bed, zipping up their shared carry-on suitcase. Steven moved his frame against the door, laying a hand on the handle. "How'd you find me?"

"Steven, if you don't get out of here, the Raptors will kill you. You gotta go, and you gotta go *now!*"

Before he even turned around to consult her, Adeline had her hand on top of his, trying to push his meaty hand down. "I believe him. Move now. *Schnéll.*"

Steven nudged Adeline back and flung the door open, ready for anything.

Instead, his old friend Vincent hastily beckoned him before turning around and rushing to an idling black Ford sedan parked in the handicap spot some feet away. Steven ran out and jumped in the front passenger; Adeline in the back. Vincent slammed the gears into reverse and sped out. Steven kept looking back to determine if anyone followed.

"Adeline," Steven said. She too was looking back.

"*Ja,*" she said, not turning around to face him.

"Keep watch."

"*Ja.*"

Steven turned forward and looked at Vincent. His olive-toned skin stood out against his dark gray button-down shirt. "Not to spoil the reunion, but—"

"Why am I here?" Vincent finished, switching to the outside left lane. "Because *someone* had to pull you outta there."

"They followed you," Steven accused.

Vincent glanced over at Steven. "I was following *them.*" He looked back at the road.

Steven exhaled a deep breath, using his fingers to massage his eyes. "Okay. How did this happen? What went wrong here?"

"Soon as I saw them start their search, I tipped the front desk off and pulled the car around to wait for the fireworks. Ole rent-a-cop did better than expected. Raptors knocked at your door, rent-a-cop called them out, they got out of dodge. Pulled up and got you outta there."

"How'd you know it was us?"

"Didn't." Vincent shook his head, but his slicked black hair didn't move. "Situation like that, better to be wrong than give the alternative a fighting chance."

"How were you even there?"

"I'm a private eye now, Steven. You made it hard using cash and all, but there are too many databases with real-time information to disappear anymore; rental car invoices, customs, airfares, ATM receipts." Vincent took an on-ramp to I-395 South. "It paints a picture. I figured you were still in the vicinity."

"Yes, but how did you know ve vere zere?" Adeline said, still scanning out the back window.

"Who's she?" Vincent asked.

"Solis Europe type," Steven said. "Vince, meet Adeline. Adeline, meet Vince. Vince was Solis America once upon a time."

Vincent smiled. "Once upon a time." His eyes glistened. "So yeah, I thought you were somewhere around here. Apparently, so did they. Picked up *their* trail as they were cruising down the stretch. Eastern Coven by the looks of them."

"Steven," Adeline said. "I zought zese Raptors vere super elite, you said."

"Oh, they're good," Vincent continued. "But I was our resident counter-intel while I was Ordo Solis. Once you figure out their M.O., it's a hard thing to unsee. Even after all these years…"

"That, and the good ole fashioned sappy lady voice," Steven said.

Vincent let out a loud chuckle. "You still doin' that?"

Steven grinned. "Wasn't sure it was going to work, either." He pointed at a sign for Washington Dulles International Airport as it passed. "There, head to the airport."

"You sure?"

"Yeah. We're leaving."

"Zank you for helping us," Adeline said.

"Yeah." Steven nodded. "Speaking of which, I remember you phasing yourself out. You here to get back in? Or is there another reason? I can't imagine you went to all this trouble to say hi."

Vincent shook his head. "I saw your video. Saw enough of the rest to know it could be real. Is it real, Steven? Is it back?"

Steven looked out his window at the passing capital city lights. "It's back. And its *name* is Nythan. I met him when they captured us."

Vincent opened his mouth, then closed it. His voice came out shaky. "Who'd they get?"

"I'm the only one left."

"Jeff?"

"Dead."

"Raeleigh?"

"Dead."

"Garret?"

"Raptor."

"Jesus."

"I don't remember him being part of the Order."

An awkward laugh filled the space.

"I don't know how I feel about it," Vincent said. "I have a good life, and I want to keep it that way."

"Well...I hate to be the bearer of bad news, but..."

Vincent chuckled, then exhaled. "Yeah, I know...if it's back...it won't matter."

Adeline didn't stop scanning their surroundings, but Steven relaxed the rest of the trip as he caught up with Vincent. They pulled into Departures at Dulles, and Adeline jumped out with their luggage.

Steven looked all around outside the car. "Do you have a way for me to contact you?"

Vincent reached into the middle console and handed Steven his card.

"How much are you willing to do?"

Vincent shrugged. "As long as it keeps me alive."

"Then I need a favor." Steven paused. "Make that two."

Vincent raised an eyebrow. "Mmhm?"

"Find out where the others are, but don't contact them yet. Something tells me Ordo America is gonna need to get back up on its feet."

"Got it."

"Two. You remember our sympathetic friend, the one from the State Department who always complained about how cold it got in New York?"

Vincent laughed. "Oh yeah. That guy from the Children's Benefit who used green beans to show Jeff how *complicated* his job was." Vincent used air quotes to stress the word.

Steven smiled, but the memory stung. "Only Jeff could see that as a prerequisite to forming a partnership. Yeah, that guy. See if he still works there and ask him if he's still sympathetic, given everything that's happened."

They were both interrupted by a loud whistle echoing throughout Departures. A middle-aged man in a yellow traffic vest stood on the curb a few feet away from Vincent's car.

Steven looked at Vincent. "Duty calls. Thanks for savin' our skin. I owe you."

"I have a feeling you're gonna owe me a lot more by the end of all this."

Steven made a mock salute. "Be seein' ya." He exited the car and walked inside. He and Adeline looked up at the Departures list.

"Where to?" she asked.

Steven winked at her. "I'm in the mood for beer and schnitzel."

CHAPTER 49

CLASH

Steven and Adeline left the Frankfurt airport and took a train to Dietzen-bach, back to the Solis Commandery. When they arrived, Steven noticed the town was abuzz with energy. Dozens of people sped through the streets. What's more, the average person looked younger, more fit, and like they had somewhere to be. It was much different than the sleepy old town he saw the first time.

Steven's interest piqued when he drew closer to the Commandery's house. Fresh paint, replaced woodwork, and tinted windows now deco-rated the place. They stopped at a makeshift checkpoint built twenty-five yards from the entrance.

The guard wielded both a baton and a harsh command of the German language. Adeline responded in the same way. After a few moments of conversation, she turned to Steven as the guard talked into his radio.

"I told zem who ve are. I'm not sure zey'll let us through."

Steven shrugged. After five minutes, the guard's radio squawked to let them pass.

Attendants ushered them through a crowded hallway and into the living room where some Grand Councilmembers lounged in armrest chairs.

"You've come back," the Worshipful Master said, swirling a copper liquid in his glass.

"And I've brought the attention of the whole world with me."

"Yes, we've been dealing with the consequences ever since."

"Good, it's about time you all did something useful for the Order," Steven snapped.

The Worshipful Master raised his hand. "Mr. Carpenter—"

"*Grand Master*, if you please. I'm here on behalf of Solis America. Per Solis Protocol, I call for the annual gathering of the Commandery."

The Worshipful Master shook his head. "Solis America is now defunct."

"No, it isn't. Jeff was the previous Grand Master. I'm the new one."

"And how many members does Solis America have?"

"Three."

"That's not enough, I'm afraid."

"I'm afraid it is, Worshipful. All I need is a quorum. That's three members."

"And who are these members?"

"Myself, Vince, and—"

"Me," Adeline blurted. Steven glanced at her. She seemed just as surprised as him at her outburst.

"You cannot have two memberships, Ms. Faehrmann," the Worshipful Master said.

Adeline crossed her arms. "I do not. I have resigned my Ordo Europe membership."

"I received no such notification."

Adeline didn't respond.

The Worshipful Master regarded Steven. "I will speak with the rest of the Commandery."

"Please do. I'll come again in a few hours." Steven and Adeline left the room. Adeline mentioned catching up with some acquaintances and went upstairs.

Steven started his tour from the living room, scrutinizing his new surroundings and staying out of the way as people came to and fro. The once creaky old house full of sleepy people transformed into something lively and abuzz with activity. Various rooms held crowded staffed meetings. He turned back into the kitchen and ran right into George.

"Heyo, chap!" George said, hugging Steven.

Steven patted George on the back. "Sup, *chap*, how you been?"

"Just great. We've been spurred into action after your introduction on the internet. Everyone is very excited."

"Almost everyone," Steven said, jerking a thumb back toward the living room. "The Commandery seems less than enthused."

George gave a hearty laugh, returning Steven's slap on the back. "Oh, don't mind them. They're happy, all the same. It wasn't what they expected, that's for sure!"

"Yeah, it wasn't what I expected either. At any rate, we need to be smart about how we play our hand. The current Commandery aren't the right people to handle this. "

"They have the experience."

"But their heart isn't in it. They've no connection with what they've pledged themselves to. The fire is gone."

"I think there's still some fire left in them."

"Too little, too late."

"Perhaps," George said. "But you should exercise patience. They see things you don't."

"Then tell me what I'm missing, because the public response from the Commandery has been subpar at best."

"They're taking advantage of the opportunity you gave them. Just wait and see."

"When we have our annual meeting, I'll figure out if they're handling this properly."

"You're too brash."

"It's one of the only things propelling us forward."

"You can't possibly be serious in thinking you're the only one in this fight."

"No," Steven said. "But I *am* the one making it possible."

"You sound just like them, you know."

"Who?"

"The Commandery you say you hate. Say the same thing you did just now."

"I'm nothing like them."

"Those are flimsy words against the full weight of history. Too many people saying the same thing and ending up wrong."

"I'm not wrong. History will prove I'm right."

"Prove it yourself. Otherwise, you'll end up realizing you're the same as these old men you despise. The only difference is you're 20 years younger and not nearly as experienced." George's green eyes reflected his sincerity.

Steven sucked his teeth at George, waving him off.

George tipped his mug at Steven. "Good luck, chap." He left the kitchen.

A couple of hours gave Steven enough time to visit the observation tower again and reminisce in front of the fireplace. An attendant tracked him down and informed Steven he had an appointment with the Commandery in fifteen minutes. He couldn't find Adeline, so he proceeded to the conference without her.

He entered what looked like a hastily emptied room with the eight old men of the Solis Commandery standing behind their chairs, forming a circle. Mr. Hoche, still dressed in his ridiculous attire, peered at him from the opposite side.

"What're you doing here?" Steven asked him.

"I belong here, just as you," Mr. Hoche said, taking a moment to straighten his vest.

"You a part of the Commandery now?"

"Quite. He's Grand Master of Solis Europe," the Worshipful Master answered for him.

Steven raised his eyebrows. "I must've missed that."

"You never stopped proclaiming your opinion long enough for me to say, Mr. Carpenter," Mr. Hoche replied.

Steven tilted his head in amusement.

"Shall we begin?" the Worshipful Master said. He took his seat, followed by the rest of the Commandery.

No one spoke.

"Go ahead," Steven said.

"You called this meeting; *you* tell *us*," the Worshipful Master said.

"What? We're not gonna open with our usual verbiage?"

The Worshipful Master shifted in his seat. "You may proceed."

Steven's jaw dropped. "Worshipful, *you* go first. Don't any of you remember how to open a meeting?"

"It's been some time since we've performed the ritual," the Grand Secretary stammered.

Steven leaned back, folding his arms. "Apparently, I can't even confirm I'm sitting with real Ordo Solis."

"Steven," the Worshipful Master said. "We've been at this for decades. Much longer than you. We've recited the ritual many dozens of times."

"I can understand that, Worshipful. But after seeing you all here, I'm not encouraged by your ability to lead the Order, much less handle the coming storm. I call for a vote to cement new leadership."

"Solis Protocol is particular about the supersession of resigned or deceased leadership. No vote will be had," the Worshipful Master stated.

"You'd be doing the right thing if you did."

"Our leadership is *not* subject to question. If you recall, none of us here asked to be in this position. It was quite an unexpected change. Not that it matters now. It's done, we're here, and we've a summit with the EU committee tomorrow to discuss real progress regarding the EU's endorsement of our organization. We won't be inviting you to accompany us, I'm afraid."

"I understand," Steven reacted. "As long as you understand that when Solis America becomes the face of the Order, it'll be nothing personal when I relieve you of your positions."

"Solis America is no more," the Worshipful Master replied, his lips compressed in a thin line.

"It definitely is *not*. I'm the new Grand Master."

"We never confirmed you as Grand Master, nor have you ever been raised to that level."

"I seriously doubt you remember *how* to raise a Grand Master. And if you recall those same regulations, the Solis Protocol is *very* specific about Grand Masters prematurely resigning or being deceased. Confirmation or not, I *am* Solis America's new Grand Master."

Mr. Hoche scoffed. "You have some nerve."

Steven took a full second to breathe in. "The war with the Soulstealer calls for nothing less. You're getting in our way. And it's time for you lot to get *out* of our way."

CHAPTER 50

SUMMIT CRASHER

Steven straightened his rental black and white suit as he and Adeline entered a spacious office lobby in Brussels, Belgium. Ever since the Worshipful Master let slip the Commandery had a meeting with the EU Special Investigative Task Force, Adeline weaseled whatever information she could about its location. They left the night before to get there on time.

Steven put his hand on the receptionist's desk. "Hello there, we're Ordo Solis, here for our appointment with the Director."

The man behind the desk inspected them with raised eyebrows, giving Steven a moment of anxiety. *Did the Commandery call ahead and tell reception not to let us in?*

The guy turned to his computer. Steven's gaze wandered up as the receptionist went through a series of clicks and keyboard strokes. Behind the desk, a row of portraits lined the wall, each labeled with a name and position.

"You're a bit early," the receptionist said. "The Chief Prosecutor doesn't have an earlier opening."

"Oh, that's fine," Steven said. "No rush. We'll wait." He glanced back to the portraits, finding the Chief Prosecutor's plaque second from the left. Engraved above the title was the name *Dane Schwandt.*

They seated themselves amid a small assortment of felt chairs, waiting for the appointed time and arrival of the Commandery council. When the Commandery arrived, the half-enraged half-horrified look on the Worshipful Master's face gave Steven every bit of pleasure he imagined it would.

"I already let the good gentlemen at the desk know we've arrived," Steven preempted.

The Worshipful Master couldn't do much except pretend the plan included Steven and Adeline from the beginning. They ascended a few floors in an elevator and were guided to a spacious conference room. A blue flag with gold stars surrounding the letters "SITF" hung next to a LED screen. Ten minutes later, the rest of the meeting attendees arrived. A man with wire-rimmed circular glasses and perfectly combed short dirty blonde hair stepped forward. Steven recognized him from the portrait downstairs.

"I'm Dane Schwandt, Chief Prosecutor of the Special Investigative Task Force. Thank you for meeting with us."

"Pleased to meet you," Steven responded before anyone else. He received dirty looks from the Commandery councilmembers.

The Worshipful Master rose from his chair. "My name is Alfie Williams. I'm the Worshipful Master of the Ordo Solis."

"Please to meet you," Mr. Schwandt said. His deep blue eyes turned to Steven. "You're the gentleman who's in those videos, right?"

"Yeah," Steven said, walking over to Mr. Schwandt, shaking his hand. "You sound American."

"Utah, born and raised. Good to see you could make it."

Steven nodded. "New Jersey, but without the accent. Thanks. Glad to be here." He returned to his chair.

Mr. Schwandt introduced the other members of the Task Force.

"Mr. Schwandt," the Worshipful Master said, "we'd like to discuss the way forward, and what your task force can do to help."

"Of course," Mr. Schwandt responded. "As you've seen on the news, we've begun investigating the violence perpetrated by the Unas. The EU resolution passed this morning. We have the cooperation of Europol now. What you haven't seen is the extraordinary success we've had locating Unas gangs within EU jurisdiction. We've located and arrested ringleaders from 12 different sites."

"That's truly extraordinary," the Worshipful Master said, scratching his chin.

Steven smiled. *Here he goes. Gonna botch it all up.*

"We *do* have a record of over 300 Unas groups in the European region," the Worshipful Master said.

"Those locations would be useful. I think we're making good progress."

"Quite!" the Worshipful Master declared, clasping his hands. "The sooner we can get to them, the sooner we can find the Satan."

Mr. Schwandt frowned. "Satan?"

"Yes. As you are no doubt aware, our Order was chartered to locate and combat the Satan. It's highly publicized."

Now it was Mr. Schwandt who scratched *his* chin.

"The Soulstealer," Steven offered.

"Ah," Mr. Schwandt said, nodding toward Steven.

"He's their leader," the Worshipful Master continued, casting a glance at Steven. "You might know him as Nythan Dwienz. The boy in the video."

"He's a teenager," Mr. Schwandt said, narrowing his eyes.

"He's no ordinary adolescent. As you saw, he has the monstrous ability to take a person's life force."

"We've yet to confirm the authenticity of that video, but we're more interested in dealing with the Unas. We have confirmed reports of their illegal activities."

"Yes, quite, but—"

Steven interjected. "But that's only one of the three radical cults that use extreme violence to pursue their delusion."

The look on the Worshipful Master's face was, for the second time that day, priceless. He raised his hand. "Mr. Carpenter, if you please—"

Steven interrupted again. "What Alfie is trying to say is that these cults think the Soulstealer is their messiah."

Mr. Schwandt alternated his attention between Steven and the Worshipful Master, amused.

Steven continued. "We've been tracking these cults for decades. There're three main ones. The Unas in Europe, the Raptors in America, and Sanhe in Asia. They were dangerous before this kid showed up, but now they're downright murderous fanatics. They think this Nythan kid is going to bring about the apocalypse, and their mission is to help him do that."

"I'm only authorized to investigate the Unas."

"Yeah, I get that. So, for what you're after, a partnership with the Ordo Solis in Europe would help you big time. Unfortunately, that incident in Prague wiped out most of our *real* leadership. But we still have information and experience you're gonna want to take advantage of."

"My leadership is pretty skeptical of involving your group. They think your claims are…bizarre."

Steven nodded. "I don't blame them. I get their skepticism. No one has believed us since we lost our endorsement with the League of Nations."

Mr. Schwandt's eyebrows raised at the mention of the UN's predecessor.

"A quick Google search will tell you all you need to know about our involvement with the League. It's all public record. In any case, we've been fighting the big three cults for a long time. They've killed a lot of us. Talking to the families of our fallen members would assist your investigation."

Mr. Schwandt looked over at one of his colleagues.

Steven kept going. "It doesn't need to be official. Hell, the CIA and FBI won't even admit they're working with us in America. But they'll need my help again before this is all over."

"You've spoken to the CIA?"

"Yeah, talked to them right before I flew over here. I'm the leader of the Ordo Solis in America."

"What about the Asian group?" Mr. Schwandt asked.

Steven shifted his weight. "We uh, lost contact with them some time ago. We don't think they made it…"

Mr. Schwandt heaved a sigh. "This is complicated."

"Yup. We're really grateful you've decided to look into the Unas. They're every bit as barbaric as you think they are and more. Soulstealer Satan stuff or not, they need to be dealt with."

"Absolutely!" the Worshipful Master cut in. "We appreciate your help."

Steven touched his fingers to his forehead and closed his eyes. "Can you just…stop that?" Steven said, shaking his head.

Mr. Schwandt again appeared tickled. "Isn't he your leader?"

"Temporarily, until it's time to vote in replacements for the leaders we lost in Prague."

"Young man, that is quite enough," the Grand Secretary cut in, coming to the rescue. "Your rude behavior stops here and now."

Steven ignored him. "You'll find that our current leadership means well, but Solis Europe and Solis America have some major disagreements over how to handle all of this. My videos on YouTube weren't exactly sanctioned by the good folks sitting in this room." He gestured to the members of the Solis Commandery.

"Ah," Mr. Schwandt said, eyeing the Worshipful Master. "Is that what you meant when you said Steven wasn't going to make it today?"

"We feel he is acting inappropriately and outside the authority of his position," the Grand Secretary said.

"You'd still be sitting around a campfire in cozy southern Germany if I hadn't," Steven retorted, turning to Mr. Schwandt. "I'm sorry you have to see our dirty laundry, but the situation is desperate. We need your help."

"We'll do our best," Mr. Schwandt said. "But we're not here to get involved in your…religious dispute. What I *can* say is that our preliminary findings have given us even more than we thought we'd find. My leadership is very motivated in continuing this investigation."

"Excellent," Steven said. "Good news is there's plenty more to find. A word of warning, though. These guys are true believers. When they catch you sniffing around, they're going to sniff right back. They don't care about rules, or who they hurt. I've been kidnapped by these thugs, and I *barely* escaped not one, but three gunfights. I've been on the run for weeks. They're out there looking for me right now, and they nearly got me back in D.C." Steven paused, gesturing to his companions. "These folks are in danger too, except that the Unas have much bigger problems to deal with now that you're here."

"Do you need protection?" Mr. Schwandt asked with concern.

Steven smiled. "Thanks for the offer; the FBI already offered. I'm going back to America to see what I can do about starting an investigation into the Raptors. *They're* the real threat. These Unas, they're the JV team. The Raptors are varsity."

"What about the third cult?"

"Sanhe. That's a needle in a haystack problem. No one even knows where to start with them. Worry about those guys when you've a handle on the Unas and Raptors."

"I know a couple of people in the State Department," Mr. Schwandt proposed. "If you need assistance, I can put you in touch with them."

"That would *really* help," Steven said. "I'll take you up on that." He dug into his coat pocket. "Here's my card with my new email address. I think the Raptors hacked my old email, so keep this close, please."

Steven handed Mr. Schwandt his card, printed only a few hours ago.

"I'll get this over to my colleague."

"Thanks. In the meantime, these fine gentlemen are the ones to coordinate your Unas investigation in Europe." Steven gestured to the Worshipful Master. "They'll be able to assist with whatever is needed."

Mr. Schwandt glanced over to the group. "How about we get a picture?" He motioned to one of his colleagues, who rushed out. Thirty seconds later, he returned with a photographer wielding a sophisticated camera and a holographic "PRESS" badge.

"Ms. Koshner, could you take the picture here, please. I'll be making a statement immediately following this meeting." Mr. Schwandt said.

"Is there a partnership between the EU and Ordo Solis?" Ms. Koshner asked.

"I'll make a statement following this meeting, Ms. Koshner. Picture, please."

Ms. Koshner made quick motions with her hands toward the group. "Come more together."

Steven, who stood closest to Mr. Schwandt, took a step closer and extended his hand. Mr. Schwandt gripped it in a frozen pose for the picture, and they both smiled as the Commandery and Task Force squeezed around them. The journalist thumbed her camera in a flurry of clicks.

"Thank you, Ms. Koshner. I'll see you outside," Mr. Schwandt said, and she left.

"You can bet that will be on the front page of a few newspapers," Mr. Schwandt chuckled. "Thank you all for your time. We'll be in touch."

Steven tried not to make eye contact with any of his Ordo Solis compatriots as they left the room. He felt the Commandery's rage-filled stares sear into his skull. He finally broke, looking at the Worshipful Master.

"Good luck, Worshipful. I'll be in Solis America."

The Worshipful Master trembled with fury. "Mr. *Carpenter.*"

CHAPTER 51

SWIFT

Steven awoke with a start as Adeline shook him awake.

"Wha, what?" Steven removed his sleep mask. His hefty frame made for a tight fit in the economy seat on the jumbo airliner.

"Look!" Adeline pointed to her in-flight entertainment screen. The muted volume did little to hide the news anchor speaking a mile a minute, but it was the scrolling headline that caught Steven's eye: *"Thousands Found Dead from Unknown Cause in Bhutan."*

Steven shot upright. The scrolling captions told about an unknown disaster that had struck a rural city in northern Bhutan, killing all inhabitants within a ten-mile radius. The Bhutan royal family declared a state of emergency, quarantining the entire region. The anchor grasped for straws, finally settling on "a sudden outbreak."

Steven looked to Adeline. "You think it was him?"

"I know it vas him."

"You sure?"

"It vas him."

Steven accessed his email, hoping for a message from Mr. Schwandt's colleague in the State Department. Nothing. He logged out, reaffixing his sleep mask. "Let me know when we land."

They landed in the U.S. a few hours later. He wasn't surprised to see

FBI agents, surrounded by TSA, waiting for them a few steps out of the gate. They politely, but assertively, led Steven and Adeline to the arrival pickup lane where a small convoy of black SUVs waited with flashing lights. On their way out of the terminal, Steven couldn't help but notice people huddled around their phones and TVs. The televisions he passed were all turned to local news stations, which flashed the headline: *"Phantom Disaster Strikes Again in Bhutan, Claiming Tens of Thousands."*

"Look!" Steven pointed.

Adeline followed Steven's finger. "It's happening. He's doing it."

"They'll see what we're talking about now," Steven said as they were ushered to a motorcade.

Before they even had a chance to get into one of the vehicles, another convoy of SUVs with flashing lights came to a speeding halt next to them. Steven and Adeline were ushered back, just inside the sliding doors. Out of the newer convoy came several people in government suits to stand opposite the dozen government suits already there.

One Suit handed another Suit a piece of paper, and an argument started between them that engulfed the group. It only ended when a much larger Suit, who had the swagger of being in charge, came into the picture and took one of the FBI Suits aside to talk one-on-one. FBI Suit—a female with her badge displayed prominently on her belt next to her gun—became visibly frustrated the longer the conversation continued. It was clear to Steven that the power dynamic favored Swagger-in-Charge Suit, who looked down at her with nothing short of indifference.

FBI Suit motioned them forward, and Steven and Adeline were led outside into the loud echoes of the Arrivals chute. They approached FBI Suit and Swagger-in-Charge Suit.

"At least let us accompany you," FBI Suit said.

"No," Swagger-in-Charge Suit said flatly.

"The FBI has an interest in this," she protested.

"Take it up with the Secretary of State. She's already had input from the FBI. You may leave now."

FBI Suit sighed, then looked at the agents next to Steven and Adeline. "Let's go."

As the FBI agents got into their convoy to depart, Swagger-in-Charge

Suit turned his lifeless gaze toward Steven. They were of similar build, but Steven was a tad taller.

"I'm Emmett Judge," he said in a southern drawl. The roar of the departing motorcade did nothing to drown out his voice. He extended a hand to Steven and Adeline. "Deputy Secretary of State for the United States."

Steven shook it without skipping a beat. "Mr. Judge. I take it you got my message from Mr. Schwandt."

"Who? Oh yeah, him. Yeah, we spoke. I'm here on behalf of the Secretary herself, who is at this moment, meeting on a related matter. As I understand it, you're the President of the Ordo Solis?" he asked, sounding like pronouncing the name was difficult for him.

"Of the American branch, yes. It's called Ordo America."

"And this is…?" Mr. Judge scrutinized Adeline.

"Adeline Faehrmann," Adeline replied, extending her hand.

"She's the Vice President, from Germany," Steven said, not bothering to muddy the situation with their exact titles.

Mr. Judge motioned toward the only convoy of SUVs left. He entered the nearest back door, pointing Steven to the other side, then motioned at Adeline. "She goes into the next one."

Adeline narrowed her eyes at Mr. Judge. Steven exchanged looks with Adeline. "Don't worry, I have a feeling big things are about to happen."

"Ve shall see." Adeline walked toward the next SUV.

Steven hustled over to the other side. The thick door thudded shut behind him. Inside, Mr. Judge studied him as the SUV lurched forward. "How big is your organization?"

"We're down to three. The Raptors killed a bunch of us not long ago."

"I'm sorry for your loss." Mr. Judge didn't appear sorry at all.

"Thanks. I don't mean to be rude, but why're you here?"

"I'm to give the Secretary a clear picture of you before you meet."

Steven slowly nodded. "Sounds like we finally found the right people."

CHAPTER 52

MS. ZEE

The convoy stopped in front of a large, bland-looking structure with the words "HARRY S. TRUMAN BUILDING" affixed to a black obsidian sign behind a yellow flowerbed. As soon as they entered, Mr. Judge left them, choosing a more exclusive-looking route. Steven and Adeline rode up in an elevator and were ushered into a long windowed room.

Steven and Adeline took their seats, awaiting the person whom Steven assumed would be the United States Secretary of State.

At last, the doors opened, and in walked a black woman with small oval glasses, pinstripe business suit, black undershirt, and a slight frown. She spearheaded a large entourage of men and women in dark suits, with Mr. Judge to her right.

"My name is Darlene Van Der Zee. Call me Ms. Zee." She extended her hand. "As I understand, *you* are the foremost expert on the Soulstealer."

"That's right," Steven replied. "How much do you know about the Soulstealer?"

"I need more. You're here to help me rectify that in the next 57 minutes."

They sat at the table, where Ms. Zee grilled Steven on everything related to the Soulstealer and his cults. She devoted a majority of her questions to the Raptors.

In the process, he learned of the gruesome events that unfolded in the past 24 hours. Bhutan, a country in Asia, suffered a total loss of life in one of its rural villages of a few thousand. An investigation couldn't uncover the cause of death. Hours later, Bhutan's second-largest city lost all but a fraction of its upper 20,000 residents with no clear reason how they died, and the only connection they could make was with the dead Unas in Prague's catacombs. The total death toll approached 30,000 people.

"Nythan Dwienz is now a person of interest," she concluded.

Finally, you show your hand. Steven glanced at Adeline's gaping mouth, nodding his head. He couldn't remember a time in history when the Soulstealer ever took so much life at once.

"Ten minutes left before your hour is up, Ms. Zee," Steven said.

"Yes. I have a working knowledge of the circumstances now."

"Then you have me at a disadvantage. What's the next step here?"

Ms. Zee stood, nodding to Mr. Judge. "Emmett can fill you in. Now, if you'll excuse me, I have an appointment."

"Actually, I'd rather hear it from you." Steven likewise stood. "We're the experts. And everyone's doing their best to leech us to benefit themselves. Not—not that I'm saying you're a leech. But no one has the bigger picture in mind. *We* know what we're doing. Partner with us…while you still have control of the situation."

Ms. Zee held his gaze for a few seconds. "Walk with me."

Steven and Adeline followed her and Mr. Judge into the hallway.

"Whatever do you mean?" Ms. Zee asked as they exited the room.

"We're at war. Our previous leader was murdered alongside his family last month. The Raptors are still hunting us. The Soulstealer is growing stronger, and you need to know how to handle something like this. That's exactly what we're good at. We can help you succeed."

"There are complicated forces at work here."

"You understand the outside political forces, and we understand the actual struggle. We know what's happening better than anyone out there. Don't pass this up. We need to keep helping."

"What do you propose?"

"A simple and effective plan to deal with the Soulstealer. I need to speak with the UN Ambassador to make it happen."

They came to a fork in the hallway, one left and one right. Ms. Zee stopped and faced Steven. "The result?"

"A powerful alliance you can take the credit for."

Ms. Zee turned to the person behind her. "Emmett, call the Ambassador. Tell her they're on their way," she commanded. "Now if you'll excuse me, I must go."

"Of course, Madam Secretary." Steven offered his hand. "Thank you for your time."

Ms. Zee didn't speak as she shook his hand and departed down the right hallway. Mr. Judge ushered Steven and Adeline down the left. Outside sat a Sikorsky helicopter with "UNITED STATES OF AMERICA" on the side. Its propellers whined as the engine came to life.

"That's you," Mr. Judge said.

"What? Not coming with?" Steven asked.

Mr. Judge shook his head. "I need to make that call, otherwise you won't make it in the building."

"Thank you," Steven said.

"Make sure this works," Mr. Judge said as he turned and walked back inside the building.

Steven and Adeline boarded the helicopter and it took off.

CHAPTER 53

MS. RAYE

The ride lasted no more than ten minutes from liftoff to touchdown in front of a stiff, blue, rectangular structure basking in the sun. They entered and went to the 20th floor, where they were guided to a spacious office. The woman talking on the phone behind the vast desk hung up as they approached and stood to greet them.

"Nikki Raye." She offered her hand. "U.S. Ambassador to the United Nations. Please." She gestured to the chairs in front of her. She wore a cropped navy pantsuit in black heels. Her medium-length chestnut brown hair was tucked behind her ears.

"Steven Carpenter. Pleased to meet you, Ms. Raye."

"Adeline Faehrmann, *hallo*."

"The Secretary mentioned you had a proposal?" Ms. Raye asked.

"Absolutely," Steven said, wasting no time. "The Soulstealer is back, his cults are entrenched, and we need to work quickly to stop more attacks."

"The proposition," she pressed.

"Our plan is to get the UN to endorse the Ordo Solis, like the League of Nations used to do."

"I'm afraid that's impossible." Her hazel eyes flickered with disapproval.

"Why would that be impossible? It's already been done, and we've all the support we need now. The Soulstealer saw to that."

"The General Assembly will never let it pass. There is far too much uncertainty about what's happening. I haven't been in this seat long, but I'm quite sure the Assembly won't fight a strange force by deputizing another strange force. The world is just now coming to terms with this monster...*if* it truly exists."

"What do you mean, *if*? There's evidence all over the place!"

"We see the smoke, Steven, we even see the burned down building, but no one has seen the fire."

"There's a YouTube video that *shows* you the fire—"

"No one has *seen* him do it, Steven." Ms. Raye raised her voice to his level. "No one has seen him. And until it's been confirmed by someone with unquestionable standing, nothing will happen."

Steven became so infuriated he couldn't speak. Adeline came to his rescue.

"Ambassador," she said. "Vhat of ze European Union task force? Zey are unquestionable, no?"

"That's a step in the right direction, but still not enough. The most they can say is that they've confirmed the brutality of the local cults."

"Zese recent attacks must have changed something. Could not ze UN put something forth zat vould investigate ze attacks?

"We could, but the EU has already done that."

"Yes, in Europe. But as I understand, ze crisis is in Asia. Ze EU cannot go zere. But ze UN can."

Ms. Raye's face went from dubious to astonished. "Yes, that...that could work..."

Steven stared at Ms. Raye with a neutral expression. *Why hadn't she considered this before?*

"So then..." Steven trailed. "Can the UN offer humanitarian assistance to that country, and we go along as consultants?"

"It shouldn't be difficult. But the Bhutan government would need to ask us for assistance first."

"Has Bhutan not done so?" Adeline asked.

"I don't...I'm not sure," Ms. Raye replied. "I'll check."

She turned to her desk and began tapping at her keyboard.

"Well?" Steven asked, folding his arms.

Ms. Raye picked up her phone. "Please be patient." After a brief conversation, she returned to the table. "Czechia hasn't accepted aid. The Kingdom of Bhutan has. The UN has already approved a humanitarian mission. It's launching from Germany in three days."

"That's just enough time to get there. Are you going?" Steven asked.

"No, I'm staying here."

"We could use a ride to Germany," Steven said. "Can you help us out?"

"I'll get you both on a flight that leaves first thing tomorrow morning."

"Actually," Adeline interjected, "Just one seat vill do. Steven is staying here."

Steven's head jerked to Adeline. "I'm what? No, we're going together."

Adeline smiled. "You need to be here vith ze Ambassador. Zis is important to us, and she vill need your help."

"But the attack in—"

"She needs your help, Steven," Adeline continued. "Ze UN is ze most important international alliance ve have, and you are ze best person to represent us. Ze task force is leaving from Germany, my native land, and I need to be zere."

"I *do* need help," Ms. Raye admitted. "I'm trying to tackle something I have so little exposure to. I need a credible advisor."

"Then *you* stay," Steven said to Adeline. "It's too dangerous there."

Adeline punched Steven in his arm. "Vhat did I tell you about zat, you American man? Life is hard, and I know hard better zan you." She pointed her finger at him. "*You* are ze one who is in danger. *You* are ze Grand Master of Ordo America. *You* stay."

"No!" Steven couldn't help but think he sounded like a child just then.

Adeline beamed. "One seat vill do, and please make sure it's for me."

Steven pointed his finger at Ms. Raye. "Don't you do it. Put us both down on that ticket."

Ms. Raye narrowed her eyes. "She's going back to her home country. I need you here with me."

"I don't care—"

"If you have any hope of UN assistance, you *will* stay here," Ms. Raye said firmly. "I won't continue to be thrown into these meetings while my new advisor goes off to play cowboy."

Steven stared daggers into both women.

Adeline ignored Steven. "Vhen can I leave?"

"I'll have Chaston get you on one of our flights there. He'll also get you a temporary badge."

Steven seethed in silence. Adeline only giggled. "You're doing better by being here vith zem."

He grunted.

Adeline and Ms. Raye exchanged looks. "He's sulking," Adeline said.

"Chaston!" Ms. Raye shouted. A young man came into the office. "Put her on the next UN flight to Germany if it can get there tomorrow, otherwise a direct to Bhutan. Badge her under my authority. Provide her a letter stating that she's a special advisor to Commander Benton and is allowed anywhere he goes."

"Yes ma'am," Chaston said. Adeline followed Chaston out, waving to Steven before the door closed.

Ms. Raye went back to her desk and turned her attention to her computer.

"Now what?" Steven said.

"Now we wait until you stop sulking and decide to join our team."

"Huh?"

Ms. Raye stopped tapping on the computer and turned her attention to him. "I've only held this job for six months, and now I've been directed to form a coalition of willing nations to respond to this crisis. It's my staff's number two priority, the first being catching up on *what we need to do* about this. I have the full support of the President. I'm going to bring us into this thing…whatever it is. But we're going to do it on *our* terms."

"Mmmhm," Steven grunted. *So you're new. Now I get it.*

Ms. Raye placed her hands on her desk, and her shoulders slouched as she looked down. "I need help." She looked back up at him. "And as I understand it, that's exactly what your group wants. So, all I need to know is, are you here to do that, or do I need to contact your friends back in Europe?"

"That sounds like a threat," Steven growled.

"Not a threat," Ms. Raye came out from behind her desk. "An opportunity. Mr. Schwandt told me about your disagreement with your counterparts in Germany."

"They're not equipped to lead us into what's to come."

"I agree with you," Ms. Raye said. "Which is why I want you here. I want you to help me navigate this issue. Tell me about your plan, the Sparrow's Roar."

Steven's eyes widened. "Where'd you hear that?"

"It was included in a summary sent by Homeland Security."

Steven slowly nodded. "It was our fancy way to get the world to wake up to the Soulstealer. It went through a few revisions, but it worked spectacularly."

"Was the idea just to make everyone believe your claim?"

"Pretty much. And I leave the rest to history."

"And you think you've succeeded?"

"I've personally met with the Secretary of State, and now I'm sitting down with the U.S. Ambassador to the United Nations. I'd say so."

"Then let me offer you a lesson in politics. Unless you do something to make it stick, it'll be a passing hashtag."

"Oh no, not that Twitter thing again…" Steven trailed. "Look, the Soulstealer's gonna make it stick for me. When people realize it's back, they'll flock to the Ordo Solis, the one institution that's been fighting it all along."

"I've been getting intelligence briefings on who Nythan Dwienz and his cult of followers are. So far, I've gathered Nythan is a 19-year-old youth and his cults are made up of violent fanatics. The cults were considered the biggest threat until the incident in Bhutan. Now we have far more questions than we can answer. But we all agree on our skepticism that a supernatural demon has possessed an American youth to take souls."

"Disagree all you want, but a few more extinct cities and your skepticism won't matter."

"Do you want thousands more to die just to tell the world 'I told you so?'"

"No," Steven answered. "But I do want this done right, and I know how to do it right."

"*That's* what I want on our team," Ms. Raye emphasized. "I want someone who knows how to do this right."

"As long as it answers to you," Steven accused.

"As long as it answers to the elected. We don't live in monarchies anymore. The Pope won't be calling for another Crusade. Democracy, not religious decree, will ensure we do this right."

Steven pursed his lips, considering her words. "Okay, let's say I'm all in. How'll you make sure that we do this 'the right way?'"

"First, we need to agree on what the right way is. *Then* I can tell you how we're going to do it."

A grin spread across his face. "That's more like it. Okay, Ms. Raye, let's talk details."

She reached out her hand. "Call me Nikki."

CHAPTER 54

THOSE WHO STOOD WATCH

Steven sat with Nikki as she met with the UN Ambassador from Germany. At the moment, they were discussing a draft UN resolution and which countries they thought would vote their way. And by "they," Nikki and Ambassador Brüne did most of the talking. Steven would pipe up when the subject returned to the Soulstealer, but it didn't happen often.

"We can definitely count on most of the European nations to vote positively on this, as well as Canada, Mexico, Nepal, Bangladesh, Myanmar, and India. I'm not sure about the Middle East, China, or Russia," Ambassador Brüne said. He sounded like a natural when speaking English. His large bald head reminded Steven of Humpty Dumpty.

"Russia will go for it if it's vaguely worded," Nikki surmised.

"Yes, however, China will not. They will want more specific lines of authority. What this group can and cannot do."

"Have you approached them about it?"

"I don't know, Nikki, you tell me. You came to me about this."

"I haven't said anything yet. Whatever we propose will open the door to failure and possible veto, and then we'll be back at square one."

Steven stared up at the white ceiling, crossed his ankles, and clasped his hands in his lap. *Why am I even here?*

"It'll take months to get this group off the ground," Ambassador Brüne said.

"We don't have that much time," Nikki replied. "There could be another attack at any moment."

"I understand why you want the UN to take a stance against this boy, Nythan, and his followers. But what is the point of this resolution?"

Nikki glanced at Steven. "We need to know his whereabouts. We have credible evidence that this young man has access to an extraordinarily destructive weapon made from unknown technology. His followers have grown considerably powerful."

Steven wanted to blurt out the truth. Instead, he heeded her warning that it would be the gravest of mistakes if he did.

"And the United Nations will assist in supplying resources?" Ambassador Brüne asked.

"Yes, eventually. But for now, all we need to do is get a coalition working together."

Ambassador Brüne clapped. "Well, then the solution seems clear. We have a humanitarian mission going to Bhutan, *ja?*"

"Yes, but—" Nikki began.

"But! The humanitarian effort is already a formal recognition of the disaster at hand. Its area of responsibility is limited to the Kingdom of Bhutan. Still, the scope is adequate enough to give unofficial birth to a group of individuals who investigate the source of the matter. You may not yet have express authorization to fund positions dedicated to a new department, but you do have the authorization to respond to the disaster in Bhutan. Should your findings lead you to outside areas of Bhutan, I believe that decision would fall under the purview of the committee and would not require the concurrence of the Assembly."

"Yes, but as soon as the Assembly finds out that our group has a military component, they'll rescind authority of the entire effort."

"Ah *ja*, I see the problem. Perhaps, then, a peacekeeping mission is in order." Ambassador Brüne smiled.

"I thought of that, but they won't have the necessary power to do what is required of them."

"And what, precisely, is required of them?"

Nikki paused, again looking at Steven. "They may encounter armed hostility."

Steven smirked. *And make them dead.*

"I see," Ambassador Brüne muttered. "I fail to understand how that would not be within the mandate of a peacekeeping force? We send our peacekeepers into contested areas, expecting them to react defensively if they are attacked."

"This is different—"

"It is not, Ambassador Raye. Our peacekeepers will be going into a member nation where there are unknown hostilities taking place. It is the unknown force that is the aggressor, not the peacekeepers. Do you see?"

Nikki nodded, as did Steven. "A compelling narrative," she said.

"Good, now when we bring this to the Security Council, that is precisely how you will justify it. They will agree. And it will require less time and votes to acquire the approval we need. Do you have personnel ready to support?"

"Yes," Nikki replied. "Steven Carpenter here will lead our team."

"Hmm. I'm unsure if the Security Council will entrust something of this magnitude to someone who is not known by them."

"He has my full support."

"I'm sure he does. He does not, however, have the support of those he has not met. As qualified as you believe him to be, you need to choose someone with whom the Security Council will not object. Otherwise, you will delay this resolution, and I understand time is of the essence." Ambassador Brüne raised a hand before Nikki or Steven could object. "Once you gain the initial approval needed, it is at that point you will find your path forward much easier. Take baby steps, as you say."

Nikki held her tongue.

Steven let out a long held in breath. "I'm the most qualified person there is."

"Nikki would not have you here if you were not. But time is your adversary. If you wish to have your peacekeeping force operating within the time you specified, you will heed my advice." Ambassador Brüne stood. "My staff will await your draft, Nikki. We will review and ensure it gets to the Security Council. You may count on Germany's support. We can work to prepare a larger resolution for the General Assembly in parallel, should it become prudent to do so."

Nikki rose, shaking his hand. "Thank you, Harald."

After Ambassador Brüne left, Steven shook his head. "They'll put someone stupid in charge."

"You're not thinking clearly." Nikki waved a hand at Steven's comment. "I was worried about how quickly we could do this, and Harald just gave us the golden ticket. We can call an emergency meeting and authorize a peacekeeping mission while we work on the larger resolution. The Security Council will want a known director to head the mission, but they're less picky about the deputy director. I'll suggest a middle-of-the-road director they'll be comfortable with. When he's approved, I'll recommend to him that you be the deputy."

"That sounds good."

"It sounds *very* good," Nikki stressed.

Chaston poked his head in. "Ambassador, a Miss Adeline Faehrmann is on the line to speak with you." Steven and Nikki walked over to her desk, answering the phone through her speaker.

"Adeline," Nikki said.

"Hallo!" Adeline sneezed. "Sorry, my allergies are severe here. I have learned much. The first site vas quiet; no survivors in ze village. But ze second site, ze city. Steven, zere have been a number of survivors. The Soulstealer did not kill zem all."

"What? How?" Steven asked.

"Zey vere in enclosed spaces, like cars, greenhouses. Vitnesses saw Nythan drive away vith one of his followers."

"That's huge!"

"*Ja.* I had zem retrace zeir actions. I zink ve may do ze same, but vith gas masks and oxygen."

"We, we, we…have to…" Steven stammered, "we have to get something up and ready."

Nikki waved a hand. "Shouldn't be difficult. I'll have my staff make a call to the purchasing department. Just get me a list of the things you need."

"What else?" Steven talked at the receiver.

"Steven, ze survivors said zey saw bright silver snakes all going to a gift shop building vith a greenhouse on top. Ve vent and did not find anything zere, but ve zink zis is vhere ze Soulstealer vas vhen he made his attack."

"Take pictures," Steven advised.

"I have, and I vill send zem. Vhat about you?"

"It's looking good. We might have a way to get official authorization from the United Nations."

"*Wunderbar!*"

"There is still a great deal of work that must be done," Nikki reminded them.

"Still," Steven said, "it's looking up."

"Might I suggest sending back one of ze experts to give testimony."

Nikki's eyes lit up. "Yes, yes, of course. Send one of the scientists to give their report. But they need to be here by tomorrow, or else they'll miss the Security Council." She sighed. "On second thought, I don't think we have that kind of enough time."

"I could use a video teleconference," Adeline suggested.

Nikki smiled. "I think that will do just nicely."

Adeline covered the phone as she gave muffled directions to someone on the other end. "I must go. Ambassador, I am pleased to know you are doing well. *Auf wiedersehen*, Steven."

"Bye, Adeline. Give 'em hell," Steven said.

Nikki eyed Steven after Adeline hung up. "She's very astute."

"Her talents weren't properly recognized in Ordo Europe. She has what it takes to be in charge."

"What about you?" Nikki nudged. "What do you get out of this?"

"Retirement. I'm not fond of all the jibber-jabber we're doing here." Steven smirked. "No offense. Adeline, however, has both the skill and appetite. You should be mentoring her as my successor."

"So should you."

"Honestly, she hasn't needed a lot of guidance from me. She knows what she's doing. And she's always been the voice of reason. She's way more qualified than I am to be deputy director. But I can tell that *you're* the one who can bring her to the next level. A level the new-age Ordo Solis leader needs to be."

"But aren't you the head of the Ordo Solis?"

"Technically. But it's really only myself and Adeline. If I had to lead a bunch of people, all my flaws would show. The type of flaws you *don't* want in a leader. Adeline's your gal."

"What a selfless thing to say."

"Well, it's not *all* selfless. It means that I don't have to be the one to do all the work. I can do what I do best."

"Which is what?"

"Stand watch. And give the occasional slap upside the head."

Nikki matched Steven's smile. "You need to have your team slapped up within twenty-four hours."

"That's not a lot of time."

"Then you better get started. Make all the calls you need. Just be sure you're ready before I walk into that meeting tomorrow at one."

Steven nodded. "You get things done. You and Adeline will do great things together."

"We're already doing great things. I expect you to remain a part of that."

"Yeaaaaaaah…you'll have my expertise until we can get Adeline in the right position. There're a few things I wanna ensure get enshrined in this resolution to the General Assembly. After that, we'd have done what I set out to do. I'm too worn out to keep going any longer."

"We'll talk about this later. Right now, I need that team of yours ready to go."

"Yeah, yeah." Steven walked into the adjoining conference room. He pulled out the contact card he'd kept, using the landline on the table to make the call. After a few rings, a voice said, "Hello?"

"Vince."

"Who is this?"

"It's Steven. I'm calling from an office in the United Nations."

"Hey, Steven. You get a new job?"

"Yup. And I need you to do the thing."

"I already did the State Department thing. You talking about the band-back-together thing?"

"The Statement Department thing worked out perfectly," Steven said. "Yeah, the band-back-together thing, and I need it done by tomorrow."

CHAPTER 55

MOMENTUM

The next day, Steven relaxed behind Nikki along the back wall of the oak-adorned room. He sat in as one of Nikki's personal assistants at an emergency session of the UN Security Council. The council discussed the report from the humanitarian team in Bhutan, accompanied by a live video chat with the lead biologist and Adeline. The biologist summarized his findings of the abnormal deaths and testimonies of how those deaths took place. The Security Council asked many questions about Nythan's "supernaturalness." However, the analysis contained enough testimony and scientific study that the Security Council decided not to argue *if* it happened, but rather about the UN's response.

The FBI report from Steven's interrogation sealed the deal. After the biologist explained the destructive potential of the "weapon" used by Nythan, Nikki and Ambassador Brüne suggested the peacekeeping mission. They met stiff resistance from the Ambassador of China, who advocated a narrow mandate for the assignment. Nikki and the Chinese Ambassador came to an agreement after making some uncomfortable compromises. At the end of the discussion, the Council unanimously passed the resolution. The meeting concluded with the biologist complimenting Adeline's superior leadership skills. Steven slipped Adeline a subtle thumbs up. A slight twitch formed at the edge of her mouth as she thanked the council for the opportunity.

Steven exited the conference room and went to an isolated lobby corner. There, he found all the former Solis Americans that Vincent could round up: Maggie, Myrka, Ra'ef, Monti, Jayce, and the Mayhle brothers. Steven glanced back and saw Nikki stopping to talk with Ambassador Brüne.

"Well?" Myrka, a short Latina with an abundance of curly hair, said with a giggle.

Steven crisscrossed his arms and held up peace signs. "We're officially a part of a UN peacekeeping mission."

Ra'ef and Vincent high-fived.

"What were the stipulations?" Jessey Mayhle asked. Of the four Mayhle brothers, Jessey had become a walking legal encyclopedia before passing the bar in New York. Vincent found him and reconnected Jessey to the group. Jessey jumped at the chance to teach Steven how to navigate legal boundaries.

"They had to compromise on another Director, seek approval for anything outside of Bhutan, and limit the peacekeeping mission to 90 days," Steven explained.

Jessey scratched his chin. "I suppose we can work with that."

"The head biologist guy talked a lot about how their bodies showed no causes of death or nothin'," Steven said to Ra'ef.

"I'd really like to get my hands on that report," Ra'ef said. "It'll help us better brainstorm that prototype I brought up earlier." Ra'ef worked with lasers and optics; the closest thing to a scientist they had.

Nikki came over to the group. "We're not out of this yet. That last-minute change to the Director means we'll need to ask her consent to secure your selection of deputy. I've heard of her. Chinese national. Ambitious, but by the book. It's not a guarantee."

"Yeah," Steven trailed, praying the new Director accepted Nikki's recommendation.

Steven and Nikki returned to her office. The others went into Nikki's conference room. Half worked on crafting an outline Steven wanted to introduce in a resolution to the General Assembly. The other half brainstormed a list of requirements for a prototype suit that Ra'ef thought could prevent the Soulstealer from getting at the suit-wearer's soul.

Nikki led Steven back into her office and called the new Director to schedule an impromptu introduction. The recent appointee arrived by herself. She was barely five feet tall with a pale complexion and crinkles around her eyes that implied an earned wisdom.

"Ambassador Raye," the woman greeted them in heavily accented English. Her straight black hair was cut at her collarbone, with long bangs hiding her forehead.

"Good to see you again, Doctor Wu. Congratulations on your appointment," Nikki said, offering her hand.

"I understand I have you to thank, Ambassador," Director Wu replied, taking Nikki's hand.

Nikki turned to Steven. "This is Steven Carpenter. He's the leader of the Ordo Solis, the group that fought hard to get us here."

"Mr. Carpenter," Director Wu said.

"Steven, if you please."

Nikki ushered them to sit down. "Mr. Carpenter here is the foremost expert on this topic. I thought that he would be a good fit as Deputy Director."

"I see." Director Wu offered no visible reaction. "Have you been here long, Mr. Carpenter?"

"Came from the field, ma'am," Steven answered, unsure of her question.

"Do you have a resume?" she asked.

"I uh…didn't have the time to look for it between getting kidnapped and shot at," Steven blurted before thinking, regretting the implication. He thought he saw a twitch at the corner of Nikki's mouth. "That uh," he stammered, shifting his weight, "that came out wrong."

Director Wu nodded. "You meant to say your experience isn't lacking."

"That's right," Steven affirmed with relief.

"I welcome your assistance. I will speak to you about your position at a later time. When you said 'we,' were you referring to others behind those doors?" Wu asked.

"Absolutely, yes." Steven hurried to open the door. "Yo, guys," he shouted, much louder than needed. "The new boss is here."

The group stood as Director Wu entered the area, smiling. She introduced herself to them all, asking about their background and how they came to be with the Order. The air grew awkward as each revealed they had left the Order until yesterday.

The Director came back around to Steven. "Please," she said, motioning him out of the room.

Steven exited with her and Nikki, suddenly remembering the important person he forgot to mention. "There's one more, Adeline, but she's in Bhutan with the mission."

"Yes, Adeline and I are acquainted. I met her in Germany before the Humanitarian Mission left for Bhutan," Wu said. "We can use our newly acquired office space for your group. They will integrate with my staff."

"Awesome. How do I contact you?"

"You can come back with me to my office. Let's discuss there."

Steven looked over at Nikki, who regarded Director Wu. "That sounds wonderful. I'll leave you two to it." She shook the Director's hand. "Your team can use my conference room for as long as you need it."

"Thank you for your accommodation, Ambassador."

The director took Steven through a labyrinth of cubicles and workspaces. She stopped amidst a cluster of dusty workstations.

"It's not luxurious," Director Wu said, "but it's the best they could do."

Steven counted a half-dozen computer workstations set in a rectangle and a small conference table.

"It's perfect," Steven whispered. His hand went to his gut as the full weight of the past 48 hours caught up with his brain. He felt relief; he felt *official*.

Only if she accepts your help, Steven reminded himself.

"What has your group been working on?" Wu asked, taking a seat behind her desk and steepling her fingers.

"Adeline told us that she thinks the Soulstealer can't get through glass. Ra'ef's been reviewing all the scientific stuff, and he thinks that it holds up with how we believe the Soulstealer uses the airways to do its dirty work. So we've been on working getting some vacuum-sealed helmets."

"And what will we do with these helmets?"

"Kill the Soulstealer."

"With the helmets?" Wu asked, straight-faced.

"No no." Steven felt a hot flash wash across his face. "When we find out where he is, we go to him, then we kill him. The helmets keep us from getting our souls sucked out of our bodies."

Director Wu's lips compressed in a thin line. "That exceeds our mandate."

"As I recall, the direction was for us to provide security for current *and* future affected regions. I interpreted that as pursuing the Soulstealer and his cult groups."

"I do not agree with that interpretation. That's far too liberal. We stay with the main force."

"But we're not just a humanitarian team now," Steven countered. "Our combined directive exceeds their individual one. It explicitly says *future*; going out to search is implied."

"Even if we could, we cannot go outside of Bhutan. The council will not agree to this."

"Can we at least try to persuade them? The Soulstealer has many targets in many other countries."

"I will give it thought."

"Don't think about it too long," Steven said, abandoning all attempts at tact. "Every minute we wait is another we're unprepared to react."

"I understand." Wu pursed her red lips. Steven felt the sting of her frustration.

"I'd like to go to Bhutan and orient myself with what we have. I wanna see what we're working with."

"That's fine. I'll have our staff schedule you a flight by the end of the week."

"Is there a way to book one sooner?"

"I need you here to oversee the operations of your team until then."

"Actually, I was wondering if you'd let Adeline come back to do that. She has the necessary field experience, and as you know, she's stellar at management. I think she'd make a fine operations person. I'm more of a field guy anyhow."

Director Wu stared at Steven. "That's acceptable. Call her and tell her to book the next flight here. When she arrives, give her any continuity you have, then you may go."

"Gotcha," Steven replied, gesturing at the people typing away on their computers. "Which person do I talk to over here about that?"

"Any of them. They're at our disposal."

I bet they are. "Okay, thanks. I've a feeling we're going to do great things together, Director." He touched her shoulder without thinking.

The Director's lips compressed so thin they could have been razor blades. She smiled, saying nothing in response.

CHAPTER 56

HOUSE OF CARDS

Steven stared through the grimy computer screen, brooding over his new circumstances.

"Hey." Maggie prodded him from behind. "Something's happening again." Steven turned as she pointed at the crowd of pe0ple huddled around a TV mounted on the far wall. He stood and pushed past them, unable to hear from that far away.

"Turn it up!" Steven demanded, eyes locked on the screen. The chyron flashed across the bottom of the screen: *Soulstealer Rumored in China.* Three people sat on a widescreen panel, engaged in conversation.

"Help us get into the mind of this young man, Nythan Dwienz. What is he doing? What is his goal?" the anchor asked. The camera angle flipped to a slender man with finely plucked eyebrows. *Dr. Michel Klinos, Psychologist, University of Leshle*, the tag read.

"I believe that Nythan's actions are motivated by a well-known phenomenon we call phobia indoctrination. It's the fear of what will happen if one disobeys the group or its leader. In this case, it's certainly the group the young man fears, although a strong argument could be made that this kid is not the leader he is believed to be. There are just too many unknown variables."

The camera panned back to the anchor. *"A 19-year-old adolescent is the leader of three dangerous cults spread across the world, and now we hear that a company associated with the Southern Baptist Convention provided security for its cult headquarters. What does this mean?"*

Steven wanted to yell at the TV. *What in the* hell *does that have to do with China being attacked?*

He devoured the scrolling chyron at the bottom: *OUTBREAK OF A HIGHLY CONTAGIOUS DISEASE REPORTED… RUMORED DEATH TOLL RISES IN CHINA… CHINESE GOVERNMENT SHUTS DOWN WEIBO AMIDST RUMORS OF COVERUP… CHINA CALLS STATE OF EMERGENCY…*

Dr. Klinos continued. *"I am skeptical of the SBC's purported involvement. It seems more like a diversion. As it is yet unsubstantiated, we shouldn't spend our time speculating. But it is important to know that we're dealing with an adolescent who's very much in over his head. These cults have been in existence for decades. This kid is 19 years old. He is clearly not the progenitor of the idol image the cults have of him. All we've confirmed was that he was there. If initial analysis of these cults is accurate, they enjoy an advanced support structures on a global scale. The one here in America encourages its members to will all real estate upon death. Clearly, these structures are beyond the machinations of this young mind."*

The other panelist shook her head in disagreement.

The camera panned back to the news anchor. *"Video surveillance shows him killing all those people. Are you saying that he wasn't making those decisions?"*

"Well, it's not clear what's occurring in those videos. To say he's a supernatural being capable of soul theft is—at best—a dubious claim serious scientists should treat with skepticism."

The camera angle zoomed out as the anchor observed the third panelist. *"That seems fair enough. Do you agree with Doctor Klinos' perspective, Allorria? Is he liable for his actions?"*

Allorria nodded her chin so hard it could've been hammering a nail. *"Absolutely, he is. It's clear from recent events that this legal adult, let me remind you, is clearly cognizant of his own actions. I studied his behavior with care. He displays a consistent level of malevolence toward both supporter and adversary…"*

"Why aren't they talking about the stuff scrolling at the bottom?" Steven barked. "Turn this s*** to another station!"

A few clicks later, they found BBC News.

"...with numerous outbreaks, resembling the recent epidemics in Bhutan. It is still unclear who or what is perpetrating these attacks. The Chinese government has called a state of emergency, telling everyone to barricade themselves inside their homes. Rumors abound about the source of the chaos. A source within the Chinese government, who wished to remain anonymous, told the AP that the attacks are connected to the Soulstealer. To speak with us about this..."

We're not going to be ready in time, Steven thought, no longer paying attention to the broadcast. He glanced over to Director Wu's office, obscured by the surrounding crowd. *She's holding us back.*

Steven stared at the ground, zooming through his thoughts.

We gotta kill him. But how? We've no idea where he is, except that he's in China. Even if I get to Bhutan, our "mandate" won't let me outside the country.

Not unless I throw the mandate in the garbage, he countered. *But should I?* Steven shrugged. *Adeline's the chosen one.* He nodded. *I gotta do it. It'll be worth it in the end.*

Steven pushed through the crowd and plopped his hefty frame back into his undersized chair. He ripped the phone out of its socket and called Nikki.

"Ambassador Raye's office," Chaston greeted him.

"Chaston, it's Steven. Is Nikki there?"

"I'll see if the Ambassador can take your call." He placed Steven on hold. He tapped the keyboard, absentmindedly punching random keys. A few moments later, Chaston came back on the line. "I'm putting you through."

Steven heard a soft click, then Nikki. "Steven?"

"Hey, Nikki. I need a favor."

"Yes?"

"I need to get to Bhutan on a short-notice flight, like what you did for Adeline."

"I'm not sure I can do that."

"Why not?"

"Because that's now Director Wu's responsibility."

"Director Wu doesn't understand the gravity of the situation," Steven told her. "I'm staring at a massive Soulstealer attack on China."

"And you came to me, hoping I'd circumvent her."

"Well, when you put it like that—"

"How else should I put it?"

"That…you'rrrrre giving me the opportunity to do what must be done."

"That's one way of saying it. I prefer the former."

"Nikki, please. Don't make me beg."

"Not this time, Steven. I'm not going around Director Wu on this. I really need to go. Good luck."

"Yeah," Steven pouted. "See ya."

The phone clicked, followed by the dial tone. Steven viewed the computer screen, noticing the long list of random letters spawned by his haphazard twitching. He swiveled his chair toward the group in front of the TV.

"Ordo Solis!" Steven shouted. His team rallied around him.

"Okay, the Soulstealer is in China, taking souls en masse. That's what that report means."

"Maybe," Ra'ef said. "We don't know for sure. The description is too vague." His light brown eyes narrowed in concentration.

"What about that was vague?" Steven challenged him.

"Everything. It's being labeled a disease outbreak, it's happening within China, and all of this is unconfirmed, which means it's a rumor."

"Yeah, but consider what they're saying. Multiple cities are being attacked by an unknown thing, killing its residents but not destroying anything else. Doing it right next to a confirmed incident in Bhutan in a country that has a motive to keep something like this a secret. China is the perfect target."

"Perhaps," Ra'ef continued. "Even if we did know for sure, what would we do?"

Find him and kill him, Steven thought. He shrugged instead.

"Adeline's right there, yeah?" Maggie pointed out.

"Yeah, if she hasn't left for her flight yet," Steven said.

"Call and find out," Vincent recommended.

Steven paused, looking back at the team as they looked at him. He thumbed Adeline's work number. After four rings, she picked up.

"*Hallo?*" she said over the speaker.

"It's Steven. You're on speaker with the rest of the team."

"*Hallo*, Steven. I'm at ze airport, vaiting for my flight."

"Hey, yeah. About that. Have you seen the news?"

"*Nein*, not since yesterday morning."

"China is under attack. We think the Soulstealer might be there."

"Zat is big news. The Bhutan kingdom officials gave us zeir report zis morning before I left. I'm just now starting it. There is a later section about vhat happened after ze incident. I haven't read it yet."

"Can you read it now?"

"*Ja*, hold please." After a pause, she continued. "It reads zat Nythan traveled north but does not state vhere he vent."

"Hold on." Steven typed in the search bar and brought up Bhutan. "China is to the north of Bhutan."

"Zen it's possible he vent zere and is ze source of ze attack in China. Vhat are zey saying?"

"It's conflicted. Some stations are saying that it's a disease and that it looks like what happened in Bhutan. China isn't talking yet."

"It sounds like ze perfect opportunity for ze Soulstealer."

"Exactly what I was thinking. We need to get over there, Adeline."

"Ve can't, Steven. Ve aren't approved to go outside of Bhutan."

"I know, but those rules are flexible; the investigation is implied in our mandate. If the Soulstealer has left Bhutan, we need to follow."

"Steven, you cannot go to China. Director Wu vill not approve."

"The director doesn't need to know. All she needs to know is that I'm on my way to the scene of the crime."

"Steven, take me off speaker."

"Whatever you've to say, say it to all of us. No more secrets."

"Fine. You are ze *leader* here. If you break ze rules, you make a bad example to others to break ze rules as vell."

Steven smirked. "Who said that's a bad example? We got here *because* we're willing to break the rules. Besides, the people who made the rules have no idea how terrible their decisions are. I don't feel bad showing them the right way to go."

"You can't just decide zat for everyone. It's not your place."

"Ohhh," Steven trailed, "but it is though. It *has* been ever since you convinced me to do those YouTube videos."

"Zat's not fair, Stev—"

"It's completely fair, Adeline. You wanted me to break the rules *then*; you even helped me. And *now* that I need to do it again, you're not here?"

"I'm here, you jerk!" Adeline yelled over the speaker. "I have been nothing *but* here!"

"Then stick to your commitment and *stay* here."

"I vill not stand by you and let you sacrifice yourself like Ludwig. Not zis time."

Steven scrunched his eyebrows, recalling her utter that same phrase atop the observation tower in Germany.

"What do you mean, sacrifice myself like Ludwig? You mean Worshipful Master von Maur? They died when they were ambushed at the meeting with the Soulstealer. What are you saying?"

"Nothing," Adeline stammered, "I didn't mean—"

"No, Adeline. Tell me what that means. How'd Ludwig sacrifice himself? And how'd you just stand by?"

Dead silence. Steven narrowed his eyes, trying to understand. When she didn't respond, Steven pressed further. "Adeline."

"Steven, it's not impor—"

"What sacrifice?"

He heard a sniff on the other end. "I, uh…zey…ze Grand Council." Adeline took her time as if waiting to be rescued. "Decided zat zey would…"

Steven's dread grew by the second. "Just say it, Adeline."

"Ludwig wanted to prove to ze world zat ze Soulstealer really had come and zat it vasn't a fake zis time. So ze Grand Council sacrificed zemselves so zat zey could prove it."

He felt like a predator who caught scent of its prey. "How did they *prove* it?"

"Ze…ze video. Ludwig planted ze camera so zat it vould capture ze fight."

"Yeah, but they were there to talk peace, establish a non-aggression pact, how could they possibly have known—" Steven stopped cold. "Motherf*****s. Was that fight part of the plan?"

More silence.

The shot that hit the antler woman. That's what set it all off. The knot in Steven's throat throbbed. He opened his mouth, but no words came out.

"Did they lose on purpose?" he managed to squeak out.

He sat, shuddering, while the silence slowly sucked out the truth.

"Yes."

The response was damning; an indictment of both the Order and himself. The evidence had been there, and Steven allowed himself to be blinded. More important, his consciousness rebelled at the thought of Raeleigh being collateral damage.

Steven disconnected the call and pushed himself back from the chair. Those behind him made room. No one spoke; they knew how Raeleigh had died.

The phone rang as Steven walked away. Myrka picked it up.

The immeasurable pain he buried in Dietzenbach threatened to surface. But now, the grief transformed into guilt, and his guilt turned his focus toward the part he played. *I kept prioritizing the mission over Raeleigh.*

In the blink of an eye, she stood before him. Steven couldn't see her face through his tears. "I didn't know," he whispered.

Raeleigh gave him a sad smile.

"I was supposed to be the sacrifice, not you."

She shook her head softly.

"This whole thing went so wrong."

He became aware of a presence behind him. An unfamiliar hand touched his arm, restarting the moving gears in his brain.

"We have them on the ropes," Steven said as his anger started to boil. "We can kill him. Your sacrifice won't be in vain."

Raeleigh's dark brown eyes grew sad, and she shook her head again.

"Steven," Maggie said. Steven turned to see most of the team standing there. "You okay?"

"I ignored the truth for so long."

"No one blames you."

"Sure."

"Adeline wants to talk to you," Myrka said.

He took time gathering himself before he spoke. Inhaling all the way in and then letting the air out.

"Tell her I'll call her back," Steven replied, wiping his eyes. "We're going to finish that General Assembly resolution and get it to Nikki's office within the hour. She'll be needing it much sooner than expected."

CHAPTER 57

ACTION

Steven's crew put the finishing touches on the General Assembly resolution when the desk phone rang. Myrka handled the receiver, listened a few seconds, then jabbed Steven with it. "For you."

"Who is it?" Steven asked.

"Ambassador Raye."

Steven grabbed the phone. "Hello?"

"I need you to come to my office."

"Uh, sure. Should I bring anyone?"

"No, just yourself. Don't run, but don't waste any time getting here."

"Got it." Steven handed the phone back to Myrka. "I'll be back."

Steven wasted no time getting to Nikki's office. He found her talking with a familiar looking man, but Steven couldn't place him.

"Hi, Mr. Carpenter. I don't know if you remember me. My name is Agent Smith. I'm the agent who interviewed you upon your return to the U.S." He shook Steven's hand.

Another anonymous Agent Smith. "Ah yes, gotcha."

"Sorry about the radio silence. We weren't authorized to share any information with you at the time," Agent Smith explained.

"Sure." Steven shrugged, looking to Nikki. "What's up?" She nodded to Agent Smith.

"What I'm about to tell you is extremely sensitive information," Smith said. "You will *never* divulge where you got this from. Nor will you even hint that you got it from anyone. Understand?"

"Yeah, sure."

"I need to hear you say you understand what I just said. There are consequences if you don't."

"That sounds like a threat."

"Yes."

Steven stared deadpan at the agent. Nikki said nothing. Finally, Steven nodded. "Yes, I understand. I won't tell anyone where I got this from."

"We're tracking the Soulstealer. He's about to board a flight to Japan."

Steven's head jolted. "Wait, what?"

"We found him in China. We know where he's headed."

Steven's breath quickened. "Where?"

"Tokyo."

"How can you be sure?" Steven asked, trying to remember Tokyo's population. He kept wanting to say ten million people.

"We're sure."

"What's going to happen? What should we do?"

"Which question do you want me to answer?"

"Both—uh—what's going to happen?"

"We're putting together a rapid response team to capture him—"

"No, no, no, no, no, no, no, you gotta kill 'em. You gotta kill 'em *now*. As soon as he sees you coming, he'll destroy everything. You saw what's happened everywhere else."

"Ambassador Raye says you have a way to fight him."

"Ye—yeah, but it hasn't been tested."

"Are you confident enough to use it yourself over there?"

Steven narrowed his eyes, darting between the agent and Nikki. "Are you asking…me…to go?"

"Yes."

Steven exhaled all the breath he didn't realize he had held in. "Wow. This is new."

"We don't have time for you to think it over."

"I mean, yeah," Steven stammered, looking straight at Nikki. "I'm confident in Adeline's report. We've sketched out suits that'll block the Soulstealer from taking the wearer's soul. It's not very advanced—but—we think it'll work. We're trying to make a prototype, but it's coming slowly."

"Give me the details. We'll get it done faster and better."

Steven exhaled again. "Well, slap me sideways. You got it. Where do I send the info?"

"You don't. Give me the details here verbally."

"Oh…okay…we're trying to attach hazmat suits to glass helmets. It has to be airtight. The Soulstealer uses air to do its dirty work."

"That everything?"

"That's it. Oh, you—uh—need a way to keep someone alive in that suit, since they can't breathe outside air. It has *got* to stop the Soulstealer from accessing the air inside. You get that wrong, you're dead."

"Got it. Plane leaves in two hours. Nonstop to Kadena Air Base." The agent scribbled something on a piece of paper and handed it to Steven. "Memorize this. Don't say it out loud."

Steven took the note, committing the address and a four-digit code to memory. "Done."

"You sure?"

"Yeah. Am I the only passenger?"

"Yes." The agent held out his hand; Steven returned the paper. The agent took out a lighter and burned the paper. It sizzled to crisp ash, leaving only a scorched aroma.

"One last thing. Director Wu can't be trusted."

"Mmmhm." Steven nodded. *I knew it!*

"Good luck." The agent walked out of the room and clicked the door shut.

Steven focused on Nikki. "What. The hell. Was that?"

Nikki smiled, shrugging. "Sounds like an opportunity."

"I thought you weren't giving me those anymore."

Her smile grew wider. "I'm not." She glanced back toward the door. "*He* is." She winked. "Don't let me keep you."

Steven trotted all the way back to the team's work area. He stopped at the entrance of the cubicle area, gripping the walls with his sweaty palms. The team stopped what they were doing and stared.

Myrka walked over. "What happened?"

"No time," Steven blurted as he tidied himself. "How do I look?"

"Like melted ice cream."

Steven let out a laugh and went straight to Director Wu's door. He knocked and entered without waiting for an invitation. The Director didn't look up to acknowledge him. Agent Smith's words echoed in his mind as he approached Wu.

"Director, I understand that you want me to wait here until Adeline gets back, but this is something I can do over video. We benefit far more if I leave now."

"Who benefits? Us or you?" Wu pressed, still not looking up from her computer.

"Us. Adeline is one of the most capable people I know. She knows what I know and can handle a transition just fine. I, however, need to know what she knows, and I can't figure that out by being here."

"You'll get there, Steven, just not as early as you expect."

"The more we overlap our experiences, the better we are. The more you make this a sequential process, the less prepared we are. China is under attack at this very moment and it's the Soulstealer. Everything about what we know points us to that. We *have* to go."

"We do not have the authority to venture outside of Bhutan, and China will never allow us to—"

"That's beside the point," Steven cut in.

Director Wu stopped typing and stared Steven square in the eye. "Please don't ever interrupt me like that again."

An awkward hush fell across the two. Steven waited for her to speak.

"We cannot go there," she repeated, returning her attention to her monitor.

"We're not going there. I'm going to Bhutan, and I need to do it sooner than you're allowing me to."

"You'll have to make do, Steven."

"Director, please. I can't stay here while things are happening so quickly."

Director Wu paused to inspect Steven. "Why the abrupt change of plans?"

"It's not abrupt," Steven said with a nervous twitch. "I just gave it more thought, is all. This is for the best."

"I think it best that you heed my direction, Mr. Carpenter."

Mr. Carpenter. A title of exile. Steven felt the distance grow between them. He resisted the urge to consult his watch to avoid raising her suspicion. *There's nothing more I can do here.*

Steven made an effort to slump his thick shoulders. "Okay," he murmured, turning around.

"Steven."

He turned back.

"I understand your passion."

Not yet you don't, he thought.

"You're going to get there, just wait a few more days." She attempted a smile.

That's not real. Steven matched her insincerity, nodding. "Okay," he repeated, leaving the office. He tried not to rush. Myrka waited nearby.

"What happened?" she asked.

"Let's go," Steven said, striding back to the crew. Before entering the workstation area, he paused and faced Myrka. "I need you to stand there and pretend like I'm saying something normal," Steven whispered.

Myrka tilted her head. "Uh...sure...why though?"

"I have to go, and I've got a feeling that when I get back, I won't be welcome here anymore." Steven jerked his head toward Wu's door.

Myrka looked at the Director's office out of the corner of her eye. "Okay, can I come?"

"Not this time."

"But I can help."

"I need you to take over and lead this shindig until Adeline returns. The resolution is ready; look it over one last time. Email it, then go straight to her office and put a copy into her hands. When Adeline gets back, show her everything, and then fill her in on what happened."

"But I don't know what's about to happen. You're not telling me," she whispered.

Steven let out a burst of laughter. "No, Myrka, I mean tell *her* what we've done so *far.*"

Myrka's eyes widened. "Ohhh. *Claro*. No problem. What should I tell *them*?" she gestured toward the group. Steven looked back and saw them all staring.

So much for a stealthy getaway.

He walked over to the work area. "Sooo…look, guys…I gotta go somewhere and do something that's gonna be a big help to the Order, but none of you can be seen within a thousand miles of it. So, I'm—uh—going alone."

He crossed his arms, waiting on someone to say something. No one did.

"Um…this thing we've got going on with Director Wu and the United Nations. They're helping, but they're not Ordo Solis. *This*…" he asserted, nailing his finger into the small round table they all encircled, "this is Ordo Solis. The people standing here."

He straightened back up. "Myrka's in charge until Adeline gets back, then she's in charge. I don't trust Director Wu as far as I can throw her." He cast a nervous glance at two of her staff working in the corner workstations and lowered his voice. "She might mean well…maybe…" He shrugged. "But I don't know where her loyalties lie, so Myrka is putting a copy of the resolution into Nikki's hands. You guys did a really, *really* good job on that thing. When it gets passed—"

"If—" Jayce interjected.

"If…" Steven corrected himself. "In either case, you've all done something so important for the survival of our Order and the world. We can never repay you for that, and you'll never get the thanks you truly deserve. But from the bottom of my heart, thank you, guys. It was truly an honor."

"Aw shucks." Ra'ef nudged Steven.

Steven bit his tongue as his emotions swelled. "It's time for me to go. It's been great seeing you all again."

"Yeah," Jessey said, shaking Steven's hand. "Watch your back, Steven."

"Don't talk like it's the last time we'll see ya. Just go do it," Jayce said.

"Whatever it is, best of luck," Ra'ef added.

"Are you coming back?" Monti asked.

"Probably," Steven replied. "But things'll change. I want to cover my bases, just in case."

"Picture!" Maggie ordered. She walked over to one of Wu's staff, handing him her phone.

The team all mushed together in the small work area. Steven heard the familiar "snap" of pictures being taken, marking them family once again. The moment lasted only a few seconds.

Steven looked at Vincent. "Thanks, dude. You did it."

"Couldn't have done it without ya."

Steven stuck his hand out, pulling Vincent in for a bear hug. "See ya, buddy."

"I'll see you when you get back."

Steven backed away from the cubicle, leaving the area. He hurried out of the United Nations building and jumped into the nearest taxi.

He recited the street name to the driver, adding, "There's a hundred bucks in it if you get me there in half the time."

"You got it, boss," the driver quipped, whipping out of the roundabout. Steven gazed out the window, watching the sights zoom by.

CHAPTER 58

THE RIGHT HOOK

Steven scanned the hazy skyline as the small formation of HH-60 rescue helicopters sped along the horizon toward their objective, the capital of Japan. Their mission definitely didn't fit that of a rescue. Outfitted with two 50 caliber machine guns and a full crew of 9 special ops soldiers each, the three helicopters could fight a small war. Before leaving Kadena Air Force Base, every person was fitted with full-body Teflon coveralls over body armor, fused to a helmet with a glass face shield, the helmet connected to an oxygen tank on their back. No one told him how they got these suits ready so fast, and Steven didn't ask. The GoPro strapped to each helmet captured everything going on around them.

One of the soldiers next to Steven flashed all ten fingers twice as the sea of buildings below them loomed larger and larger. Twenty minutes out.

Steven dared not adjust the scrunched material under his body armor that made his sides ache. Instead, he prayed the maker of their suits made it airtight as instructed. If not, he expected this to be a short trip.

Up ahead, a massive cloud of silvery mist across a shrouded meadow of skyscrapers beckoned them closer. He knew what it was, even if seeing it in person for the first time.

Souls. *Millions* of them.

"Holy shizat," Steven said. "You getting this?" He glanced over to the soldier next to him. The soldier made no response.

Steven looked back out across the metropolis. An infinite number of ghostly streams spiraled up from the ground and arched toward the city center. He spied dark figures lying still on the streets below. Traffic didn't move, and some cars burned like flares.

As they went deeper, the streams converged into a giant fog. Soon, Steven could only see five feet out from the cabin, and he lost the outline of the other two choppers. He feared they might collide, but the pilots didn't seem concerned. The wind from the propellers pushed the souls away from them enough to form a small bubble. Up close, the souls became indistinct filaments; a silver beam that flashed like a ray of sunshine.

The soldier at the front of the helicopter held up five fingers. Five minutes out.

The souls moved with them. Sometimes Steven thought he saw the clouds pulse, like a heartbeat. He held his breath as if he might lose it any second. Steven wondered how the suits worked. More importantly, *why* it worked. Why did airtight helmets shield a person's soul? Was there something special about what they used?

Steven patted the glass jar at his feet. His team came up with a theory based on the longstanding belief that when the Soulstealer's vessel died, it left through the mouth in search of another host. After talking with the survivors of Nythan's massacre, Adeline posited that solid material like glass and steel had blocked Nythan from taking their souls. She took it a step further and proposed that if it could block, it could trap.

It's worth a shot.

The soldier held up a fist, slamming his hand down on the shoulder of the guy next to him. That guy slapped the shoulder of the guy next to him, igniting a chain reaction until each person felt the hit, including Steven. He couldn't tell if he participated in tradition or the slapping served a relevant purpose. Steven's stomach lurched as their helicopter descended. He peered out and down toward the impenetrable abyss.

Five seconds into the descent, a wave of small arms fire erupted from somewhere up above. Steven's body tensed, expecting something to hit them. The guys closest the now-open doors concentrated on covering their field of view, but none of them returned fire.

Probably because they don't know where to shoot.

Then, a deafening pair of guns from the helicopter above began firing back. They sounded like one continuous *brrrrrrrr.*

It's like shooting blindfolded.

Small sounds of impact peppered the top of the helicopter. Steven tightened his grip on the inner railing, one hand going to the pistol strap. He glimpsed bronze shell casings falling all around them from the aircraft's guns above. Steven surprised himself as he began laughing, and surprised himself still when he couldn't stop. He tried to pull himself together, but it took the helicopter knocking against the ground for the laughing to disappear.

The guy behind him pressed Steven out of the helicopter cabin. Steven stumbled forward a bit before he could straighten back up on the hard pavement.

"HELL YEAH, IT'S GO TIME, BABY!" Steven yelled. No one paid him any attention as they sped past, guns at the ready.

CHAPTER 59

THE RETREATING DARKNESS

As the turbulence of the helicopter settled, Steven made out luminescent souls climbing toward the sky. At eye-level, a path of souls pulled forward, as if sucked through a straw. "Follow the trail!" Steven shouted into his headset. "It'll lead you to him!"

They ran to a building within seconds. The revolving door and luggage racks identified it as a hotel. Steven noted how much thinner the haze got as he took his first step inside. A few shots echoed, and a couple of soldiers in the front doubled over as incoming fire hit them from the reception desk. Steven marshaled his considerable weight and dove behind a nearby couch as a flash battle ensued. It must not have been a very intense fight, because all gunfire ceased fifteen seconds later. Feeling the adrenaline spike through his veins, he hustled over to his team. They towered over one of their unmoving squad mates amid dead figures dressed in colorful kimonos.

"This must be what Sanhe look like," Steven said, glancing up. "The Raptor's Asian counterparts." An injured soldier clutching his side caught Steven's eye. They widened as he pointed at the guy's side. "Close that up! Quick!"

"Already done," the guy said, lifting his hand for a brief instant. A sealed patch rested over the blood-stained hole.

Steven breathed a sigh of relief. "You lucky bastard. You okay?" Steven asked.

The guy nodded, wincing. "Hit me good, but better than buying it."

"Let's move," the mission commander said. "Sanchez, Brown, you stay here with Steven. We take the stairs until we find them. Key the elevators and be ready when called."

"Rog," one of the soldiers said.

"But—" Steven began to protest.

"You stay here," the commander ordered.

The team lined up on the wall to the stairwell. They tapped each other before opening the door and charging up.

Brown walked over and queued all four elevators. When one opened, he stuck his foot at the edge of one of the sides, preventing the door from closing. Sanchez did the same.

Steven went over to the three dead Sanhe. He knelt and inspected them. They wore a robe, with a V-neck overshirt, a half-coat, and a kilt-like garment that extended down to their feet. All of them wore V-shaped dragon masks; tiny horns lined around the edge from the forehead to the chin. The mask's scaly dark green-blue texture appeared different from various angles.

The *burrrrrr* of the heavy guns on the helicopters continued to sound up above. Steven listened to the windy scream of a propeller as one helicopter touched down outside the building. Another team sprinted through the lobby, stopping before Steven.

"Where's Echo," one of them said.

Sanchez coughed. "Up the stairs."

Every ten seconds, the sliding elevator doors attempted to close again before being jarred back open.

"Standby till the enemy is located." Brown pointed to the elevator doors.

Ten minutes later, the call they all waited for came. "Floor 24."

The other team hurried into Brown's elevator, pressing a button. Steven tried to enter with them, but the outside guy pushed him back out.

"Damnit," Steven muttered. He spun around as the third team bolted into the lobby.

"Over here!" Steven yelled. He hopped inside the next elevator, passing Sanchez, touching the number 24. The third team jammed into the tight space; Sanchez slipped in at the last second. As they got closer to the 24th floor, a crescendo of reverberant gunfire went from a whisper to earsplitting. The elevator doors dinged open. One soldier from the first team was immediately outside the doors, providing cover fire for the others who cut across the opening.

Steven seized in fear as his eyes locked onto a grenade thrown across the opening. The soldier at the entry point jumped inside and on top of the people in front of Steven. His hands went to cover his ears, only to have his hands clunk against his hardened helmet. One of the soldiers behind him yanked Steven into the corner of the elevator. Steven clutched his jar for dear life as he fell backward into the wall.

The grenade blast shook the elevator and forced the wind from his lungs. Fragments peppered the exposed entry. A shard ricocheted off a soldier's face shield, splitting the glass right down the middle.

He waved his hands at his team. "I'm okay, keep going!"

His team charged out, and a few soldiers from the second team ran across the opening to join the others.

Steven struggled to roll back up, managing to get on his hands and knees. The soldier with the cracked helmet began thrashing and clawing at himself. Steven stood petrified as a silver vapor exited the guy's mouth and filled the inside of his helmet. The soldier grew still as the vapor eked through the break in the glass, joining the silver wave journeying down the hall.

Steven scrambled out of the elevator, turning left down to a T intersection. The noise from the shootout reverberated with enough force to guide Steven at each turn. He pushed forward, passing many dead Raptors and Sanhe along the way. The Sanhe in their colorful kimono attire were in stark contrast to the Raptor's black tuxedos. Steven reached down and swiped a handgun off one of the dead Raptors.

At last, he rounded a long corridor where the teams stacked up, then piled into a room. A few soldiers dove back out as a grenade exploded, throwing shrapnel and dust everywhere. The rest of the team took the opportunity to charge back in, guns blazing. Steven crouched next to the doorway, trying to catch his breath.

About half a minute later, the fighting stopped. Steven shook his pounding head and entered through the swinging traffic doors. He found himself in a laundry room amid dozens of dryers and washers. The teams huddled around a cluster of dryers toward the middle, some with weapons trained at something on the ground.

"Is it him?" Steven rejoiced as he maneuvered over the Raptor and Sanhe corpses, trying not to slip on the water and blood slicking the floor. "Move! I want to see him," Steven demanded, shoving his way past the soldiers.

He knelt next to the two people on the ground. The first, a pale bald Raptor without a mask, wore a tuxedo riddled with bullet holes. His eyes drooped as he repeatedly whispered, "Be at peace, my Lord."

Steven stared with righteous triumph at the motionless teenager next to him. Nythan Dwienz looked much worse in what was left of his tuxedo. He was missing part of his leg.

One of the soldiers took Nythan's pulse. "He's alive."

Steven grinned with wild abandon. "Smile, b****, you're on camera!" Nythan twitched. "Yeah, I know it can't be easy for you right now, but tough s***."

I told you I'd do it. I promised Raeleigh I would.

Steven stood. He gestured to the surrounding corpses. "Take a good look, boys. This is the face of your enemy." Steven's fingers tightened on the handgun, pointing it at the ceiling. He pulled back on the slide, just like Raeleigh had taught him.

"This is for the Ordo Solis…and all those you made suffer." He aimed the gun at Nythan's face and whispered the words he had rehearsed a thousand times. "For Raeleigh."

Steven fired the weapon straight into the Soulstealer's forehead. He dropped the gun as he remembered part two of the plan. Steven took the glass jar and jumped on top of Nythan, maneuvering the jar over the boy's lips.

If they guessed correctly, the Soulstealer would go into the jar and be trapped. Steven waited a few seconds, looking for any sign of the Soulstealer. He saw none, but Steven capped the jar to seal it just in case. He stood, holding the jar with both hands, bumping his way out of the circle. "S'cuse me!"

Steven left the soldiers there to do whatever soldierly things they did after a battle. He returned to the elevator, stepping over the bodies littering the ground. Steven peered up at the silvery stream of souls lurking above his head. It no longer moved with a sense of purpose.

As he reached the bottom floor, Steven spoke into the microphone. "Hey guys, you can come pick me up now, please." No response. Steven walked outside. "Helicopter guys, come on down here." The density of the souls was packed so tight he couldn't see the glass container in his hand. He craned his head up, trying to spot the helicopters. "C'mon, guys. I can hear you swirling about up there," Steven begged. After minutes of radio silence, Steven sulked back inside, sitting on one of the lobby chairs.

"All I did was kill the world-ending apocalyptic monster," Steven muttered. He smiled, his words dawning on him. He killed the most dangerous thing on the planet. The thing that had earned the title of *Humanity's Bane*. His eyes jerked to a form in his peripherals, only to see Raeleigh seated a few chairs over.

"Hey, babe." Steven gave her a somber smile. He held the jar up and wiggled it. "We did it." She flicked her hair. "You look lovely." Raeleigh only smiled at him.

"Ya know, I never figured out what you really are," Steven said. "I mean, how's it that I see you? You're gone. I know that. But I see you as clear as day. It shouldn't be possible."

Raeleigh stuck her tongue out, causing Steven to laugh.

"Yeah, I suppose a soul-sucking demon shouldn't be possible either, but here we are." Steven gestured at the silvery mist all around. "Speaking of which, I wonder how long it'll take for all these souls to go away. Do you think they go back to the people they bel—" Steven paused when his gaze fell on Raeleigh's empty seat.

"—long to," he finished. "Like you."

Steven's eyes started welling with tears. "I know where you are. You're here," he choked, touching his chest. "You're just in here, and you'll always be."

Steven laughed. "We got him!" He wobbled his head to shake off the tears.

His mind raced backward in time. He thought of Jeff, Sara, Trista, and how Jeff never got to see their life's work fulfilled. Of Lawrence Tucker, the first Freemason to give his life. He thought of Guthrie, the one who believed in him. Elmer, that ornery bastard, and the rest of the Templars. He even thought of his beloved bike, the Anvil, and how it must be sitting in some chop shop or dung heap tow yard. His final thoughts settled on Raeleigh.

Steven looked back over, seeing her once more. Raeleigh tilted her head and smiled brightly.

"Yeah. It wasn't all bad." He thought of Rod, the friend who helped Steven smuggle his videos through the mail. And Nikolaj, the wealthy Belgium who took him and Adeline on a voyage across the Atlantic.

And, of course his friends: Jessica, Maggie, Jayce, Myrka, Ra'ef, the Mayhle brothers, Monti, and Vincent; all the old Ordo Americans who came back to help. He thought of Nikki Raye, the ambassador extraordinaire who spent long hours getting the support of the United Nations and working with him on the resolution. Last but not least, he thought of Adeline, that whip-smart German woman who'd be running the Ordo Solis in no time.

All those people helped him pull that trigger to put an end to evil.

Steven rested his hand up against the glass jar, hoping the Soulstealer swirled inside. He didn't get his hopes up. Odds were the Soulstealer was already searching for its next victim at that very moment. Still, Steven felt an enormous weight off his shoulders. The victory didn't come from the hope of what Steven held in his hands. Victory came from how they caught the attention of the entire world.

The *whomp whomp* of a helicopter sounded as the elevators dinged open. The teams of soldiers came out, totting body bags. Steven grabbed the jar and stood, facing the silver glazed doors. He stole a glance at the empty seat Raeleigh sat in moments before, marking the end of his moment of silence.

It's time to finish what we started.

CHAPTER 60

HOME TO ROOST

Steven stood in front of Director Wu, who sat at her desk with Adeline at her right. Adeline had refused to speak to him since he had returned from Tokyo.

"...and furthermore," Wu continued, "I cannot allow your disobedience to go unpunished. Effective immediately, you are removed as deputy."

Steven smirked, unfazed. "Who's replacing me?"

"That is not your concern. Your job now is to assist in whatever is asked of you."

"That seems rather ambiguous."

"Your actions have led us to this place."

"That's not true."

Wu pursed her lips. "This is not an argument, Steven."

"Good, cuz there's no argument here."

Adeline chimed in. "You complicated so many zings, Steven. Ve have many questions to answer now."

Steven resisted the urge to scoff at someone he still considered a friend. *Needs to be good enough to convince Wu and careless enough to get Adeline going.*

"Hardly," Steven retorted. "This is the first recorded return of the Soulstealer, and *I* killed him. That same Soulstealer, mind you, that massacred eight *million* people in four countries and nine cities. *I* gave us the time we needed to prepare for the next return. If I hadn't, we probably wouldn't even be having this conversation."

"That was not your—" Wu began.

"Yes it was, Director Wu."

"I told you to—"

"Never interrupt you again, yeah yeah." Steven waved. "Look, Wu. I've been in this fight my entire adult life. You've been in it less than a month. While I appreciate your sensitivity to the bureaucracy, when it comes to a fight between your rules and my oath to the Ordo Solis, the Order wins. Especially since I know your allegiance lies elsewhere. I can't have you politicking behind our backs. *Our* mission trumps *your* interests."

Adeline trembled in fury, but Steven couldn't be sure who exactly she was angry at.

"Steven Carpenter," Wu proclaimed with rage. "You are hereby dismissed from this organization."

Steven saluted her with a wink, sucking his teeth. He turned around and walked out of the office into the team area. "She canned me, boys," Steven declared.

"Whelp, can't blame her," Ra'ef said, jerking his finger at a live broadcast of Tokyo. "You *did* sneak to Japan and shoot the Soulstealer." The city loomed below the helicopter, enveloped in a soul-filled mist.

Steven chuckled. "True. That's true, I did do that."

"So, shouldn't you be scared? I mean, the Raptors probably won't like that you killed their god."

Steven shrugged. "The FBI has a security detail on me."

Jayce laughed. "Uh huh, and in every Hollywood movie, the two FBI agents parked down the street are the first to die, right before the witness. Also, the Prey, so there's that."

Steven's confidence evaporated. "Damn, Jayce, way to pop my balloon."

"Better popped then dead," Jayce chirped.

"Whatever. Nythan's gone. The CIA, FBI, ATF, and Homeland Security are all over the Raptors. That's what matters. In any case, I need to make a phone call, and then I'm out." Steven waltzed to the nearest phone and dialed Nikki.

"Ambassador Raye's office," Chaston answered.

"Chaz, my man," Steven hailed. "Is Nikki available?"

"The Ambassador is out to lunch. May I take a message?"

"Yeah, tell her that the opportunity she didn't give me earned me a dismissal. I'd like to finish up with the draft resolution if that's okay. Don't call this phone anymore; lemme give you my new cell." He recited the number.

"I'll tell her."

"You're a good bro, my man."

"Have a good day," Chaston replied without emotion.

Steven hung up, smiling. He gave one last wave to the team before strutting out.

A short while later, Steven had almost finished his lunch at a nearby cafe when his old school flip phone rang. He opened it and pressed the green call button. "Yeah?"

"Steven, you a**vipe! Do you know how much trouble you caused?"

Guess that answers my question.

"Why hello, Adeline." Steven smiled into the mouthpiece, mid-chew. "I only have one question for ya: Did you get my spot?"

Adeline howled in frustration.

"Well...did you?" Steven pressed, kicking his feet up.

"Of course yes. I can't believe you acted like zat toward her!"

"Aw c'mon, don't be like that. You know I did the right thing."

"*Nein*, Steven. You made it more terrible. The Security Council is very angry zat you broke ze rules, Wu is on ze warpath, and now ze Soulstealer can plan his return yet again."

"Except this time, we have the UN at our back and all the evidence we need to ensure the world knows it's real. Just turn on any news station. They're only talking about Tokyo and the Soulstealer. As for the spy, don't worry about her. Got one last poker in the fire that'll deal with all that."

Adeline took a deep breath. "Steven, you've done enough, just stop."

"Don't worry, darlin'. This one you'll actually like. It'll be my coup de grace." Steven's chuckle turned into a full-blown belly laugh. "And ya know what? I ain't even gettin' paid!"

A low-tone rung in his ear. Steven glanced at the screen and smiled.

"Gotta go. Duty calls," Steven said amidst Adeline's protest. He thumbed accept.

"Mr. Carpenter's phone." Steven giggled.

"The Ambassador is ready to take your call," Chaston said. Steven swore he could hear Chaston smile through the receiver.

"My man!" Steven shouted, slamming his feet back down on the ground.

A brief snippet of elevator music played before Raye came on the phone. "I just got off the phone with Director Wu. She very curtly informed me of your dismissal."

"Well dang, she got to you before I did. Look, it was well worth it. We have a slam dunk case against the Soulstealer. I can't imagine you having any trouble getting our friendly UN resolution passed."

"I agree. Harald and I are meeting within the hour to review it one last time before we submit it to the queue. Would you like to join us?"

"Absolutely, I'll be right there."

Nikki hung up and Steven jumped up from the table, startling his nearby FBI detail.

"Don't worry boys," Steven said, pulling up his pants. "Nothing to be afraid of; I have it all under control."

Steven decided to strut the ten-minute route back to the United Nations, where Chaston told him to wait. The twenty minutes did nothing to blunt his enthusiasm. He felt like he was on top of the world. As far as he could tell, he *was* on top of the world.

Ambassador Brüne arrived, and Steven followed him into Nikki's office. They walked over to the long conference table. Nikki rose from her chair to greet Brüne, acknowledging Steven with a smile.

"Shall we?" she gestured toward the seats.

"Steven," Nikki began. "Ambassador Brüne and I spent a great deal of time reviewing your suggestions to this resolution. We first want to thank you for being especially thorough on the details."

"*Ja*, very thorough. Like a German," Ambassador Brüne said.

Steven held his breath. He waited for the damnable 'but' to follow.

Nikki continued speaking. "We had to simplify the language, but—"

Steven tensed.

"—your suggestions were fully integrated. Ambassador Brüne and I feel that it's ready for a vote by the General Assembly. The Secretary-General assures us that it will have an immediate vote."

Steven pounded the table and grinned from ear to ear.

"The intent of your recommendations breathed life into this resolution," Ambassador Brüne said. "It now has the proper context and call to action that a successful bill requires."

"The team's recommendations," Steven corrected. He stopped trying to contain his glee. "The Ordo Solis team wrote them. They deserve the credit."

Ambassador Brüne nodded. "Would you like to hear the final version?"

In the blink of an eye, Raeleigh appeared on Nikki's left across the table. Steven stared at her, biting his lip as he drew them in.

"Yes, please," he whispered.

Ambassador Brüne smiled as he took the paper from the table. He cleared his throat rather ceremoniously.

"Resolution A/ES-18-L36, Question of the Soulstealer," Ambassador Brüne began.

Steven felt the tears long before they appeared.

"The General Assembly…*reaffirming* its strong commitment to peace and security…*acknowledging* the abundant record of the Soulstealer in historical archives…*acknowledging* the League of Nations' endorsement of the Ordo Solis to contest the Soulstealer and its nefarious agents…*acknowledging with appreciation* the historical and current efforts of the Ordo Solis, the Catholic Church, and Knights Templar of the Freemasons…"

Steven stared at Raeleigh while he listened in silence.

"…*recalling* the Security Council resolution concerning the peacekeeping mission to the Kingdom of Bhutan…*noting with grave distress* the Soulstealer's re-emergent threat to humanity…*expressing outrage* at the mass devastation of life…*noting also* the inhumane acts of its nefarious agents: the Raptors, the Unas, and Sanhetuan Group…*recognizing* the imperative need for a defense against the Soulstealer and its followers… *proclaims* the actions of the Soulstealer a 'Crime Against Humanity'…*recommends* the Ordo Solis be integrated as an organ of the United Nations… *recommends further* that the organizational leadership be comprised of individuals having demonstrated Ordo Solis experience and the utmost integrity…*establishes* funding for its operations pursuant to its purpose… *calls upon* all member states to cooperate with the Ordo Solis in its mission to defend Humanity against the Soulstealer and its followers…*requests* the Secretary-General to keep the General Assembly informed of the implementation of the present resolution."

Ambassador Brüne set the paper down, looking to Steven.

Raeleigh's dark eyes were filled with joy. She raised her hand to her mouth and blew him a kiss. Her ethereal form dissipated outwards as if she were the kiss she blew.

"Goodbye, darling," Steven said under his breath. He returned his attention back to Nikki and Ambassador Brüne, wiping his nose. "Thank you."

Nikki beamed. "I'm glad you approve."

"What about the rest? The Solis Protocol, the Baneslayer, and the Vanguard?"

"It will be used as a suggested template from which the Order is to be constructed."

"How soon before it goes to vote?"

"Soon," she responded. "The Secretary-General has called an emergency session. It's the only item on the list as far as I'm aware."

Steven clasped his hands together. "Do you think it'll pass?"

"What's the latest?" Nikki asked Ambassador Brüne.

"We have not surveyed all member nations, but what feedback we have puts us in a positive place."

Steven shut his eyes and let out a ferocious holler. Then settled on Nikki and Brüne, both wide-eyed.

"Sorry. That was eight hundred years' worth of blood, sweat, and tears. Many people paid the ultimate price to get us here. Thank you both."

Nikki gave a sad smile, reminding him of Raeleigh. "I'm so sorry you had to suffer alone."

Steven tried to match her smile. A flutter across the table confirmed Raeleigh's presence.

"I was never alone."

CHAPTER 61

EFFECT

Steven viewed the procession from a front-row seat in the upper balcony of the General Assembly auditorium. Down below, at the front, three people sat at a podium. The man in the middle spoke.

"I now give the floor to the Secretary-General of the United Nations, his Excellency, Polokahm Tu Fah."

Mr. Tu Fah ambled down to the podium. He touched the mic before speaking.

"Distinguished Heads of States of Government, Excellencies, ladies, and gentlemen. When I was sworn in December, I said that our most serious shortcoming was our inability to prevent crisis. I noted how the United Nations was born from war and that we must be here for peace. Today, we must be here for peace once more to thwart further disaster. The extraordinary circumstances that confront humanity compel us to act."

"In times past, your principled leadership has helped secure the future of the UN. Your commitment has been to peace and security, through your initiative to put human rights at the heart of all work. We defend those same values that unite us. In the words of my predecessor, this is not 'textbook or academic.' This menace, known as the Soulstealer, threatens us all. It offers neither peace nor security. It offers no life but pain and suffering."

"I call upon all nations, no matter their prosperity, to work with one another to face this grave threat. We cannot allow this evil creature to continue its widespread practice of death."

Mr. Tu Fah raised his hand to the front row.

"His Excellency, Harald Brüne, of Germany, with the assistance of her Excellency, Nikki Raye, of the United States of America, drafted the resolution, on which the General Assembly will now vote. It authorizes an international cooperative group, so named the Ordo Solis, who will search out and bring this Soulstealer to justice. Its demented followers will answer for their crimes against humanity. It falls upon us to protect those who cannot protect themselves."

"We call ourselves the international community; we must act as one. Because, only together, as the United Nations, can we fulfill the promise of the Charter and advance peace and security for all. Thank you, *shukran, xiexie, merci, spasiba, gracias, beata.*"

The pressure in Steven's chest grew the longer it took for the voting to start. He drummed his fingers on the armrest and tapped his foot to distract himself.

Mr. Tu Fah left the podium and walked back up to his platform chair. "The assembly will now take a decision on draft resolution A/ES-17-L36, entitled 'Status of the Ordo Solis.'"

Steven leaned forward.

Mr. Tu Fah adjusted his glasses before proceeding, "For your information, the draft resolution is closed for sponsorship. I now give the floor to the representative of the Secretariat."

The woman next to him queued her microphone. "Thank you, Mr. President. Since the submission of the draft resolution and in addition to those delegations listed on the L document, the following countries have also become co-sponsors of A/ES-17-L36: Nicaragua, Guyana, Brazil, Chile, Oman, Czechia, the People's Republic of China, Bhutan, Japan. If any other countries wish to co-sponsor, please signify now by pressing the microphone button."

The woman paused, looking up at the auditorium. Steven wanted to pull his hair out.

Just vote already! he mentally screamed, though his face remained stoic.

"Belgium and Canada have also joined the list of delegates cosponsoring the resolution. Any others?" She paused. "No. Thank you, Mr. President."

"Thank you," Mr. Tu Fah began. "A recorded vote has been requested. We shall now begin the voting process. Those in favor of draft resolution A/ES-17-L36, please signify…those against…abstentions."

The woman next to him queued her microphone again. "The General Assembly is now voting on…" She droned on as Steven stopped listening. He glued his eyes to the large screen showing the countries as they voted yay, nay, or abstained. Steven guessed the green plus signs were "yays," the red lines were "nays," and the yellow X's were "abstains." He watched in delight as an overwhelming number of green plus signs lit up. It took less than a minute for the screen to fill up with colors.

"The voting has been completed. Please lock the machine."

The screen went from showing the individual votes to a summary display.

> VOTING RESULT:
> IN FAVOR   107
> AGAINST   19
> ABSTENTION   46

The room experienced five seconds of silence, then underwhelming applause filled the hall.

"The result of the vote is as follows," Mr. Tu Fah spoke, "In favor…107, against…19, abstentions…46. Draft resolution A/ES-17-L36 is adopted." The President clunked the gavel on the pallet, prompting a much more enthusiastic ovation.

Steven jumped to his feet, eyes wide with the biggest grin. He strutted out of the balcony to the back area from where he expected to see Nikki. He didn't break stride when he came upon Adeline and Director Wu waiting as well. Wu pretended not to notice Steven. Adeline stared at the door, sneaking glances at him with a sly grin.

"So…" Steven trailed. "Good news for you." He rocked back and forth on his heels. "Well, I mean. For the Order, not exactly for you." Steven nodded toward Wu. Neither of them responded. "The Order is going to do so much more good now. It's official."

"Your dismissal stands, Mr. Carpenter," Wu said without looking at him.

Steven feigned a gasp, putting his hand to his chest. "I should be so offended at the implication, Director," he said with emphasis on all the consonants. "But I do believe," he continued in a terrible British accent, "that your machinations have been properly attended to in paragraph eight of the resolution. Your puppet masters won't be able to stick their little fingers in it this time."

Wu showed the briefest of snarls before regaining her composure. She turned and left the vicinity.

"Steven," Adeline chided him. "Zat vas unnecessary."

Steven chuckled. "Yeah, maybe it was. But still. The point is to get *you* in that position, Adeline. You're the best person for the job. They don't see it because they look at you and refuse to admit that you're more than a babe. You belong there, not Wu."

"She is a fine lady," Adeline stated, ignoring his remark.

"Not really, her nose is a bit big—"

"Zat's not vhat I mean."

Steven smirked. "I know what you meant."

"You mustn't treat everything as a nail and you a hammer."

"It seems to work just fine."

"You rot the foundation and create enemies."

"As long as they're *my* enemies and not yours, I have them exactly where I want them."

"Must you always view zis as a sacrifice?"

"Absolutely! We're talking about the survival of the planet. You saw what happened. It's the best way I know to get what I want *and* ensure that I'll retire at the end of it all."

"Oh, is zat vhat zis is?" Adeline crossed her arms.

Steven beamed with pride. "You betcha. I didn't come all this way just to get dragged back in the middle of everything. Somewhere along the way, I saw how good you were for the Order. It all became about killing Nythan and getting you in the top spot."

"Vell, I appreciate the confidence, but I do not need you to do so."

"Well good thing it's already done then, eh? Pretty soon you'll be rid of me, then you can run it however you want."

Adeline shook her head. "*Arschloch*." She rolled her eyes.

"I remember when you first called me that back atop the observation tower. Seems like such a long time ago."

Nikki approached without either one of them taking notice. "Catching up?"

Steven grinned. "Yup. Also saying our goodbyes."

Adeline jerked her attention to Steven. "Huh?"

Nikki alternated between them. "You didn't tell her, did you?"

"Tell me vhat, Steven?" Adeline said icily.

Nikki's eyes widened. "I'll leave you to it."

"I'll be in touch," Steven said to her.

Nikki touched his shoulder. "Take care, Steven. And thank you." She walked from them toward Director Wu.

Steven flinched under the daggers Adeline's eyes shot at him. "Uh—"

"Spill it," she demanded.

"It's nothing you don't already know. I'm retiring from all this. That's all."

"*Ja*. Vhen though?"

"Right after I give you this." Steven took her hand and gave her a device he had held since the passing of the resolution.

Adeline looked down at a small oval thumb drive. "Just like zat, you're leaving?" Her face hardened before immediately softening. "I need to talk vith you."

"All the documents and records I could dig up for the Ordo Solis. Everything I developed. All the operating procedures, strategic plans, and purchase recommendations the team came up with. There's even recommendations for department chants that I found in my email archive, courtesy of Trista, Jeff's daughter." He pointed at the small device. "It's all right there. You're holding the future of the Order in the palm of your hand. Use it, throw it away, strip it bare. It's your call now. No more interfering from us."

"Us?" Adeline said, her eyes starting to well.

"Yeah, uh." He scratched his head. "There's a few of us leaving at the same time. Jayce, Monti, one of the Mayhle brothers."

"Steven, I—"

"Na-ah-ah," Steven interrupted with a grin and wiggled his finger. "You've been a great thing for the Order. And to tell you the truth, you never really needed me. I just made sure you got to where you're going at lightspeed, rather than a crawl." He gave her a tiny nudge with his index finger. "*Ze Ambassador* iz vaiting for you." Steven chuckled. "And she has a conference call with some very important people that the future Director of the Ordo Solis is gonna to wanna meet."

Adeline glanced over before returning her attention. "Zis von't be ze last time ve see each other."

Steven shrugged. "Maybe, maybe not." He paused, smiling at her. "Now go on and lead the Ordo Solis. And Adeline…don't look back. Don't ever look back. You're not going that way anymore."

Adeline wiped her eyes. She jumped up and hugged Steven. She whipped around and strode toward Nikki as Director Wu sulked away.

Steven watched Adeline and Nikki exchange a few words before boarding the elevator. He continued staring at the polished doors long after they closed, grinning from ear to ear.

CHAPTER 62

THE CLOSING DOOR

Steven flipped through Washington state news channels as he sat in Larissa's living room. He had spent the last five months of his retirement with her. It served as one of the few places he still called home.

"Eggs?" Larissa shouted from the kitchen.

"Yeah!" Steven yelled back.

Every news station he turned to was covering the same topic. Some organized "expert" panels, others ran historical lessons on the Soulstealer and the Ordo Solis. Most featured Tokyo, their cameras panning a vast stillness. The silver mist still infested the city, leaving only the skyscrapers visible.

"Of its nine *million* inhabitants, only three million survived the unimaginable genocide caused by the Soulstealer and his cult. It is, as of yet, still unclear *how* the Soulstealer was able to cause such mass destruction in Japan, China, Bhutan, and other countries. Many nations in the area surrounding Bhutan have declared martial law, and several European and South American countries have issued a state of emergency. President Kiden made a statement confirming she was *not* declaring a state of emergency, but has since directed her intention to bring the Soulstealer and his co-conspirators to justice. The FBI has begun a nationwide search for those affiliated with…"

Steven turned down the volume as a frail black woman with braided white hair entered the living room, bearing a pan of eggs.

"Can't get enough, huh," she teased.

"You know how obsessed I used to be with the Soulstealer? Now they're even more obsessed than I was!"

Larissa half coughed, half chuckled as she sat and grabbed her pipe on the end table. She took a waft of a plant Steven couldn't remember how to pronounce, then shoved the pipe in his direction. "Want some?"

Steven caught a whiff of watermelon. "Not now. I don't wanna deal with any more demons jumping out at me."

"Oh Steven, this one isn't even like that. It's much more…subdued." She gave him an exaggerated wink. "Besides, you're officially retired." Larissa lowered her head. "Your watch is over," she said in a spooky tone, before shrieking, "Live a little!"

Steven sighed with satisfaction. "Larissa, I've lived quite enough for now."

"Nonsense!"

Steven's interest in the TV resumed when an image of the blue monolithic United Nations building popped into view. He thumbed the volume back up.

"…the United Nations re-established the Ordo Solis—an organization which had been in stark decline since the end of the League of Nations—and gave it broad authority to oversee an investigation into the Soulstealer. The Ordo Solis, supported by a coalition of many world powers…"

A knock sounded against the front door. Steven looked to Larissa. "Expecting someone?"

She shook her head, looking at the door with raised eyebrows as she took another draw from her pipe. Steven went to the door, grabbing the shotgun propped up behind the umbrella stand. He spied through the peephole to see a beautiful blonde. Steven put the shotgun back in its place before opening the door and stretching out his hands.

"Adeline!"

"Steven!"

"Come in, come in."

Adeline entered, taking off her long black coat. She peered past Steven to Larissa and gave her a soft wave.

Larissa squeezed her eyes shut and outstretched both hands. Adeline went to her and the two grappled each other in a tight hug.

"Good to see you, darling," Larissa said. "Have a seat. Want a puff?"

Adeline laughed. "*Nein*, zank you."

Steven alternated his attention between them. "Did I miss something? Since when did you two become best friends?"

"Vhen I came looking for you here just after you left, and instead met Larissa."

Larissa winked at him.

"Alright, alright. What can I do for you?" Steven asked, seating himself.

"Vell, hmm…" Adeline smiled. "Vould you come back to us?"

"And give up this vacation from all the crazies? *Nein!*"

"Vell zen, I came to catch up and say hallo. I haven't seen you since the resolution vas passed, and you never told me vhere you vere going! I vas angry for a long time because of zat."

Steven gestured around him. "It was the right thing. I knew you wouldn't have trouble finding me when the time came."

Adeline nodded. "Do you vant to know vhat has happened?"

"You mean, other than you becoming Director of a UN-backed Ordo Solis? Wait, I know, you figured out the Soulstealer really was in that jar!"

"*Nein*, empty of course. Last week, ve vere approved for another branch of ze Ordo Solis to find ze next Soulstealer. It gets tricky vhen explaining it to the oversight committee. Zey still zink ze Soulstealer has a weapon. But anyways, ve have a new group zat searches ze globe for ze Soulstealer. I call zem ze Hunters."

"The Hunters hunt," Steven smirked. "But how's that different than the Vanguard? Aren't they hunting the Soulstealer too?"

"I have repurposed ze Vanguard to be a specialized attack force. Zey are training to attack ze Soulstealer once found, like you and ze soldier team."

Steven winked. "See? It wasn't all bad."

Adeline rolled her eyes and moved her long blonde hair out of her face and behind her shoulder.

"So then, who'd you put in charge of the Hunters?"

"Ra'ef. He seems good at it. Myrka is still Director of ze Vanguard. Ve have two teams now. Amethyst and Beryllium."

"I heard," Steven said. "I talked to her last week. Her and Ra'ef are really hitting it off."

"You did vhat? And you never called me!"

Steven's face turned into a frown. "Yeah, it still stung too much. I wanted a clean break."

Adeline matched his expression. "Steven—I—I vanted to explain, I had no..."

Steven waved her off. "No need. You couldn't have known."

"*Nein*. I need to say zis. A vhile ago, Enzo, the Grand Secretary, vent missing from his home. Ve zought ze Unas had killed him. But a couple of days before ze meeting, Enzo called. I vas ze one who answered. He told me about ze meeting vith ze Soulstealer. I convinced ze council zey should hear vhat Soulstealer had to say. But zen Oliver asked me to help out more, and I gave zem ze rifle zat shot ze deer lady."

"Uh oh," Larissa chirped. They both ignored her.

Steven's expression didn't change. Somehow, her words soothed his suppressed need for closure. "Were you there...when it happened?"

"*Nein.* I just gave ze rifle. I told zem to just go listen. But I knew. I knew vhat zey vanted to do. I knew vhen he asked me to get ze long-range gun. I'm very sorry for zis." Her gaze fell to her hands in her lap.

Steven smiled, wrapped his arms around her and gave her a big bear hug. "It's okay. We all thought we were doing the right thing, and she's in a better place now. If it's any consolation, I forgive you."

They pulled away from each other, sharing an awkward silence.

"Zere's something I vanted to get your advice about."

Steven nudged at the empty air between him and Larissa. "Here it comes, here's the *real* reason she came."

Adeline playfully punched Steven in the arm. "Ze Worshipful Master called me yesterday. He said zat ze Commandery voted to combine vith us and hibernate zeir operations."

Steven clenched his fists, shaking them. "About time!"

"He told me zat zey're encouraging everyone to join our Ordo Solis, without condition."

"Yessssssssssssssss!" Steven shouted. "That'll help big time. When we were last in Dietzenbach, those new volunteers looked ready and willing."

"I also spoke on ze phone vith George; he said to tell you…" Adeline cleared her throat, and in the worst possible British accent, said: "History proved you right, old chap."

Steven laughed at Adeline's attempt at the Queen's English. "Music to my ears. And the advice?"

"How to mend zis rift?"

"Well, you mend it in some ways, and you don't in others. We were right to do what we did; the others are catching up. However, I don't recommend you stick it in their faces. How you integrate them without causing you to adopt the same principles that led us to ruin, *that* should be your focus."

"But von't zat change now zat zey know its back?"

"Sort of. First, not everyone's convinced that it *is* back. Second, the majority accepts it, but there's an untold number of lackadaisical people in the Ordo Solis who'll slow you down or outright keep you from moving forward."

Adeline raised an eyebrow. "Vhat is lackadaisical?"

Larissa snorted. "What'd I tell you about using those big words, Steven. Ya big dumb!"

He pointed to the pipe. "Take another huff there, puff mama."

Larissa scrunched her eyes and stuck her tongue out at him.

"It means lazy, careless, inappropriately relaxed," Steven explained. "The point is, they don't pay attention. So, when I talk integrating them, what I'm talking about is separating the wheat from the chaff."

Adeline gave him yet another puzzled look.

"Identify who has the traits we need…get them in the right place. Identify who has the traits we don't need and push them out."

"You make it so harsh," Adeline said.

"It's a harsh business we're in. This isn't the Girl Scouts."

"*I* was in the Girl Scouts," Larissa commented, smoke shooting out her nostrils. "And I can still kick your a**."

Steven ignored Larissa, speaking to Adeline. "I know it's harsh. But if you get this wrong, you *will* give the organization a disease. It'll have a lasting impact that'll either result in more Ordo Solis deaths or the Soulstealer winning."

"Also, some of ze Commandery vant to come in—"

"No," Steven said, waving her off.

"Let me finish!"

"No. Out with the old. There may have been one or two good people in there, but you need to cleanse the leadership. Send a message that this is something new, not a variation of past failure."

"I don't like vhere zis is going, Steven."

Steven shrugged. "You asked my advice. That's it. I'm retired for a reason. I'm reckless and I know it. It's why I'm sitting in the middle of nowhere next to a crackhead granny."

"Hey!" Larissa croaked mid-draw, coughing.

Adeline and Steven shared a laugh.

"Another," Adeline said, "the Ambassador recommends I appoint a specific person as Vanguard deputy commander. I zink she has a connection to zis person."

"Is this person qualified?"

"As far as I can tell. But I don't like being pressured into zis. I feel as zough it may not be right."

"You're within your right to reject the nomination. But you should remember, she used that same method to get me to deputy director and you as actual director. She has a good eye for who should go where."

"Hmm," Adeline muttered. "*Ja*, I see vhat you saying." She tapped her fingers together. "Zat's all I came to say about vork. But I do vant to visit. Vhat shall we do?"

"He's had a thing for nature walks lately." Larissa coughed. "Have him take you on one of those."

"*Wunderbar*! Ve vill!"

"How about you go with me, eh?" Steven said to Larissa. "Those lungs of yours could use a break."

"These lungs have been working long before you were born, buddy."

"Well, they won't be working much longer if you don't stop smoking all that pot."

"Ya know what? You're big and you're fat. What do you think about that?"

Both Steven and Adeline laughed. Adeline stood and put her coat back on. Steven followed her to the sliding glass back door, grabbing a banana on the way out.

He stepped outside, stopping on the edge of the porch that overlooked a dense forest. The cold air pricked his face and arms. After they walked down the steps, Steven felt at home going out onto the grassy forest floor. The only sounds came from a slight wind rustling the branches overhead.

"Vhat vill you do now?" Adeline asked, breaking the silence.

"I don't know. And you know what? That's more than okay." Steven unpeeled the banana and chomped. "What about you? Where do you plan on taking the real Ordo Solis?"

Adeline looked down as they kept walking, kicking a pinecone out of her way.

"All I see is a vision. It's ze same, every time."

"Yeah?"

"Ze Vanguard. Zey wear battle armor and have powerful weapons. Hunters are finding ze Soulstealer. Another branch is finding ze Sanhe and Raptors."

"Was it a dream?"

"*Nein*, not a dream. I see it vaking. It's something I imagine."

"Is it something that you want to happen?"

She nodded.

"What would it take to make it a reality?"

"Money and technology."

"Based on what I've heard, you've plenty of the former."

"*Ja*...ve have manufacturers making our first anti-Soulstealer armor suits."

Steven smiled. "Seems like you're well on your way to making it happen."

"Zis is future though. Something ve do not have. Like in ze movies. An army, disciplined, experts, finding ze Soulstealer and stopping it."

"With the right people in the right place, you can *build* that army."

"*Ja*," Adeline said. She didn't seem fully engaged.

Steven waited for her to catch up.

"I'm scared."

Steven raised an eyebrow. "Tell me more."

"Ze Raptors, Unas, and Sanhe are still very powerful. Ze Soulstealer has proven zat it can kill *millions* at a time. At ze UN, zere are so many different allegiances who vant different zings. And in ze Order, ve all disagree as to how ve should fight. I don't know who to trust, I don't know vhat I'm doing, and I feel like ve're going to implode from all ze intensity directed at us." She became quiet and stared at the ground, nudging the dirt with her shoe.

Steven bent down, trying to see Adeline's face. "Do you know why I kept saying that you're the right person for this job?"

Adeline eyed him without moving her face.

"Your eyes. And I'm not talking some 'you're so beautiful mumbo jumbo.' You are, but still. While the weak see only beauty; those who matter see a professional. Within a few seconds of meeting you, I saw your eyes go from 'bimbo with room-temperature IQ' to 'tear my throat out.'" Steven bared his teeth. "Lethal. *That's* when I knew. The Ordo Solis was *desperate* for that kind of leader. And you know what that word doesn't include? Knowing everything. Being fearless. Not a stubborn a** like I was."

He pointed at her. "*That's* why you're the right person for the job. And all your micromanaged trust issues can't hide how good you are at what you do. Be who you are and keep your ear to the ground for what comes next. *That's* my advice to you."

"But zere's so much happening. So many people. How can I plan for all of zis?"

Steven careened his head before looking back at Adeline. "Well, a wise, cranky ole bastard once told me, 'You can't change what people are going to do, you just need a way to deal with what comes after.'"

Adeline grinned. "I like ze cranky old man."

"Yeah, me too. He was a good man. They all were."

The two of them shared a moment of silence.

Adeline touched Steven's shoulder. "Do you still see her?"

Steven nodded. "Yeah. Not quite as often though."

"Vhen vas the last time she appeared?"

"A few minutes ago."

Adeline offered him a sad smile. "She must have been a formidable woman to have survived ze afterlife for zis long."

"Ohhh yeah." His eyes flickered with joy. "Raeleigh was a lioness. Sharp, dedicated, had a good sense for what was up. She reminds me a lot of you, which's why Raeleigh hasn't left. She's here now."

"Oh? Vhere is she zis time?" Adeline asked, eyes glancing left and right.

Steven tapped his chest. "In here." Then pointed at Adeline's. "And there."

CHAPTER 63

THE EMERGING LIGHT

Steven sat at what used to be his and Jeff's usual spot in the tiny cafe on Lexington and 38th Street. Although he had quite a bit more facial hair from the months spent at Larissa's, he once again wore a t-shirt with the original 1960s Star Trek cast. His long dark hair was pulled back in a ponytail with a purple bandana around his mocha-colored forehead.

He clutched two photographs. The first was an old picture taken of the team a decade ago, the second a reunion taken right before Steven left for Tokyo. He admired the photos before finally setting them down. This time six months ago, Steven and Jeff embroiled themselves in Soulstealer debates, or Jeff would brag about how well Trista did in school.

"We did it, you know," Steven whispered, looking at the empty red booth Jeff had occupied a thousand times. He willed his imagination to allow Jeff to visit him as Raeleigh did, but that didn't seem to be in the cards. Raeleigh hadn't appeared since his talk with Adeline.

"The world remembers. It knows what's happening. Everyone understands how important this is. The Ordo Solis is officially with the United Nations, and every news station on planet Earth talks about the Soulstealer."

We did our duty.

Steven admired his Victory Hammer S motorcycle double-parked in the lot. He unearthed the Anvil in the worst place imaginable, Craigslist.

He repurchased the bike for a third of what he would've let it go for. Steven resisted the urge to negotiate the price up to its appraised value, just to regain the Anvil's honor.

Outside the cafe, two men stood across the street observing Steven, one leaning against the pedestrian signal pole. The first looked like an all-around average guy with brown hair; a glint from a gold necklace shone around his neck. The second loomed taller but slender, with light skin and black bangs.

"I don't think he's coming out. You ready to go in there, Ahgo?" the first said, looking to his paler companion.

"Let's mash this worm," the black-haired man said, hands twitching toward his sides.

The brown-haired man grinned, revealing a chipped front tooth. They waited at the crosswalk for the light to change and the white pedestrian signal to begin blinking.

At the opposite side of the crosswalk stood three warriors of the newly formed Amethyst Vanguard. They dressed in lavender business suits and white ties, standing as rocks amidst a sea of bystanders scurrying across the road.

As the unmasked Raptors drew close, the lead Amethyst turned to his teammates. "By the Ordo Solis, *purge* them."

You reached the end! I hope you enjoyed reading *Soulstealer: Steven* as much as I enjoyed writing it.

I ask that you please **rate and review** wherever you bought the book, especially if it's Amazon. I'd also appreciate a review on Goodreads. **It's so helpful to me as a self-published author**.

Your review will let others know **they should read the** *Soulstealer* **series too**, and your rating will move us to the **#1 spot!** Thank you so much for your support!

☺

Scan the QR codes below or type the link into your browser.

bit.ly/SoulstlrBk2AmznRvw   bit.ly/SoulstlrBk2GR

GET CONNECTED!

SoulstealerBook.com

@SoulstealerBook

fb.me/SoulstealerBook

@SoulstealerBook

ACKNOWLEDGMENTS

This seven-year labor of love wouldn't have happened without the help of so many others.

There's a long list of extraordinary people who made this story what it is today.

I kept track as best I could as time passed. I apologize if I missed you!

A huge thank you, in no particular order, to:

My family	Trisolaran5151	Greg H.
Kelhi D.	maisels	Dr. Hal T.
Sydny M.	SuperCarbideBros	Andrew J.
Pamela C.	Uqbari	Grace J.
Cassy B.	Rks1157	Jenna C.
David S.	Vignaraja	Zella B.
Amy T.	national_sanskrit	Damonza
Ashlesha G.	Hunt B.	Michelle C.
Myrka & Ra'ef M.	Xiaobo G.	Leo R.
Steven from USPS Concord	Kimberly Q.	Sharon N.
Phantagor	C36 of SOS class 18C	Maggie M.
Jake A.	Donsun N.	Jeremiah H.
Allorria H.	Lauren F.	Alexandra G.
Oscar S.	Dr. Mary H.	Vince B.
Brian M.	Paris S.	Jeremy Y.
Shawn D.	Daniel W.	Rebecca W.

THE AUTHOR

SHANE BOULWARE is an unconventional idealist from Orlando, Florida. *Naturally*, he commissioned as a Contracting Officer in the United States Air Force in 2012, where he promptly got tased, was hit with pepper spray, participated in a mock riot, jumped out of an airplane, and lived in a combat zone. These experiences tempered his creative instinct and led him to publish two music albums, found an innovation company, break a Guinness World Record, and learn over sixteen dance styles.

Having grown up a huge fan of *Dune*, Star Wars, Stargate SG-1, Warhammer 40K, Harry Potter, *Avatar: The Last Airbender*, and *The Lord of the Rings*, Shane always wanted to create and share a world of his own. His imagination set him on a path to write the supernatural thriller, *Soulstealer*, and its sequel, *Soulstealer: Steven*.

When he's not negotiating contracts or salsa dancing the night away, you can find Shane taking his creative passion out on an unsuspecting keyboard. If you want to know when his next book will be available, visit his website at ShaneBoulware.com, where you can sign up to receive release updates on what's coming next!

Made in United States
North Haven, CT
21 May 2022

19409577R00174